LOGAN

A REVENGE ROMANCE

GIULIA LAGOMARSINO

Copyright © 2017 by Giulia Lagomarsino

All rights reserved.

No part of this book may be reproduced in any form or by any electronic or mechanical means, including information storage and retrieval systems, without written permission from the author, except for the use of brief quotations in a book review.

Cover Design courtesy of T.E. Black Designs

www.teblackdesigns.com

Created with Vellum

To my sister, who edits my books with humor that leaves me laughing months later.

CHAPTER 1

CECE

"THAT'S THE LAST OF IT," I said as I hauled the last box up to my new apartment. I was moving in with Vira, my best friend who I had met at a summer job during college. Vira was a few years older than me and a confirmed man-eater. She had a steady boyfriend, but she insisted on an open relationship. She vowed to never be tied down to one man. I didn't share her way of thinking, but Vira was wild and crazy and full of terribly delicious ideas.

"Is that all?" Vira asked sarcastically. "You only brought enough to fill both our bedrooms. Since when do you have more shoes than me, Cece?"

"Since you turned me into a shoe fanatic. You know, I used to only wear comfortable shoes. I was an outdoor girl that wore flip flops all summer long and wouldn't be caught dead in a pair of high heels. Now, heels are part of my everyday attire and I hardly ever wear flip flops."

We were both sweating profusely and went into the kitchen for some water. There was a time when I would have chosen pop over water. Sugar had always been my best friend, but then I was always on the less-toned side of skinny. I had never paid attention to my body before. I had always been active, so I enjoyed all the sugar and fast food I wanted. I didn't care about a slight pudge or whether or not my legs were in shape. Then I went out with a guy for several months and I fell madly in love with him. When he broke up with me, he told me I reminded him too much of a little girl. He said that if I acted like a woman, dressed like a woman, and took care of myself like a woman, I would have been more attractive. It broke my heart and I was absolutely devastated. I met Vira soon after and never looked back. Vira taught me how to enjoy life and experience all that I could.

"Oh my God. I don't think I can move anymore. My muscles are so sore. I need a massage. What do you think? Movies and wine tonight?" I started to rub my calf muscles that got quite the workout from hauling boxes up the stairs.

"That's no way to celebrate you moving back here. We need to go party. Let's go to the disco club and you can shake your groove thang. We can get all dressed up and drive the guys wild."

Vira walked over to me and started dancing and shaking her hips against me. She was so bouncy, it was irritating. I didn't have that energy, but Vira never backed down from a night of fun. I had learned a long time ago to go with the flow when it came to her, because I usually had a great time when we went out.

"I don't have anything unpacked yet. All my stuff is in boxes."

"I gotcha covered. I have the perfect outfit for you to wear. I'll even do your hair for you. It'll be pretty." Vira fluffed my hair. "You're prettier your own way." I started laughing at the *Dirty Dancing* reference. It was one of our favorite movies to watch, and that was a line we repeated multiple times a week.

"Go get showered and I'll get out some clothes for you."

"And shoes! I need a sexy pair of shoes to wear," I shouted on my way back to my new bedroom. I grabbed my shower stuff out of the box labeled "bathroom" and grabbed a towel and washcloth out of the linen closet. I showered, washed the grime of the day off my face, and then slathered body lotion all over. In my younger days, I never bothered much with body lotion. I put it on when my skin felt really dry, but other than that, I didn't care. Vira saw that one day and taught me all about the benefits of having silky, smooth legs and what they could do for me when seducing men. I learned quickly that Vira always had the best insights into the male mind.

I walked out of the bathroom wrapped in a towel and headed to Vira's room.

"Hey, I laid an outfit out on my bed for you. I'm gonna jump in the shower really quick. You remembered to shave, right?"

"Yes, Mom."

I rolled my eyes, but really, this woman had done a lot to change my way of thinking. Always be prepared. You may not get laid, but you might end up in an accident. Either way, you wanted to be prepared for someone seeing your coochie. I picked up the outfit, or lack thereof, and smiled. This was definitely going to be a fun night. I went back to my room and grabbed a thong. That was really all I could use anyway. Vira had picked out a pair of skin tight, black short shorts. They were just long enough to cover my ass and a shimmery, silver halter top with an open back. There would be no wearing a bra tonight. Looked like the girls were going to be shining bright tonight. I was curious to see what had been picked out in the way of heels. I made my way back to Vira's room as I brushed out my hair.

"Hey, chica! What'd ya pick out for shoes?" I shouted to Vira in the shower.

"They're next to the bed."

I walked back into the bedroom, and there next to the bed were a pair of black suede, thigh high hooker boots. I squealed in delight and sat down on the bed to put them on. The stilettos were at least three inches high, and as I zipped them up, I felt very naughty. I was gonna get lucky tonight and these boots would be my golden ticket. I stood and went over to check myself out in Vira's floor length mirror. Damn. I looked good. I wasn't being conceited. Vira just taught me to appreciate my own body.

"Damn. I did good on that outfit. You look sexy, bitch!"

"Thank you. How am I gonna do my hair?"

"I think you need to leave it down in waves. That way you can lift it off your neck while you're dancing. Men want to see your neck, ya know, something for them to nibble at. That's the way you draw them in while you're dancing. Let me get dressed and we'll do our hair and makeup. Go throw some mousse in your hair and let it air dry."

We finished getting ready and looked in the mirror one more time. "Damn, we look sexy." Vira was dressed in a black, halter jumpsuit with wide legs and a vertical cutout between her cleavage. She paired it with four inch open toe stilettos. Vira always said that it was best to be covered and leave something to the imagination. I felt like we were out of an Austin Powers movie, but I had to admit that the look was just what I needed for tonight.

I had only been back to this town for short visits, but now I wanted to let loose and shake the past off my shoulders. Ever since I returned, thoughts of Logan swirled in my mind. I wondered if I would run into him and what he would say about my new appearance. I was nothing like the girl I used to be. I had changed a lot since he last saw me ten years ago. Gone was the slightly pudgy girl with short, frizzy hair and no style at all. I was fit and looked hot now, whereas before I couldn't care less. I always dressed to impress these days, and it wasn't just for work. When men saw me, they saw an attractive woman that oozed confidence. I would never be mistaken for a naive little girl again.

We left around nine and got to the club a little later. There was a line to get in, but when the bouncer saw us get out of the cab, he waved us over. It helped that Vira was a regular and any time I came to visit, we had a night out here. It was a great place to blow off steam and the men were hot. It was where you came to dance if you weren't into all the crap they played on the radio nowadays.

We entered the nightclub that I had grown to love in the years we had been coming here when I visited. Disco balls hung over the dance floor and people were shakin' it to *Car Wash*. We danced our way over to the bar and ordered drinks. After the first round was finished, we hit the dance floor. *Turn the Beat Around* came on and we started dancing and singing. We spent a good hour on the dance floor before we went back for more drinks. The thing was, it was fun to drink while we were out at the club, but we had so much fun dancing, we really didn't think about alcohol all that much.

We were at the bar ordering another round of drinks when I stopped right in the middle of a story, and my mouth dropped open. Standing ten feet away was the man that had broken my naive, little heart. I had been madly in love with him, but he hadn't thought twice about how much he was hurting me. No, not hurting me. He had crushed me. He had been my first, and I gave myself over to him, trusting him to take care of my heart. He had promised that he would always take care of me, but after a few months, he dropped me like a hot potato.

My heart beat accelerated as I watched him from where I stood. Tall and extremely handsome, he had changed in so many ways also, but I would always remember that smile. Would he still recognize me? Was there anything about me that was unforgettable? I was scared to know. I didn't think I could handle it if I had remembered him ten years later, remembered every kiss, touch, and sweet word spoken, but he didn't remember me at all. What if he came over to talk to me? Could I hold it together? I wasn't sure, but I knew I couldn't break down in front of him. I could never let him have that control over me again. Vira noticed my sudden change in mood and looked behind her.

"What is it?"

"It's him."

"Who? You mean..." Her mouth dropped as she searched. "The asshole? Where?"

I cleared my throat and finally pulled my gaze from him. "Behind you, about ten feet. White t-shirt. Short blonde hair. Totally ripped."

Vira looked over at him and let her eyes peruse his body. I could see the appreciation on her face, but it didn't bother me. Vira checked out every guy. It was a natural reaction for her.

"Did he look like that when you were seeing him?"

"No, but he was just as good looking, just not quite as large. His muscles are huge now. I think I just got a lady boner."

"So, how do you want to approach this?"

"Well, I definitely don't want to see him, but I don't want to leave just yet either." My eyes widened when he glanced over and stopped mid-drink. His eyes locked with mine, and that old twinkle that was always there sparkled in his eyes. "Oh, shit. He's walking this way." I reached over to the bar and grabbed my drink, downing it in one swallow. He walked up to me with his signature sexy grin.

"Damn, sweetheart. Are you trying to give every guy in here a heart attack?"

The nickname stung. He used it on me all the time while we were together. The fact that he used it so casually now really infuriated me. I had given him everything, and he casually strolled up to me like he could just pick up where we left off? I was pissed and I was about to let him know when he totally shocked me.

"What's your name, sweetheart?"

I stood there stunned for a minute. He didn't know who I was. He had meant everything to me ten years ago, and just as I suspected, I was forgettable. That was a blow to my ego, but I straightened my shoulders and vowed to not let him see me falter. I plastered on a fake smile and pushed my chest out a little.

"You can call me Sugar." I shook his hand and ran my tongue around my upper lip, then bit my lower lip.

"What's your name, handsome?" I tilted my head to the side playfully and ran my eyes down the length of his body. I made sure to linger over his package.

"Logan, but I'll answer to handsome also."

I smirked at him. He was even more cocky than I remembered. "Well, Logan, do you come here to dance or just to pick up ladies?"

"I can dance, if that's what you're asking."

I curled my fingers in his front pocket and pulled him closer. "Good. Let's see your dance moves," I whispered seductively.

I took his hand and pulled him out to the dance floor. *Hot Stuff* started playing, and I wrapped my arms around his neck as I shimmied against him. My hips started gyrating against him as the tempo pulsed. I took one hand and ran a finger down his chest to the waist of his pants. I stared into his eyes as I slowly licked my lips and ran my hand back up his chest. I turned around in his arms and bent at the waist so that my ass rubbed against his cock. Slowly, I ran my hands up my boots and then up my center until my hands brushed my breasts. I lifted my hair off my neck, leaving it exposed for his mouth. I wasn't disappointed when a second later, I felt his hot, wet tongue run from my neck to my shoulder.

I started rocking my body against him, shaking my hips and wrapping my arms around his neck. Small breaths huffed out across my neck and my pussy slickened in response. I was trying to turn him on, show him what he had been missing, but my body was responding to his and I felt my desire build inside. I turned to face him again, grinning when he wrapped his arm around my waist, grabbing my ass and pulling me closer. I could feel his hardness pressing against me. I gasped and wrapped my arms around his neck, pulling him in close. He had always been aggressive, but this Logan was hot and knew what he was doing. The song came to a close and *Bad Girls* came over the sound system.

I felt two hands wrap around me from behind, and a sexy grin crossed my lips. I knew exactly what was happening. Vira had come to put on a show with me. I was pulled back against Vira's body and closed my eyes as if in ecstasy. Vira wrapped one arm around my chest and the other lay across my belly. I was spun around to face her, and we danced together with less than an inch between us. We stared at each other as we ran our hands over each other's bodies. Vira grabbed my ass, pulling me flush against her body. She was really laying it on thick for Logan, and I gladly played along.

Our bodies gyrated together in a tantric rhythm. Vira turned in my arms and bent down running her hands up her legs until her ass was in the air, then I slapped her on the ass and ran my hand up her back, gripping her hair and yanking her back against my body. Vira opened her mouth as her head was pulled back and turned to face me. We shook our hips and continued our exploration of each other's bodies. I ran my hands over Vira's breasts, groping them roughly. When I saw the look of desire on Logan's face, I couldn't stop if I wanted. We were driving him crazy, but it really heated up when Vira wrapped her arm around my neck and pulled me in for a kiss. Our tongues tangled for a minute as the song died down.

When the song ended and we broke apart, there was quite a crowd gaping at our lewd act. We didn't care. We weren't gay, we just liked to have fun. Logan was staring at me with lust in his eyes. He stalked over to me like a panther and grabbed my arm, pulling me across the dance floor to a dark corner of the club. He threw me up against the wall and grabbed my ass, kissing me with a passion I'd never felt before. His hands were all over me and my eyes slid closed as his mouth sucked at my neck. He pulled my leg up and I obligingly wrapped it around him.

This is wrong. I shouldn't be doing this. It's asking for trouble.

But when his hand grazed my thigh and slid up to my ass, I lost all train of thought. It didn't matter that this would only hurt me, or the fact that he was apparently fine with what looked like two hookers kissing on the dance floor. He wanted me, and despite knowing I was one of a thousand, I still wanted him.

His hand slipped beneath my shorts, his groan right against my ear as he slid his fingers under my shorts and realized I was only wearing a thong. His lips blazed a trail down my neck, over my top, to my breasts. My nipples were straining against the material, and his teeth bit at the taut peaks.

I gasped as his hand came around to the front of my shorts and unzipped them. In the next instant, his hands were inside my thong, rubbing at my slick pussy. My hips started moving against his hand, begging for the orgasm I could feel building inside. His mouth moved up to meet mine as I gasped in pleasure when his fingers entered me. His fingers slid in and out of me, pushing deeper and deeper with each stroke. My leg tightened around his waist as I felt myself tipping over the edge. I opened my mouth to scream, but his mouth covered mine, swallowing the sound. I rode the waves of my orgasm with his fingers buried inside me. I had never felt more alive than I did in that moment.

When the sounds of the club finally came back to me, I realized no one really noticed anything. He had shoved me up against the wall and made me come harder than I ever had, and no one had stopped to watch. In that moment, I was grateful that no-one cared enough to look. I had let loose a lot since I met Vira, but sex in public was something I hadn't yet encountered. I was still flying high on alcohol and lust. I could feel him pressing his erection against me and my pussy clenched with desire. He started to stroke me again with his fingers and I reached down to grip him through his pants.

His eyes darkened as I stroked him. When my mouth opened slightly, he dove in, shoving his tongue in my mouth as he fucked me with his tongue. It was overwhelming. It was sexy as hell. It was— He ripped himself away from me and dragged me down a dark hall. He pushed me up against the wall as he lost all control and pulled my shorts down. My pussy needed him, clenching every time I thought of him entering me. Glancing around, I could tell we were well hidden, not that I cared right now. I just needed him. The sound of his zipper being yanked down rippled in my ears, and then my thong was torn from my body. I lifted my leg from one side of the shorts and let them fall to the ground. He grabbed my ass and pulled me up around his waist. His kisses were hard and punishing against my skin. He couldn't seem to get enough of me, and as his hard cock pressed against me, I knew this man would ruin me all over again. In one swift move, he was inside me, thrusting hard and telling me how much he wanted to fuck me.

"You are so fucking sexy. I saw you dancing and I knew I had to fuck you tonight."

I moaned, hating myself for loving his words. He was a pig, fucking me in the club all because he saw me dancing sexy with Vira.

But I couldn't deny him either. His thrusts were hard and punishing, and I relished the feel of his cock thrusting inside me. With every pound, I felt myself slamming against the wall.

"Oh, God. Fuck me hard. I need this!"

He continued to thrust into me, his hand moving to my clit to bring me to orgasm again. I felt my walls tightening around his cock and he slammed into me a few more times before he stilled, coming inside me.

"Fuck. You are so fucking sexy. I'm gonna need to have you again as soon as my cock recovers."

That brought me out of my sex haze. I had just had sex with my ex-boyfriend, and he didn't even know it was me. I needed to leave before he realized who I was.

"That was fantastic, but I need to go." I leaned down and put my shorts back on, pulling them up around my waist. "See ya round, cowboy."

"Wait." He pulled me in close and nuzzled my ear. "Tell me your name, Sugar. I need to see you again." He was running his hands over my breasts and nipping at my ear. "At least give me your number." My head was thrown back in desire as he explored my body, but I pulled myself from his grasp and sent him a sexy grin.

"Until next time, handsome." With that, I turned and walked back to the bar, finding Vira talking with a hot guy. She was sending off all the signals that she was available for the night, and I knew she wouldn't be going home alone. Vira gave me the predetermined signal and I headed for the door to grab a cab. I was just about out the door when I saw Logan coming after me. I ducked out the door and rounded the corner to the alley to hide. I watched as he came running out of the club looking around the parking lot for me. He finally gave up and walked over to a dark colored sports car and climbed in.

I hid in the shadows, but he passed me as he drove away. I caught his license plate and smiled. Still cocky as ever. SXMCHN1

CHAPTER 2

LOGAN

THE WOMAN from the other night had me all tied up in knots. She was sinfully sexy and had me hard as steel within five minutes of meeting her. When I saw her drinking with her friend, I thought maybe I knew her, but she showed no recognition when I approached her. She exuded confidence when she talked to me, and her body, oh man, her body was smokin'. She had blonde, curly hair that hung to mid back and gorgeous, blue eyes. Her lips were full, and I wanted them wrapped around my cock. Her ass was nice and tight and gave me a chubby just thinking about how she shook it on the dance floor.

When her friend approached her and started dirty dancing with her, I about blew my load. It was the sexiest thing I had ever seen. It was dirty, but sensual. They explored each other's bodies like they were already well acquainted. Maybe they were even lovers, but the way she took my cock said that she craved me. She was so perfect in my arms. She molded to my body like she was meant to be there. Then she left me standing there craving more. She practically ran away from me, and by the time that I kicked myself out of my sex haze, she had disappeared out the door. I needed to see her again, so I showed up the next night to see if she came back. I stayed for four hours before finally giving up and going home. I had offers from other women, but they didn't even tempt me. All I wanted was the sexy vixen that had taken over my thoughts.

I went into work Monday morning completely distracted. My partner Ryan had been trying to tell me something for ten minutes, but I couldn't keep my mind off that woman.

"The Winslow project is running smoothly, but they want to meet about possibly adding on to the building. Their projections are changing, and they think they're going to need more space. Since we're still in the early stages of building, I think we can add on without too much trouble."

"Uh-huh." I grunted as I stared out the window. I wasn't really paying attention, and I knew I should, but my interest was elsewhere. I was trying to figure out how to find this girl, and other than searching for her at the club, I couldn't figure out a way.

"So, Sarah came over last night and told me she might be pregnant."

"That's good." I murmured as I thought of pressing Sugar up against the wall of the club. "That's really good."

"Yeah, she told me it might not be mine either."

I thought of how she had latched onto my cock with her pussy and squeezed me tight. "That's fucking great." The images of her with her head thrown back in ecstasy were swirling in my mind, making me hard.

"So, then I told her that I was totally cool with that, and maybe this dude could move in with us too."

I needed to get out of the office or I was going to embarrass myself in front of Ryan. I stood in haste and headed for the door, trying to conceal the rather large bulge that had taken over my pants. Shit. This was a disaster.

"That's cool, man. Listen, I got shit to do, so I'll catch you later."

"Logan, what the fuck, man? I just told you my girlfriend might be pregnant by another man, and you didn't hear a word I said."

"Sarah's pregnant?"

"No! I just said that to see if you were listening. What the fuck is wrong with you this morning?"

Sighing, I lowered my folder in front of my hard on as I turned to face Ryan.

"I met this chick at a club Friday, and she was hot. I fucked her up against the wall, and she bailed on me without even giving me her name."

"Maybe you need to work on your seduction skills."

"No, she was just as into it as I was, but then she thanked me and walked out the door."

"I'm no expert on women, but I'm guessing that if you fuck a woman against the wall of a club, neither of you is looking for a relationship."

I scoffed. "I didn't say I was looking for a relationship."

"So, you got laid and it was a good time. Move on. That's what you normally do."

I walked over to the chair and sat down, running my hand down my face. "This girl was different. She wasn't just sexy, she exuded this raw sexuality, and we fit together in every way. It was....amazing. Like, blow your mind, never gonna meet anyone like that again, amazing."

"So what you're saying is that you want to fuck her again."

"No, what I'm saying is that I want to see her again, not just fuck her. I think I met my match with this girl. She's my fantasy woman." I thought back to when I first locked eyes on her. "It's weird because she looked so familiar, but she didn't seem to recognize me."

"Maybe you've fucked her before and this was payback."

"No, I would've remembered her. She actually kind of reminds me of a girl I used to know, but they're nothing alike."

"You do realize that makes no sense, right?"

"I mean they looked similar, but they have totally different personalities, different styles. I kinda thought for a while there that she would be the one I ended up with."

"What happened to her?"

"I was a dumb shit and broke up with her. I could see she was in love with me, and I wasn't ready for all that. I wanted to be free to stick my dick in other pussy."

"She didn't put out?"

"No, she did, but I was her first. She didn't really know what she was doing, and it wasn't that great. But it was obvious she was in love with me. Man, I could see the crazy in her eyes."

He stared at me incredulously. I knew what a dumb fuck I had been, but I was young and stupid. "Are you stupid? It's your job as her man to teach her. Do you realize that you could have molded her to what you wanted during sex?"

"I know that now, but at the time I just wanted someone that knew what they were doing. When I felt her getting too clingy, I thought, *well it's not like she's that great in bed,* and I didn't want to be stuck with someone, so I broke it off with her. Looking back, it was fucking stupid. She was pretty amazing, but that's in the past," I waved off the memory. "This girl I met the other night is fucking incredible."

"All you did was have sex with her. She could be a total psycho."

"I'm not saying I want to marry the chick. I just need to find her and see if there's something more between us."

"I guess I know where I'll find you from now on. Just do me a favor and don't spend all your time at the club. We still have a business to run."

"Don't worry about it. I'll get my shit together." I stood and walked toward the door. "I've got a few calls to return and then we can head over to the meeting."

"Take your time. We don't have to leave for an hour," Ryan said as he sat down at his desk.

I headed to my office and vowed to get my shit together enough to concentrate on this meeting. An hour later, we were on our way to an office downtown. It was a small building that was quite cramped. It was clean and decorated with small feminine touches, but it wasn't overdone. We were meeting with VAS, Veteran Assimilation

Services. The woman running the organization was Cassandra Crawford. She was raising funding for a center for veterans where they could get the care they needed all in one center. There weren't any VA hospitals within a hundred miles, so this had the potential to be a huge business in the area. We didn't really have any details yet on what was to be expected, but based on the size of this office, I doubted we would be starting off big. This would probably end up being a cheap rehab center that would take us a few months to complete. There wouldn't be much money in it, but still, every job put our business out there. Besides, it was a good cause, and I had two friends that had been to war. I knew what kind of services were available, and I would do anything to help.

We walked over and introduced ourselves to the receptionist, telling her we had a ten o'clock appointment. The receptionist was a twenty-something blonde with a nice smile.

"Ms. Crawford is expecting you. You may go in. Can I get you some coffee or water?"

"Coffee would be great, beautiful." Ryan had a steady girlfriend, but apparently had no problem flirting with other women.

We walked into the office and saw a woman in a tight pencil skirt bent over picking up some papers that were on the ground. She had on black stilettos that had a strap around her upper ankle. My eyes were glued to those heels for a brief second, but then I turned to see Ryan's eyes trail up her long legs to her tight ass. This woman was sexy as hell, and it seemed that Ryan took notice. She stood up and turned around, looking shocked to see us.

"Oh, excuse me. I didn't know anyone was here." A blush crept over her face as she straightened her skirt. One of her buttons on her blouse had come undone, and I could see the skin of her creamy breasts. Her white, lacy bra was showing as well. Fuck. This girl was sexy, and if I didn't have it bad for another woman, I would be all over her.

Ryan stepped forward and whispered in her ear. There was no mistaking the seductive tone that I could just barely hear. And when his hands slid to her blouse and slowly started to do up the buttons that had come undone, I had to turn and hide my chuckle. It was obvious he had a thing for this woman, and apparently, she liked him too. She flushed, brushing her hands down the front of her blouse to make sure everything was in place, then cleared her throat.

"Are you here from Jackson Walker Construction?"

"Yes, ma'am. I'm Logan Walker, and this is Ryan Jackson." We shook hands and exchanged pleasantries.

"Well, how about we get down to business. As you are aware, VAS is looking to construct a building that can accommodate a veteran's every need under one roof. There aren't any VA hospitals close by, and there are many veterans in the area in need of physical, mental, financial, and other services. What we are looking for is a building with at least four separate wings. One will be just for physical needs, a rehabilitation center. There would be a section for inpatient and outpatient treatment. Another wing would be for mental health services. There would be a wing that would be dedicated to helping veterans get their finances in order and help with job placement. The fourth wing would be a staff wing. We are hoping that the center would be open twenty-four/seven with the night time hours being dedicated to the inpatient veterans and emergency calls that we may receive."

Ryan leaned back in his chair, thinking out loud. "A building that provides that many services would not be cheap to build or maintain."

I was thinking the same thing. Based on this tiny, little building, where would she come up with the funding for something like that?

"We have quite a few donors on board. They've all requested that before any money is given, they'd like plans drawn up for the center. I would need not only building plans, but interior design sketches. They all agree that a center like this needs to be top of the line. We have several companies that have agreed to have employees come work here for free as long as we advertise that we are using their services. I have doctors, nurses, and physical therapists that have agreed to come once a week and donate their time. There's a firm that is willing to send over several lawyers to work pro bono with the veterans every week. I have an interior designer on board to work with you at no cost, and that's just the beginning of the list of people willing to donate their help to this project. So you see, we are doing everything we can to keep our costs down. I've worked for two years to line up the funding for this project. What I need now is a good construction company to take on a building like this. The question is, are you willing to do it at cost?"

I ran my hand over my jaw and smirked. Damn, she was feisty. This girl had spunk and was obviously passionate about this project. I glanced over at Ryan and he nodded his head.

"We can draw up some plans for you, but Logan will have to sit down with you and get some specifics on what exactly you are looking for in this building. We have an interior designer on staff that can help. She works on all our buildings with us, and is very good at what she does. If you hire us, we'll do it at cost."

"I thought you were just a construction firm?"

"We do construction, architectural, and interior design at our site," Ryan said.

"Wow. I didn't realize that your company was so extensive. Well, how about we set up a time to get together and go over plans for the building. I'm not an architect, so I can only tell you what I am looking for, but I have some volunteers that have worked in constructing this kind of center that would like to be able to attend to help plan. Would you be open to working with them?"

I could tell that she really wanted this deal to go through. Based on her office, she had dedicated a lot of time working on this project. She had samples of other centers hung on the wall and file cabinets all along the wall that were labeled VAS. This project meant a lot to her, and I wanted to help her make it happen. I stood and walked over to her, handing her my card.

"Let me know when they can all get together, and I'll bring a small team along with me to get the ball rolling on this project."

She took the card from my hand and breathed a sigh of relief. Ryan stood and we all said our goodbyes, heading for the door. When we stepped outside, I grabbed Ryan's arm to stop him.

"What was all that in there?"

"What are you talking about?" He cocked his head to the side as if he truly had no idea what I was talking about.

"You know what I'm talking about. When we walked in, you had your hands on her and you were whispering in her ear. You have the hots for her."

"I have a girlfriend."

"That doesn't mean jack shit and you know it."

Ryan sighed and shoved his hands in his pockets. "Sarah told me she wants to see other people. Apparently, she met someone new and he's wonderful." He used air quotes around *wonderful* and rolled his eyes. "He doesn't work long hours, and he thinks that they have something special."

"That sucks, man. What did you say to her?"

Ryan huffed out a laugh. "Well, I sure as shit didn't stop her. She pretty much made it sound like she had already moved on. I'm not gonna fight for someone who doesn't want me."

"Had she ever said that she wasn't happy with the way things were going?"

"She told me she didn't like me working so much. She was always nagging me about taking the next step, but honestly, I'm not sure I wanted to. It sucks that it went down this way, but it's probably for the best. I don't think she was the one."

I patted him on the shoulder. "Well, at least now you don't have to feel guilty about going after Cassandra."

"Never mix business with pleasure. I fully intend to go after her, but it's gonna have to wait until this deal is done. If we do this building right, it could bring a lot of business our way."

"No shit. Let's get back to the office so I can get a team together. We can come up with designs for her to look at when we get together. Then we can go off that."

"I'll get the research team looking into how many potential veterans are in the area that would need this clinic. Then we can at least judge how big this facility is going to need to be."

"Sounds good."

We got back in the car and headed to the office. We had a lot of work ahead of us, and as much as I wanted to sit around and day dream about my mystery woman, it looked like she was going to be put on the back burner until the weekend.

CHAPTER 3

CECE

WHEN I WOKE up Saturday morning, I felt completely satisfied from last night. Logan was much better than I remembered, and he had definitely improved his seduction skills. There was no way that he would have remembered me from our previous sexual encounters because I had a lot more practice and had learned a few things along the way. When I met Logan, I was a virgin and had zero experience besides kissing. I was shy and didn't know how to ask for what I wanted. Logan had been good in bed, but I always got the feeling that he wanted more from me. The problem was, I didn't know how to ask for guidance. I didn't watch porn, I didn't read trashy novels, and my friends weren't too much more experienced.

As I lay in bed, I thought back to our relationship together. He had really fucked with my head. I had thought we really had something great, but he just wanted some hot piece of ass that could screw better than me. The real killer though, was when he told me I didn't act enough like a woman. It had crushed my spirit. For such a young girl, it was like being told that *I* wasn't enough. I changed completely over the summer, thanks to meeting Vira. And even though I loved who I was now, I felt like his words had taken away some of my innocence, and influenced me to be someone that I might never have become.

In some ways, it was a good thing. I learned to explore who I was and what I wanted. But in other ways, there was nothing wrong with that young girl that dressed in comfy clothes and hated makeup. She was pretty awesome. So, as I laid there staring at the ceiling, I wondered how things would have been different had he not said those cruel words to me. Would I have stayed the same, or would I have eventually learned to come into my own?

I finally got out of bed and went to the kitchen to make some coffee. I sat down and checked my email and tried my hardest to forget about last night. About a half hour later, Vira came stumbling out of her room with the guy that she was talking to at the bar last night. He was tall with dark hair and stubble along his jaw. His eyes were dark brown, and he was looking at Vira like he was ready to throw her over his shoulder and take her back to the bedroom for another round. Vira didn't do seconds though. She had a one night policy and the guy never got to stick around for more in the morning.

"Hey, Cece. This is...." She turned back towards the man waving her hand, but couldn't come up with a name.

"Jeremy."

"Yeah. This is Jeremy, and he was just leaving."

He frowned, looking surprised by her dismissal. "Ouch. Just kicking me out without a cup of coffee?"

"Sweetie, last night was fun," she patted his cheek, "but let's not drag this out."

"Sure. Let me grab my shit and I'll be out of here."

He didn't seem pissed, just surprised that she wasn't expecting more. He came back, pulling on his shirt and grabbing his jacket off the back of the chair. He walked over to Vira and gave her a scorching kiss. "Until next time, baby." Then he smacked her ass and walked out the door.

"He is hot, Vira."

Vira waggled her eyebrows at me. "He's great in bed too."

"So, why'd you kick him out?"

"He was gonna want to come back for more. I'm just not interested," she shrugged. "I think I'm going to break up with Kyle," she said, suddenly switching gears.

"Why?"

"Meh. He just isn't doing it for me anymore. At first, he was really cool about having an open relationship, but then he didn't like it when I wasn't available for a quick fuck." She put her hand on the counter and leaned forward conspiratorially. "Lately, he's been talking about changing the terms of our relationship. Says he thinks we should consider being monogamous."

I reared back. "Shut up! He knew you weren't into that. Break up with him before he goes out and buys a ring."

"I know, right? Why can't they just stick to the rules?" She grabbed a cup and poured some coffee. "So. What happened with dickhead last night?"

"Well, he pulled me over to the side of the club and fucked me against the wall. It was the hottest sex I've ever had. Then, of course, I came to my senses and left his ass. I saw him come running after me, so I ducked into the alley and hid from him."

"Smart move. You don't need him coming back."

I snorted at that. "You've got that right. I need that man like I need warts."

"Oh, honey," she sighed. "You still have it bad for him."

"No I don't," I argued. "I just...it keeps coming back to me."

"The shit he said to you?"

I nodded. "I was laying in bed this morning, and I was thinking about what he did. You remember what I was like back then."

She threw her head back and laughed. "Gangly, no style, but still the most awesome chick I knew. Girl, there was nothing wrong with the way you were."

"I know," I sighed. "You've told me that so much over the years, but those scars run deep. He made me question everything about myself."

"And he's an asshole for it. Men like that, they don't care that what they're seeing is only skin deep. He knew what kind of person you were and he still threw you away. Trust me, you don't need that in your life."

"I know." I plopped my elbow down on the counter and rested my head in my hand. "I just wonder, you know?"

"Um...not unless you tell me."

I looked at her and revealed my deepest, darkest secret that I had held onto all this time. "I wonder what I would have been like if he hadn't changed me."

"Did he change you?" she asked, quirking her head. "Or did you become the person you were meant to be?"

I shrugged. "I don't know, and I guess I never will. I'd like to think that I would still become this badass woman with a killer best friend," I smirked, "but the truth is, I was never this confident. You helped me with that. Without you, I would probably still be that awkward girl, just hoping a boy would kiss me."

"Listen, you don't need to be who I think you should be. You should be comfortable in your own skin, and girl, you were rockin' that skin last night. You had him wrapped around your finger."

"Yeah, but he didn't know it was me. He thought I was just some hot chick. He fucked me up against the side of the wall!"

"You've never cared about being crazy like that before. Why does this have to be different?"

I picked at the countertop. "Because it was him. He ruined me. He made me think he loved me, but all he wanted was better sex."

"And now you can give that to him," she smirked. "Who says he has to know it's you?"

"What do you mean? It's not like I'm going to tell him it's me. And if he didn't recognize me last night, it's not likely he will."

"Well, you've changed a lot, for the better," she said quickly. "You've got killer legs and you take care of yourself. You've finally got some makeup on your face and you do your hair. He won't be able to stay away."

The devious look on her face told me she had some plan in mind, but whether or not I would agree to it was yet to be seen.

"Look, I've never steered you wrong, right?"

"Right."

"I taught you how to attract the men and get them to do whatever you wanted."

"Yes," I said hesitantly.

"So, what if you took it one step further with this one?"

I frowned, trying to figure out where she was going with this. "I already had sex with him in the club and then left. What more could I do?"

She stared me down, her face splitting in an evil grin. "What if you could do what every woman out there wishes she could do?"

"I already have sex like a man."

She shook her head. "Not that. What if you could take revenge on the man that fucked you over?"

My eyes widened. "Vira, what's going through your head right now?"

"I'm talking about taking what every man does and dishing it back."

"That would make me a bitch," I pointed out.

"Right, but it's okay for a man to be a total dick to you? Face it, a man can walk all over you, spit in your face, and leave you hanging high and dry, but if you even yell at him, you're pathetic and should have just walked away."

I thought about it, and it was true. How many times had I heard about a woman that cried to her ex or talked bad about him after what he did? She was instantly the pariah, the woman that couldn't just walk away with her dignity. But why should she? Why shouldn't women be able to act like men?

"Okay, let's say that I'm on board with this—"

"Which you are because you know what I'm saying is true."

I grinned. "Let's say you're right. Tell me you have a plan. And not something stupid like slicing his tires or ruining his shirt. I mean something that can really get me revenge. Something that will finally make me feel like I'm leaving the same scars on him that he's left on me."

"Oh, honey, we're not going to just play with him. We're going to fuck with him, and make him wish he never met you."

"Alright, I'm in," I said, leaning over the counter, anxious to hear what devious ideas she had.

"Well, we need to start by finding out as much about him as possible. Do you know anything about what he's doing now?"

"No, but I did catch his license plate last night. Does that help?"

Vira got up and walked over to the coffee pot for another cup. "Well, I happen to have a friend who's a police officer. How about we get him to check out his police record and give us any important details about dear Logan. Where he lives, arrest records, maybe we can fuck with him a little, get my friend to follow him around and fuck with his head. Maybe he can give him some parking tickets, traffic tickets, shit like that."

"I like the sound of it, but what I really want is to draw him in, get him really attached to me, and then crush his fucking heart like he did mine."

"Sounds good, chica. Let me give my friend a call and then we can strategize. You know you're gonna have to spy on him. If this is gonna work, we're gonna need as much information on him as possible."

"That's fine with me."

Vira called her friend and then we mapped out times that each of us could take a shift watching Logan's movements. We decided we would start on Monday because I needed to get my stuff unpacked. Each of us would take a shift at night watching for him. Vira's cop friend, Eric, gave her his home address and where he worked. It turned out, he owned a construction company and was doing quite well for himself. I was going to go to his job after I got off work and see if I could follow him home. Vira didn't work until the afternoon, so she was going to stop by his house early and try to follow him to work. We planned to do this for the first week and get whatever intel we could on him.

I spent the rest of the weekend in my new apartment unpacking. I started my new job on Monday, and I was pretty excited to get started. I'd gone to school for marketing and had interned at a prestigious firm during college. I worked there for six years after college, but had decided to move closer to home. I found a job quickly, and even though it wasn't a huge firm, it was closer to Vira. One of the stipulations of taking the job was that I did some work off the books with a new foundation that was providing services to veterans. They were still in the planning stages, so I had at least a month to settle in before we would need to start working on that campaign.

The week flew by and I was really enjoying my new job. Everyone I worked with was very nice, except for one woman who appeared to be the office slut. She must have seen me as competition because she made sure to tell me to keep my hands off Jeff, my boss. Yeah, like I would ever go there. I was all about having fun and being carefree, but I would never jeopardize my job by sleeping with my boss. There were some lines you just didn't cross.

After work every day, I followed Logan from his construction company to his house. He lived in town in a secluded subdivision. It was a pretty nice house with a few acres for each lot. I didn't get to pull up real close because he would have noticed my car. I could practically feel the eyes of nosy neighbors on me, so I made sure I didn't stick around. I did drive back later each night to see if he was still at home.

On Wednesday night, when I drove back, he was just pulling out of the driveway, so I followed him out of town. I had to hang way back because there weren't really any other cars on the road and I didn't want him to spot me. He pulled into a driveway that was already packed with other vehicles. I had to keep driving, but turned around down the road and drove past the house a second time. It seemed to be some kind of get together, but I couldn't really stop by and see without giving myself away. I headed home and resumed my stalking the next night.

Saturday morning, Vira and I talked over coffee about all we had noticed for the week. We sat in our living room, sipping our coffee and lounging about. Neither of us had anywhere to be this weekend, so we could be lazy all day if we wanted.

"Okay, so at night, he pretty much goes home directly after work, except for Wednesday. He went to a house in the country and met up with a bunch of people."

"Do you have an address? I could ask Eric to look into who lives there."

Eric was her cop friend and had already gotten a bunch of information for us.

"Um. I don't know the address. I'll have to look it up on Google Maps."

"Alright, well when we get it, we can find out some more about his friends. We do have one minor problem."

"What's that?"

"He's friends with another cop. Sean something. This could make it a little difficult for us. I already talked to Eric about having a little fun with this guy and he had no problem with it. He said he even had a few friends that could watch for his car and give him parking tickets and bogus traffic tickets. However, if this Sean guy is his friend, there's only so long that'll last before he puts a stop to it. We need to come up with some other good ideas."

"Well, I think we should go back to the club tonight and scope him out. If he's interested in seeing me again, he'll go back there to look for me."

"And what do you plan to do when you see him?"

"I don't know yet. Seduce him? Have him take me back to his place so I can check it out? If I can get an invite back there, I can snoop through his stuff while he sleeps."

"Not a bad idea, but you need to know what you want out of this. Sleepovers are dangerous if you want to avoid affection. Don't make a habit out of it."

"I know, but I need to find out as much about him as quickly as possible. If I'm going to manipulate him, I'm gonna need as much fire power as possible."

"Okay, well as far as his morning routine goes, he leaves for work every day by seven-thirty and is in the office by eight. He stops by the cafe on Madison and grabs a black coffee before heading into work. I've never seen him grab any food. I think you need to meet up with him Monday at the coffee shop. Start getting him to buy your coffee every morning. Make sure you order an expensive drink."

"What's that going to accomplish?"

"Not a whole lot, but in the end, he'll have bought you a delicious coffee every morning and he'll be kicking himself. Every little thing you do will chip away at him. Remember to be thankful that he buys your coffee, but you have to keep up the air of indifference. Like it really doesn't matter whether this man buys you coffee or not. If he suspects that you expect him to buy your coffee, he'll think you're using him. We want him to be on his knees for you."

We sat and drank our coffee in silence for a few minutes, absorbing all that we had discussed. I was trying to think of some more ways to get back at Logan when Vira interrupted my thoughts.

"We might have one other problem. He doesn't recognize you now, but he may put two and two together when you tell him your name is Cece. It won't take much for him to link Cece with Cecelia."

"I have that covered. My last name used to be Clark, but when my dad cheated on my mom, I changed my last name to her maiden name, Baker. He may link the names, but he has never known me as

Cece Baker. Even if he suspects, I think we can pull off quite a bit before he figures it out. Besides, I'm nothing like the girl I used to be."

"Well, we better make some plans for what we're going to do to him so that we're ready. We don't know how much time we have, so we need to work like we're running out of time."

"I think you're going to have to seduce the cop friend."

"Sean?"

"Yep. We need an inside man, and he's it. He's just not going to know it. I'm sure when Logan starts getting tickets, he's gonna go to Sean. If you're dating Sean, you can pull some information out of him and get him to tell us what he knows."

"I can definitely do that. Nobody does seduction better than me."

"I'm well aware."

"I think we need to go after his car also. You've seen it. He treats it like it's his baby. So let's hit him where it hurts. We'll need to talk to a good mechanic and find out what we can do without totally destroying the car. We don't need to ruin it, but we can make life difficult for him."

"I think we should also look at his business," she said offhandedly.

"What do you mean?"

"Well, you're in marketing. You have a lot of contacts. You could make business very difficult for him. Word of mouth is a good thing in his business. A few bad reviews about his business could make getting new projects very difficult."

I internally grimaced. I loved Vira, but going after his business would be taking it too far. He had a business partner and all those employees. It just wasn't right.

"No, that's out. I can't destroy his business. That's taking it too far."

"It can be a backup plan, in case you change your mind. I'm just spitballing ideas here."

"Let's keep it on the back burner for now. I mostly want to make him fall in love with me and then crush him."

She nodded in agreement, but I could tell part of her wanted to take things further. "Let's plan on going to the club tonight, and if he shows, you get an invite back to his place."

"Sounds good."

I turned on the TV ready to veg out on the couch for the rest of the day. I didn't have anything I had to do, so a day of relaxing in front of the TV sounded like heaven. Vira suggested we watch *Heartbreakers* to get us in the mood. About halfway through, Vira paused the movie.

"I need you to be honest with me about something."

"Of course."

"Are you sure you can be cruel to this man? I mean, you loved him. Are you sure those old feelings won't resurface?"

I thought about what she said for all of five seconds. Logan was a snake in the grass. I would be doing ladies everywhere a favor by teaching him a lesson.

"I'm sure."

"It's just...I saw how heartbroken you were with him. Last weekend he was all over you. I saw the way he was looking at you. He wanted you big time."

"Vira, you don't have to worry about me. I know what I'm doing."

"I'm not suggesting you don't, but sometimes the heart is a fickle bitch. I just want you to be aware that if you do this and you fall for him, he may not forgive you."

"Who says he would find out?"

She looked at me with sad eyes. "Honey, the truth always comes out. He will find out who you are and when he does, he'll probably never speak to you again. I just want you to be prepared."

"I appreciate your concern, but there's nothing to be worried about. This man told me he loved me, promised to take care of my heart, and then carelessly tossed me aside. He was so cruel to me that I changed who I was to be sure no man would ever treat me the way he treated me. He broke something inside me that I may never be able to fix. I hate him. So there is nothing that he could ever do to make me fall in love with him again. I'll have my revenge, and I'll cut him out of my life the way he cut me from his."

Vira must have seen something in my eyes, because she nodded and turned back to the TV. We spent the rest of the day vegging on the couch, watching movies. After dinner, we prepared for our night out. I was ready to exact my revenge, and maybe then I could finally move on with my life.

CHAPTER 4

LOGAN

THE WEEK HAD BEEN difficult to get through. All I wanted to do was figure out a way to find my mystery woman, but work was crazy and I didn't have the time to dwell on it. Ryan and I met with the different departments and spent long hours doing research on veteran needs in a one hundred mile radius. Ryan asked Cassandra to send over her files on the research she had done for the needs of the veterans and what she hoped to have in the facility so we could put some kind of plan together. Our research was pretty similar, though hers was definitely more detailed. She had obviously spent a lot of hours working on this project.

After our research teams had gone through all the paperwork, they laid out a detailed spreadsheet of what was needed in the facility and the dimensions of the different spaces. From there, my team got together and made some rough sketches of our ideas for the facility. We finished that on Friday, and we still needed the interior design team to look at the sketches and put together some designs so Cassandra could see what we had in mind for the space. Our meeting was on Thursday next week, so the design team had a few more days to get some ideas laid out.

"Hey," Ryan asked as I was getting ready to walk out the door on Friday night, "are you coming in tomorrow?"

I sighed. "Yeah, I have to help the design team with some questions."

He nodded. "I'll be in too. I'm behind on some shit because of this project."

"Thank God it pays well, right?" I joked.

He huffed out a laugh. "Are we idiots, taking on this project that we'll get nothing for?"

"Possibly. I've spent more time on worse things."

Ryan pushed the door open, holding it for me like I was a chick. "The project is really good."

"You just like Cassandra," I teased.

"Not until this project is over. She's off limits until then."

"Even for me?"

"Especially you," he laughed. "Besides, you have the club chick. What do you need mine for?"

"Oh, so now she's yours? I didn't realize that you could call dibs."

"Well, technically I can't since neither of us can date her yet, but I call dibs when this is over."

"That's assuming that she wants you. She may take a look at you and realize what a wuss you are."

"Hey, I am not a wuss."

I shook my head slightly, giving him an *I don't know* look. "Well, you're no Sebastian."

"Neither are you."

"Or Sean for that matter. Now, that's a manly man. Big gun, strong muscles..."

"Are you trying to tell me that you're gay or that you stare at our friends way too much?"

I paused for a moment. "If I had to answer that question, I'd say definitely the second."

"You know, the fact that you even paused makes me question everything I know about you."

"Hey, I paused because I realized that maybe I *do* check out our friends just a little too much. Not like, check them out in *that* way. But in a healthy *That's a good looking man* sort of way."

He stared at me and started laughing.

"What?"

"Nothing."

"No, seriously. What is it?"

"Just...the way you explained it. If I didn't know you, I would think you're trying to hide something."

"Hey, I can appreciate the male form. There's nothing wrong with that."

"I would never suggest there was," he choked out, smothering a laugh.

"Whatever, I'm going home."

"What about club chick?" he shouted after me.

I raised my middle finger and kept walking.

I paced around my house all of Saturday afternoon. I shouldn't go to the club. It was ridiculous. She was just one woman, and she had sex with me after the first night at the club. That wasn't something that she should be proud of. God, I sounded like a jackass.

Rubbing my hand down the back of my neck, I sighed in frustration. I needed to get laid, and I knew who I wanted. The problem was, she definitely wasn't the girl to stick around. I knew what all my friends expected of me. I was the jokester of the group. Everyone thought I was an asshole, and mostly I was. Especially after the way I took that woman at the club. No one would think very highly of me for that performance. But things were different for me now. I wasn't in my twenties anymore. I was at that age where I wanted the same woman in my bed every night. Not that I could tell the guys that. They would laugh at me if I even said anything remotely like *time to settle down.*

I wanted more out of life now. I didn't want to sleep with random women anymore. I'd seen what Jack and Cole had with Harper and Alex, and I wanted that. My thoughts drifted to the one woman that I might have had that with. Cecelia. All those years ago, I had a woman that wanted me, and only me. But she was too young, too naive. She had this perfect dream of what we would have. It was like she had our lives planned out from the moment I had sex with her. That was the problem with sleeping with virgins. I could feel her clinging to me, and as much as I thought I loved her, I wasn't ready for all that commitment. She was a sweet, innocent girl, but I was too young to realize what I had. I knew when I broke up with her that it was a mistake, but the things I said to her were cruel, and I knew she would never take me back.

I became the player that was carefree and fun-loving so that I didn't get myself into that situation again. If I was being honest with myself, I really didn't feel I deserved to find someone after the way I treated her, and since then, I hadn't attempted anything serious again.

I didn't have the ability to put another person before me, not then and probably still not now. But I wanted to try. I picked up my phone and scrolled through the numbers, trying to figure out who would be best to go to the club with. Jack and Cole were both out. Drew never picked up women, so he wouldn't be interested in going. That left Sebastian and Sean, because Ryan would rag on me the whole time.

I decided to try Sean, since I knew it was his night off. I was so fucking nervous calling him, not because of what I was asking, but because I was finally taking the next step: trying to get a woman to stick around. It was terrifying.

"Hey, I just got off work. What's up?"

"Uh..." I cleared my throat several times. "I was thinking, you know, if you don't have anything going on, maybe we could go to the club or something."

It was really quiet on the other end.

"Are you there?"

"Are you asking me out on a date?"

"What? No!"

"Thank God, because I've seen the way you look at me."

"I don't look at you like anything. I check out your physique sometimes, but in a totally heterosexual way."

"Right, that explanation almost made it worse," he grumbled.

"That's what Ryan said."

"You talk about me to Ryan? I mean, about my body?"

"No, it was just the one time," I said in frustration.

"What did you talk about?"

"Does it matter?"

"Well, sort of. I mean, if you were the topic of conversation between two dudes, wouldn't you want to know what was being said?"

I shouted in anger and took a deep breath. "Look, there's a chick that might be at the club tonight, and I want to see her. I need a wingman."

"So...you're not trying to get me to go to the club for gay sex?"

"Jesus Christ! It was a stupid conversation!"

"Alright, alright. Fine, I'll go, but I can't stay out late. I'm beat."

"Yeah, I wouldn't want you to stay out too late, Grandma."

"Hey, I'm doing you a favor. You should be more grateful."

"Right, you can say that when you get laid tonight."

"Wait, did you want me to pick you up? I'll even bring you flowers."

I heard him laughing right before I hung up. I was making the right choice here. I was choosing to move forward with my life. This was a good thing. I had to stop living based on choices I made as a stupid kid, because even in your early twenties, you were still a kid, just a little hairier. I still deserved to find a woman to love. I deserved the happily-ever-after and the white picket fence.

I stopped pacing and thought about what I just said, then slapped myself across the face. "Shut the fuck up, man. You're losing it!"

Finally around eight-thirty, I went to the club and scoped out the place for my mystery girl. I headed to the bar and ordered a beer while I scanned the dance floor. Sean made his way over to me when he walked through the doors. He looked a little out of place here. He listened to country music and I was pretty sure disco wasn't his thing, but the point of tonight was to find Sugar, and he agreed to be my wingman.

"Any sign of her yet?"

"Nope, but it's still early."

"So, what were you doing here last weekend? This isn't really your kind of hangout."

"I know, but I had a client that likes this shit, so I brought her here to have a good time. She found someone halfway through our night, so I decided I should at least find a hookup while I was out."

"So what has you coming back looking for this girl?"

"If you had seen her, you would understand. She had a friend with her that was pretty hot. Maybe they'll both be here tonight." I waggled my eyebrows at him. He just rolled his eyes, but I had a feeling he was interested.

We stood around for another half hour, shootin' the shit while I scanned the club. The moment I saw her, I swear my heart stopped. She stepped into the club in a skin-tight red dress and red *come fuck me* shoes. Her hair was down again, and when she turned to talk to her friend, her hair brushed over her breasts. Damn, she was even hotter than I remembered. I felt something poking me in the arm and realized that Sean was trying to get my attention.

"Hello? Are you even listening to me?"

"She's here. Just walked through the door. Red dress."

"Holy shit. Who's her friend?"

"Didn't catch her name."

Her friend was in a matching skin tight black dress and matching shoes. She looked good also, but I only had eyes for my lady in red. They were glancing around the club and when she saw me, she stopped and a big grin spread across her beautiful face. She stalked over to me like a predator going after her prey. I would gladly let her eat me up any time she liked. Her friend was eyeing Sean, and I glanced over to see him practically eye fucking her.

Sugar walked straight up to me and wrapped her arms around my neck, then crushed her lips to mine. I was so stunned, it took me a few seconds to respond. My hand slid to the back of her head, while my other hand wrapped around her waist, pulling her in close as I kissed her like it was my dying breath. My hand fisted her hair as I devoured her mouth. She tasted sweet, and my tongue swiped hers to get every last flavor. She pulled back and her teeth latched onto my lower lip, pulling it out as she broke the kiss. Her hand was skimming up and down the back of my neck as she stared into my eyes. Now that I could see her again up close, I swore I was looking at the ocean. She had the most beautiful blue eyes I had ever seen.

She took my hand, pulling me out to the dance floor. I didn't bother to look back at Sean. He could handle himself, and I was pretty sure he would have no problem with the friend. We spent the next hour dancing to disco music. She was quite the dancer, but I already knew that from last weekend. During the fast songs, she shook her ass on the dance floor and a smile was permanently plastered on her face. It was obvious she was really enjoying herself. Not like *yeah, this is a good time,* but like *this is my music, and I love dancing to it.* She was a natural. During some of the slower songs, she clung to me and rubbed her body against mine. It felt like we were having sex on the dance floor. She was amazing.

We headed back to the bar for a drink where Sean and the friend were already getting one. We ordered a few beers and she introduced me to her friend.

"Logan, this is my friend Vira. Vira, you remember Logan." She smirked at her friend when she said my name, like I was her dirty, little secret and she knew all about me. Vira wrapped her arms through Sean's as she made introductions.

"This is Sean. He's a cop." She popped the p as she said it, and I saw Sugar's smirk grow. Was she interested in cops? There was a glint in her eyes, but then she wrapped her arm around my waist and my jealousy was replaced with lust. She slipped her right hand into Sean's, giving him a firm shake.

"It's nice to meet you, Sean. I'm Cece."

Finally a name. I hadn't even thought to ask her because she had me under her spell the moment she walked in the door. Something niggled at the back of my mind, but I couldn't figure it out. My brows furrowed as I tried to figure out what it was, but then Cece leaned over and ran her tongue along the shell of my ear and all was forgotten when she whispered in my ear.

"You wanna get outta here?"

I could feel her warm breath on my skin, and my pants got a little tighter as lust swept through me. I wanted this woman so bad, but I didn't just want a one night stand with her. If I could get her back to my place and get her to stay the night, I could get a date out of her. She was throwing off all the vibes that she wasn't interested in more than tonight, but I was determined to change her mind. I looked over at Sean to let him know I was leaving, but he already had Vira wrapped up in his arms.

"Tell your friend you're leaving."

She smiled at me and walked over to whisper in her friend's ear. They exchanged a few words, and I gave a chin lift to Sean as we turned and headed out of the club. I walked her out to my 1969 Ford Mustang Boss 429 in black jade. It was a car that I restored with my father in my early twenties. It was my baby, and I took extra special care with her.

"Nice car."

"Thanks."

"A 429 Boss. You could get a lot of money for this car. It's quite rare. Why would you drive it where it could be stolen?"

"You know your cars." She raised one eyebrow, like it was a stupid comment. "My dad and I restored it together. He wanted me to have it when we were done, but he told me that what made this car special was that we had worked on it together. He said a car like this was meant to be driven, and if I kept it in a garage and never drove it, I wasn't worthy of owning it."

I laughed to myself as I remembered the day Dad and I talked about it. I readily agreed because the car was awesome, but when all was said and done, I didn't want to drive it. She was a beauty, but eventually I got over it and started taking her out more and more.

"Well, she's beautiful. You did a good job restoring her. How did your dad get his hands on it to begin with?"

"A friend of his worked for Ford and had it sitting in storage. He was going to sell it, and my dad talked him into selling it to him."

We pulled into the driveway and I got out and opened the door for her. When she stepped out, she didn't go for modesty. She put one sexy leg out the door and gave me a nice view of her shapely legs. My dick swelled as I envisioned those legs wrapped around my waist. I yanked her up against my chest and crushed my mouth to hers. I couldn't stop kissing this woman. She was so desirable, and her kisses ignited a fire inside me.

I pulled back and grabbed her hand, taking her inside my house. We didn't even make it to the stairs before she was ripping my shirt off me. I kicked my shoes off and undid my pants, but she was right there with me, yanking them down the moment the zipper was undone. She was down on her knees in front of me, stroking me through my boxers.

"Shit. Cece, you gotta stop or I'm gonna blow my load right now."

She pulled my boxers down and my cock jumped to attention as soon as it was free. She looked up at me through her lashes as she wrapped her lips around my cock. See? Every man's wet dream. I got harder with every lick of her tongue. It was the sexiest thing in the world to see a woman down on her knees pleasing me. The feel of her wet mouth around my cock was enough to make me want to come right then, but I wanted to savor every inch of her. I hauled her up and kissed her like it was our last time. I spun her around and moved her hair over one shoulder as I slowly lowered the zipper of her dress. Her creamy, soft skin begged to be touched as I lowered the thin straps of her dress off her shoulders. Her body shivered under my touch as I guided the material down her body where it pooled at her feet. She was facing away from me in nothing but a thong. I couldn't wait to see her in nothing at all.

I ran my fingers under the thin material of her panties. She pushed her ass back and I felt her cheeks brush against my cock. In one swift move, I yanked the panties from her body, the material shredding in half. I picked her up and started to carry her up the stairs, but her pussy was brushing against me and I had to be inside her. I set her down on the stairs and ran my fingers through her wet folds. She was more than ready for me. I could take my time with her later, but right now, I needed to be inside her.

"Get inside me. I need you."

I swallowed her pleas as my mouth descended on hers. As I slid inside her, I swear stars exploded behind my eyelids. Her warmth wrapped around me and I had to stop so that I didn't come on the spot. She was amazing. I started thrusting inside her, her nails scratching my back as I pounded into her. There was no being gentle right now. I needed her hard and fast, and luckily that's what she wanted.

"Harder. Fuck me harder, Logan."

I felt her fingers work into my hair and then she was pulling it so hard that I might end up with a bald spot. The pain shot straight down to my groin, sending tingles all throughout my body. I fucked her harder every time she yanked on my hair. Her other hand raked down my back, her nails scratching into my skin.

"Goddamn, woman. Put away the tiger claws."

I picked her up and threw her up against the wall, pounding into that sweet pussy. I felt her back hitting the wall with every thrust. I wrapped my hands around her hair and yanked her head to the side, sucking the delectable skin of her neck into my mouth. She would have my mark all over her by the time I was done with her. Her legs were wrapped tight around me, her pussy squeezing my cock almost to the point of pain. It spurred me on faster and faster. I nibbled along her jaw until I got to those sweet lips. Electricity buzzed through me as my mouth met hers, our hot breath mingling with every kiss. She grabbed my lip with her teeth and bit down hard, drawing blood. I pulled my damaged skin from her mouth and glared at her.

"What the fuck, woman?"

I stepped down to the carpeted stairs and threw her down to her knees. I bent her over and slammed into her pussy from behind with so much intensity I thought my dick might fall off. I brought my hand back and smacked her ass, leaving a handprint behind. I grabbed a fist full of hair and yanked her head back. Leaning over her, I sucked on her neck and whispered in her ear.

"You want me to fuck you hard and smack your ass?"

She moaned as her eyes closed. I pulled back and slammed into her again.

"Answer me. You want me to spank you?"

"Please..."

That was all I heard as I reared back and laid another hard smack on her ass. She moaned and my cock twitched inside her. I pulled out of her and spread her legs even wider. I fingered her wet folds and then drew my hand back, spanking her clit as hard as I could.

"Oh, fuck yes!" I spanked her again. She obviously wanted it rough, and I was more than happy to oblige. Her right leg swung back and she twisted her body, knocking me to my back on the floor, where she now straddled me reverse cowgirl. She lowered herself on me and started rocking on top of me. Her hands grabbed my balls almost painfully.

"Careful with the goods, sweetheart."

She rode me hard and I felt my balls start to tighten as she played with them. I reached around her and thumbed her clit. She gave my balls an extra hard squeeze, so I grabbed her nipple and pinched it hard. Her pussy squeezed my cock as she came all over me, and moments later I followed. She was breathing hard as I pulled her back against me on the floor. She laid with her back on my chest, her hair splaying all over my face. I ran my hands over her breasts and gave them one final hard smack for good measure. Fuck, this woman was a wildcat.

I held her to me as my breathing started to return to normal. I ran my hand up and down her stomach, relishing in the feeling of a woman spread out on me. I usually left not too long after sex, so this was really nice. She crawled off me and started gathering her clothes. No way was this woman leaving yet. I was thoroughly exhausted, but a short nap and I would be ready to fuck her again. She was staying the night, even if I had to chain her to the bed.

I got up and grabbed the clothes from her hand, throwing them to the floor. I bent down and threw her over my shoulder as she yelped.

"You aren't leaving yet. I'm not through with you."

I climbed the stairs, not surprised at all when I felt her lay a hard slap on my ass. Yep. This girl was definitely made for me.

CHAPTER 5

CECE

HOLY SHIT. Who knew Logan was so amazing in bed. What I experienced on the stairs with him was just a preview to what we did upstairs. I liked it rough in bed, but I never would have guessed Logan would also. Based on our first time in the club, I knew he was good, but tonight brought my opinion of him up a few notches.

We laid down for a few minutes to recover from our previous sexcapades and Logan had said something about a nap, but my libido took over and soon we were having wild monkey sex again. I had to admit, part of the rough play came from my anger toward him. He was great in bed, but my *claws*, as he called them, came out when I allowed myself to think of how different it was this time around with him. I didn't want to think of how we used to be, so I started clawing and biting to get rid of those images. Funnily enough, he was into it and gave just as good as he got.

When I started up with him again, he contorted my body in ways that I would be feeling for days. At one point, he restrained my hands and wouldn't allow me to touch him. I was writhing on the bed while he fucked me mercilessly. I wouldn't stand for it, though. I was able to get on top of him and I yanked the cord from the lamp out of the wall and tied his wrists to the headboard. When I woke up in the morning, he was still in the same position.

I purposely left him tied up. He assumed it was so I could wake him in some kinky fashion, but actually I needed this time to search his house. I needed some information on him if my plan to screw with him would work. I crept downstairs and started in his study. I went through all his drawers, but there was nothing of interest in those. He had filing cabinets, but they were all locked. On his desk, he had a file folder marked VAS. I scanned through it and it looked to be reports, plans, and projections for a new project of his. Vira had told me that he owned a construction company with a friend, so I was assuming this was a new build.

When I found nothing else of use in his study, I looked through the drawers in the kitchen, but found nothing there. I went to the backdoor where the mudroom was. Cabinets hung above the washer and dryer, all filled with little baskets. One was labeled spare keys. I snatched it off the shelf and rummaged through the keys. I found a spare key to his house and quickly grabbed it and put the box back. When everything was back in place, I went over to my purse and stashed the key inside.

I went through his refrigerator and noted the huge supply of beer, but also a shit ton of health food. I could appreciate that, as I also liked to eat healthy. He had protein powder for shakes and some granola bars in one cabinet. The others had canned goods and other pantry staples.

His house was clean and modern, and he didn't have a lot of personal items around. His dvd cabinet was filled with historical movies and action flicks. He had every *Fast and Furious* movie, and I had never seen one. I had no interest in cars, and the only reason I knew his was a 429 Boss was because I remembered him telling me a long time ago that his dad was looking at it for them to rehab. At the time, I wanted to learn everything about it so I could talk about cars with him. Turns out, we broke up before his dad bought it. So now I had a lot of information on one type of car and really didn't know much else.

My next stop was his bathroom upstairs. The master bath was attached to his bedroom, so I took my time snooping in there. His bathroom was pretty standard for a man. He didn't have a lot of stuff, just a few extras for when he ran out of what was already open. I went to the bathroom and washed my hands. I was about to go back out to the bedroom when I heard the sound of shattering glass. I opened the bedroom door and saw Logan on the bed, struggling with the cord from the lamp that was now on the ground in pieces.

I sauntered out of the bathroom, pulling his t-shirt over my head and throwing it to the ground. His eyes narrowed in on my breasts and he stopped struggling.

"I never said it was time to get up. I'm ready for round three."

I climbed on top of him and soon we were both moaning with pleasure. I rode him hard and made sure he enjoyed every minute that he was inside me, because when I was done, I would be leaving him in a bit of a predicament. While he was catching his breath, I leaned forward and distracted him with my boobs hanging in his face. He thought I was undoing the cord from his wrists, but I was really making sure it was tight enough. When I got up and started pulling my clothes on, he finally realized what was going on.

"What the fuck are you doing? Untie me now."

"I like you all tied up like this. I'm sure you'll find a way out."

"Cece, this isn't funny. Get your ass over here and untie me."

I waved my fingers at him and headed downstairs. I wasn't actually that mean. I went to the kitchen and then headed back upstairs. I saw a look of relief cross over his face as I approached him. I took the coffee filter and opened it up to make a teepee and then stuck it over his cock.

"Now you won't be embarrassed when someone comes to help you."

I kissed his cheek and he turned his head quickly to bite my lip. I tasted blood and kissed him deeply. My hand trailed down to his cock and I felt him thicken under my touch. When I had him good and hard, I pulled back and replaced the teepee.

"I have to get going, but I'll see you soon, lover."

"Cece, the next time I see you, I'm gonna spank that ass raw."

"I'm counting on it."

I turned and walked out the door, sending Vira a text that she needed to send Sean over to release Logan. I laughed the whole way to my cab and all the way home. I had never had such a fun night or left a man so satisfied. This was going to be a lot of fun.

When I walked in the door to my apartment, Vira bombarded me with questions.

"What do you mean, release Logan? Sean was hounding me with questions this morning. Please tell me this was something kinky and I don't need to worry about finding a place to bury a body."

"Relax, Vira. I just tied Logan up with a cord and left him naked on his bed."

Vira burst out laughing, covering her eyes with her hands as tears leaked out. "Oh my gosh. Sean is going to walk in on him naked and have to get him untied. That's hilarious."

"I didn't leave him totally naked. I left a coffee filter covering his dick."

Vira's phone started pinging with messages. She went over to check them and read them off to me.

Tell Cece I said thanks.
That was definitely not the way I wanted to see my friend.
What did they do to the bedroom? It's trashed.

Then she started laughing.

"What? What does it say?"

"Nope. The last text is just for me."

I walked over to the coffee pot and poured myself a cup and added cream and sugar. "So, I take it last night went well with Sean?"

"Oh yeah. He's yummy. I think he could be my new fuck buddy."

"You want to replace Kyle?"

"Hell no. He's definitely gone, but I have no desire to find another man to start clinging to me. I like my life the way it is, but Sean is definitely good enough for seconds and thirds."

"Well, you're gonna have to keep him around longer than that. We need him to be our ears, so don't screw him over yet. You have to keep him in your good graces for a little bit longer."

"No problem there. I can take one for the team on this one. It's definitely beneficial for me also."

"Aww. I love you more than my luggage."

"I'd dodge a bullet for you."

"I'd bury a body for you."

"You may need to by the time our plan is finished. So, come on. Tell me all about your night and what you found out about your new main squeeze."

I walked over to the living room and sat down on the couch, pulling my knees up to my chest. "Well, I didn't really find out a whole lot about him. He doesn't have any personal items laying around and his paperwork is all locked up in his filing cabinets. I didn't have the time to snoop properly. I did, however, get a copy of his house key."

"Nice."

"I have a few ideas of things I'd like to do."

"Such as?"

"Well, I was thinking of flooding his house. I could sneak in and clog his drains or something and run the kitchen faucet. When he gets home from work, he'll have a big surprise. I'll find a way to do it so it looks like an accident, and since I have a spare key, there will be no need to break in. Plus, he doesn't have a security system, so that's one more thing I don't have to worry about."

"Make sure you don't park on his street. Park a few streets over and sneak through his neighbor's yards."

"Definitely."

"What else you got?"

"He has this really nice car. It's a Mustang Boss 429. It's quite special to him. When we were dating ten years ago, I remember his dad was thinking of buying it for him so they could restore the car. Anyway, they did and it's his baby. I don't want to destroy it, but it's something special to him, so I need to find out something to do to his precious baby."

"Man, you're going for the throat. Isn't that car worth a lot of money?"

"Yep. By the time I'm done with him, he's gonna wish he had never messed with me."

Vira raised her coffee mug in the air and I did the same, clinking my cup against hers.

"To revenge on cruel men," she said with a smile.

"To revenge."

I hadn't heard from Logan the rest of the weekend, which was fine with me because I didn't need him taking up all my time. If I thought about him too much or saw him too much, I might end up going down the same path I had gone down before with him, and there was no way I could allow that to happen. He was a part of my past and my new version of Cecelia didn't allow shit like that to happen to her. I was stronger, but I needed this to help me move past the memories he left behind.

When Vira told me on Monday that Logan had called Sean, asking for help getting my number, I knew we were on the right path. The next phase of my plans were going into effect today. I had spent the weekend not thinking about him, but now it was time to get things back on track. I just had to keep drawing him in.

I didn't have to be at the office until nine, so I headed over to Logan's around eight-fifteen, since he usually left about seven-thirty. I drove past his house once and saw his truck was gone. He always parked his car in the garage, but his truck was what he drove to work. I parked a few blocks over and walked to his house, slipping in the back door. His neighborhood was very quiet and I didn't see a lot of prying eyes. I made sure to wear a hat so no one could recognize my hair color, and I wore sweatpants and a sweatshirt. I looked like I was out for a morning walk.

I made quick work of setting my plan in motion. Lucky for me, Logan had left his dishes in the sink this morning. I made sure the drain stopper was pushed all the way down and saw that his plate was already covering the drain. I used my sleeve to push the faucet handle up and let the water run. It wouldn't take long to fill and soon, it would be overflowing onto his floors. I smiled in satisfaction. It didn't take long, but it would be a bitch to clean up.

I let myself back out, making sure to lock the door and headed back to my car. I brought a change of clothes with me and I changed in my car on a side road before heading to work. By the time I pulled into the parking lot at work, nobody would have guessed that I spent my morning getting revenge. I looked like the perfect marketing professional.

I still had time to spare before I had to be at work. That went a lot faster than I thought, so I gave Vira a call to fill her in.

"Hello?"

"Hey. It's me. I did it."

"Everything went okay? You're sure you weren't seen?"

"Well, I might have been seen, but I was dressed like I was out for a morning walk. I don't think anyone would suspect a thing. I was in and out in under five minutes."

"Good. I talked to Eric this morning and told him that you had an ex-boyfriend harassing you. I told him you didn't want to press charges, but maybe we could have a little fun with him. I gave him Logan's name and asked him to keep an eye out for him. He said that he and a few of his friends could keep an extra close eye on him."

"Perfect. Thanks for your help, Vira. I gotta get to work. See ya later, chica."

Checking the clock again, I still had time to kill. I pulled out of the lot and headed into the downtown area for a cup of coffee. Imagine my surprise when I saw Logan parking just down the road from the cafe. He shouldn't be here this late in the morning, but it would work to my advantage. When he got out, I casually got out of my own car and headed towards the cafe, looking at my phone.

I strolled into the cafe and waited in line behind him, still looking at my phone. After a minute he turned and did a double take when he saw me. Gotcha! He turned all the way around and crowded my space, pulling my phone from my hands. I feigned indignation, like I didn't know he was standing there.

"Hey! Excuse me, that's my phone. Give it back."

I looked up at him, masking my face in shock. Then I let a slow smirk spread across my face. He was still the sexiest man I knew. Part of me wished that things would have turned out differently between us. We would have made a great couple. However, if things hadn't gone the way they had, I wouldn't be the woman I am today, and we wouldn't have the explosive chemistry that we did.

Besides, once he found out who I really was, we'd lose everything that gave us that spark. I was here for revenge, and that was it. He would no longer see me as the innocent girl from his past, but the woman who played him. And I was okay with that, because making him suffer was all I cared about at the moment. He was still the cocky asshole that I used to know. Although, back then I didn't consider him an asshole. Well, at least not until he broke my heart.

I leaned into him and slipped my finger slightly inside his pants and ran my finger along the band.

"I see you were able to free yourself. I hope it didn't take too long to get loose."

"A friend stopped by and helped me out."

He ran his hand up the back of my neck, under my hair and grasped my neck tightly. His mouth brushed against my ear and my pulse quickened in excitement. Even if I was having my revenge, I could still have some fun in the meantime.

"Next time, I'm going to tie you to the bed and I'm gonna make good on my promise to spank your ass raw."

His tongue darted out and licked the shell of my ear. A shiver ran down my spine at the promise in his threat. I clenched my thighs together to control the throbbing in my pussy. I turned my head, brushing my lips over his, and nipped at his lip.

"I'll be waiting. Don't disappoint me."

Then I stepped back and snatched my phone, ignoring the smoldering glare that he gave me. The barista called for him to step forward and after a beat, he finally turned and ordered his drink. He gave the woman a twenty and told her to pay for my drink also, and then keep the change. He moved to the pick up area and snagged his coffee, shooting me a sexy grin, before heading out the door.

I stepped up to the counter and ordered my drink, then headed back to my car once I got my coffee. As I stepped out of the cafe, I placed my sunglasses back on my face and sauntered back to my car. I had him right where I wanted him. Revenge was sweet.

CHAPTER 6

LOGAN

SEEING Cece in the cafe this morning had my pulse skyrocketing. She was so confident when she talked to me and didn't seem the least bit concerned that I might be upset over the way she left me the other night. Her sultry voice drew me in and had me begging for more. I was going to get payback next weekend, and I had a whole week to plan out what I would do to her. I didn't have time to think about it now with all the new projects in development at work, so it would have to wait until I got home.

I headed to work after I left the cafe and my thoughts drifted to her leaving me tied up on my bed. The little minx had turned me on and then left me completely naked. Well, she did leave a coffee filter covering my dick. Thank God, because Sean let himself into my house a half hour later.

"What the fuck is going on? Why are you tied up?"

"Cece thought it would be funny to tie me up and leave me naked. What are you doing here?"

Sean walked over to the headboard and started undoing the cord wrapped around my wrists. "Cece sent Vira a text that I needed to come release you. I wasn't exactly expecting this."

The blood flowed freely through my hands once again as my hands were untied. Sean threw sweatpants at me and turned around. I was grateful that she had left my dick covered. No man needed to see another man's junk.

"She's a wildcat. I wasn't expecting it from her, but damn, it was a good night."

"A good night? She left you tied to a bed."

"Yeah." I sighed with a smile. "It was well worth it. Don't worry, I'll get her back."

"I'm not worried. Just don't involve me in your kinky shit."

"So, I'm guessing you had a good time with Vira last night?"

He laughed and ran a hand over his jaw. "Yeah, she's definitely a good time."

"Enough said." I smacked him on the shoulder and we went downstairs. After he left, I spent the rest of the day trying to get stuff done around the house, but my thoughts kept drifting to the sexy woman that I couldn't get enough of.

I was pulled from my thoughts by the sound of sirens behind me. I pulled over to the side as I looked down at my speedometer. I didn't think I was speeding, but honestly, I was lost in my thoughts and wasn't really paying attention. I stopped the truck on the side of the road and got out my license and registration. I rolled down my window and waited for the officer to approach. Fuck. It was the douchebag, Officer Sawyer.

"Do you know why I pulled you over?"

"No, officer, I don't."

"You were going forty-two in a forty mile an hour zone."

Seriously? He's pulling me over for going two miles over? I told myself to stay calm. Punching this asshole would only land me in jail.

"Sorry. I didn't realize I was going that fast."

"You didn't pay attention to how fast you were going?"

The officer had his hands on his hips and was glaring at me through his sunglasses. This was the dick that had arrested Harper, Jack's wife, at Thanksgiving. He was a total asshole and I knew it was best not to push him, but my mouth wasn't getting the message.

"I just didn't realize I was going a whole two miles an hour over."

"Maybe next time you should pay more attention to your driving and think less about getting your dick wet."

"Excuse me? You want to say that again, asshole?"

Although partially true, there was no way this guy could know what I was thinking about. This guy was all about how many tickets he could get in one month. Sean hated the guy and told all of us to avoid him and his friends at all costs. He would push the law as far as he could and use any excuse to arrest you. That was something I found out moments later when my door opened and I was dragged out of my truck.

I was thrown to the ground on my belly and my arms were yanked behind my back. His knee dug into my back as he wrapped the cuffs tightly around my wrists. That was twice in a matter of days that I was tied up. I didn't appreciate this one. He hauled me up by my arms as he read me my Miranda rights. I knew better than to open my mouth and say anything further. I knew what this cop was doing wasn't right, but I would be out in no time. He didn't have anything to bring me in on.

I was tossed, none to gently, into the back of the cruiser while he called for a tow truck to haul away my truck. This was a hell of a way to start my day. I had shit to get done at the office and this was going to put me behind. Not to mention, Ryan was gonna chew me out for getting myself arrested. He was going to have to come bail me out, and it would piss him off.

An hour later, I was walking out of the police station. Sean had been at his desk when I was brought in and immediately got in Sawyer's face wanting to know why I was in cuffs. When Sawyer told him that I had mouthed off during a traffic stop, Sean stormed into his boss' office. I heard his raised voice as he told him exactly what he thought of Sawyer and his abuse of authority. I was tossed in a cell while the chief got the story from Sawyer. Apparently what Sawyer said pissed off the chief because I was released with his sincerest apologies.

I waved him off because I knew it wasn't his fault he had an asshole police officer on the force. The chief gave Sean permission to drive me to retrieve my truck.

"Okay, I heard Sawyer's version of what happened. How about you tell me what really happened."

I relayed what happened and told him I was dragged out of the truck and thrown on the ground. Sean was fuming by the time I was done with the story.

"Dammit, Logan. I've told you that guy's an asshole. Next time, don't poke the bear. He's gonna have it out for you now because you made him look bad in front of the chief."

"Seriously, I was going two miles over the speed limit. That was a dick move on his part."

"Yeah, it was, but two miles over is still speeding and he can legally pull you over for it. If he pulls you over again, just shut your mouth and only respond with polite statements. He's gonna look for any reason to get you now."

We pulled into the lot of the towing company and I got out of the squad car. "Thanks for the lift. I'll keep your suggestions in mind." I shut the door and went inside to get my truck. This day had turned to shit real fast, and I was already ready for it to be over.

I was ready to call it a day. When I got back to the office, the day just got worse. My morning coffee was left in my truck, and by the time I got it back, it was cold. The office coffee was crap and I couldn't be forced to drink it if you poured it down my throat. I seriously needed a good cup of coffee, but as soon as I walked through the door, I was bombarded with problems.

Ryan's secretary had been waiting for me by my office and

insisted I go straight to his office. I set down my bag and headed over there right away.

"Where the hell have you been?"

"I got pulled over and hauled into the police station for calling Sawyer an asshole."

I plunked down in the seat across from him with a sigh. I really didn't need to get my ass reamed right now.

"Logan, seriously, we can't deal with this shit right now. We're trying to make the company grow. Getting arrested does not look good for our image."

"The chief dropped the charges and I was free to leave. Besides, I've never done anything to give this company a bad image."

"You're excellent at your job and I couldn't ask for a better partner, but one of these days, your extracurricular activities are going to get us in trouble. You screw anything in sight, and you don't give a shit about anything. Everything just rolls off your back. One of these days, it's going to screw us over."

My friends were always underestimating me. I wasn't a screw up, but they had very little faith in me outside of work. Maybe I earned that in some way, but to decide that today's traffic stop was my fault without the details was harsh. The anger was building inside me, and I needed to get out of there before I said something I'd regret.

"Can we get this meeting over with? I have a lot of shit to get done today."

Ryan shook his head, but moved on to the next subject.

"We got underbid on the new building downtown. That's a big loss for us. The recognition for that building could have brought in a lot of business for us."

"We can't do projects at cost. I know we agreed on the VAS project, but that's different. That's for a good cause. I looked over the project numbers myself and they looked pretty good. We can't win 'em all, Ryan. There's no point in staying upset. Let's move on."

"That kind of attitude will not help us."

"No, that kind of attitude will keep us from underbidding

ourselves and devaluing the company. If we don't make enough to pay our employees, we're gonna have a hard time taking on new projects."

"Shit," he sighed, rubbing his eyes. "I know you're right. I just really wanted that project."

"There will be another project. Besides, the VAS project could be very good for us if we do it right. Speaking of which, I need to check in with the design team and see how it's going."

I stood, eager to get out of his office. Ryan was lost in thought, staring out his window, so I made my exit quickly. I got back to my office and checked all my emails before returning phone calls. It took me until lunch to catch up on my early morning routine. I worked through lunch so I could stay on top of what needed to be done. The design team was almost done on their end, so I made an appointment with them for three o'clock.

After that, the day flew by. I had several more meetings to attend, and I had to work late to make up for my late start. I headed out the door at seven, later than usual, but I was still usually the last to leave, along with Ryan.

Driving home, I was extra cautious about my speed to avoid any more problems with the police. I was mentally exhausted after today and just wanted to go chill on the couch with a beer and watch a game. I didn't care what game, just something that didn't require me to think. I stepped inside the front door and slipped immediately, falling on my ass on the tile floor. Shit, that hurt. What the fuck?

As I stood up, water dripped from my clothes in thick droplets to the floor. I flipped on the entryway light and saw water all over my floor. I flicked on some more lights as I walked through the house, stopping in the kitchen when I heard the water running. I turned on the kitchen light and saw my sink overflowing with water. Stepping over to the sink, I saw my plate from this morning covering the drain, the other sink plugged with the strainer, and the faucet turned on part way. I shut the water off, pulled the plug in one side, and removed the plate from the other.

I walked through the house to see the extent of the damage. The place was sitting in a thin layer of water for most of the first floor. I shut down the power to the house and searched for the number for a cleanup crew. I could do it myself, but I didn't have the time for it. I had a big meeting tomorrow and I couldn't afford the distraction.

I scrolled through my phone, but I couldn't find the number of the guys we normally used. Sighing, I called Ryan.

"What do you want?"

"I need the number of the cleanup crew."

He let out a deep breath. "Shit. Which project?"

"None of them. It's for my house."

"Your house? What happened?"

"Fuck if I know. I came home and the whole downstairs was flooded."

"How?"

"The water in the sink was running and both sides were plugged up."

He let out a small laugh. "Are you fucking with me? You left the water running?"

I ran my hand over my face. I really wasn't in the mood for this right now. "Do you have the number or not?"

"Hold on," he chuckled. "I'll grab it for you."

"Thanks, man."

"Okay, here it is. I'll text it to you. Hey, do you mind doing a three way?"

"I hope you're talking about a phone call."

"Well, I'm not doing a three way with you," he grunted.

"Do I want to know why you want to be in on the call?"

I could hear the grin in his voice before he even spoke. "No reason. I just want to listen in as you tell them how you flooded your own house by leaving the water on."

"Fuck you very much."

I hung up and called the cleanup crew, leaving out any major details that could get me harassed any further. Fuck this day. I headed to the hotel in town and grabbed a room, but it was still bugging me that the water was left on. I couldn't remember even turning on the water in the sink this morning. I tossed and turned all night, trying to figure out how the hell that had happened.

The next morning, I headed off to the cafe as usual, but when I walked through the door, I saw someone I wasn't expecting. My little sex kitten. How was it possible that I had been coming to this coffee shop for years and never managed to run into her before? I walked up behind her and wrapped an arm around her waist, drawing her closer to me.

"How is it that I've never seen you here before?"

I felt her relax into my body and she wiggled her ass against my crotch. Damn. I didn't need a boner right now. I had to get to work, and I couldn't afford the distraction, but she was too tempting.

"I just moved to town. This has become my new morning coffee shop."

Her hand rested on my arm and her nail scratched against my hand when she started moving her fingers against my skin.

"I'm staying at the Hillside Hotel for the week. Room three-twelve, seven o'clock tonight. Don't be late."

I nipped at her ear and then stepped around her to place my order, paying for hers also. Then I left and got to work. I made sure to drive the speed limit all the way to work and watched for police cars the whole way. Our meeting with Cassandra from VAS was at ten, so I went through my routine of checking emails and returning phone calls. The head of our interior design department, Cheryl, brought the final designs by my office at eight-thirty, and I looked them over, making sure everything was in order.

Ryan and I left at nine forty-five and I parked in front of their offices. The meeting was with a few veterans, some other designers from other veteran buildings, and Cassandra. She had wanted their input on our plans, but they looked great, so I wasn't worried that she wouldn't be one hundred percent satisfied.

When the meeting was over, an hour later, Cassandra was thoroughly pleased with our plans. She still had to take the plans to the investors for approval, but she promised to call us next week after the meeting. Ryan and I were feeling pretty good when we walked out of the office. That is, until I saw a ticket under the wiper blade of my truck.

"What the fuck? What could I possibly have gotten a ticket for?"

I snatched the ticket from the windshield and read the citation. Apparently I was parked in a no parking zone. I looked at the sign and saw the front end of my truck was about six inches past the sign. The officer's name was Calloway, but I had no doubt he was buddies with Sawyer.

"What's the ticket for?"

"Parking in a no parking zone."

"Dude, you're not even a foot past the sign."

"I know," I said as I climbed in the truck. I threw the ticket on the dashboard and started the truck, pulling out into traffic.

"Did you piss someone off?"

"Other than Sawyer? Not sure, but he had a hard on for me as soon as he stopped me yesterday. I hadn't even met the guy until yesterday."

"Maybe you fucked his sister."

"Why is it that as soon as something happens, you automatically assume that I screwed up? Fuck you."

I wasn't in the mood to deal with this shit. I needed to get back to the office and get away from him before I destroyed our partnership. I was on the verge of saying shit that didn't need to be said, and it wouldn't be good for our business or our friendship. We drove in silence the rest of the way to the office and went our separate ways. I avoided him the rest of the day and left the office at six. I'd had enough shit happen this week to last me a year, and I was ready to get the hell out of there.

I drove to the hotel and got cleaned up, awaiting the arrival of my guest. She showed up right on time, wearing a trench coat tied at the waist. Her hair tumbled over her shoulders and her makeup was flawless. She carried a small overnight bag, which meant she would be staying the night with me.

I opened the door all the way to let her in, watching her sway her hips as she walked further into the room. My cock hardened as I thought of all the possibilities of what was under that trench coat. I needed to let off some steam and her ass was my target. I shut the door, smiling at all the fun I would be having tonight.

"Take off your coat," I commanded.

She undid the belt of her coat and then slowly slipped the buttons through the holes. She pulled at the collar and opened her coat, revealing a red lacy bra and matching panties. She had on garter belts attached to thigh highs. I groaned as I took her in, my dick becoming painfully hard. She looked spectacular. The coat slid from her shoulders and down past her fingertips, falling to the ground. I prowled over to her, ready to attack, coming within an inch of her body. I could feel her breasts brush against me as my chest rose with every harsh breath.

I brushed my hand across her hip, my fingers trailing along her hip bone and up the side of her breast. Tracing the mounds of her breasts, I slid my hand up her neck. Her skin was so soft, and begged to have my tongue all over her. But first, she had to be punished. I had a feeling that she left me tied to that bed to see how I would react, and she was about to find out.

I brushed my lips along her jawline and over her beautiful, plump lips. Her breathing became ragged with every little touch. My lips skimmed over her ear, tantalizing her with every breath, but then I stepped back and smirked at the confused look on her face.

"Get on your knees on the bed, ass in the air."

My tone was harsh and I could see the excitement dance in her eyes. I didn't normally have rough sex, but it was good with her. She walked over to the bed and brought one knee up to the bed as she looked over her shoulder at me. She fluttered her eyelashes at me with a come hither look. I didn't take the bait. I knew exactly what I wanted to do to her, and she would go along with it. She finished climbing on the bed and got on all fours with her sweet ass facing me.

I took my shirt off and shucked my pants, standing nude behind her. I traced my hand over the curve of her ass, then drew it back and slapped her hard.

"Ahh," she cried after the first smack. I pulled back again and repeated it, slapping a little harder every time. Her moans filled the room and I felt my anger from the day leaching from my body. My handprint made a red outline on her ass, so I moved to the other side.

"You think it was a good idea to leave me tied up to my bed?"

"Yes." That earned her another hard slap.

"Why'd you do it?"

"Because I wanted to leave my mark on you."

I caressed her ass before pulling back and smacking her again. "Well, now I'm gonna leave my mark on you."

I smacked her a few more times before running my fingers along the back of her thong and down underneath her panties. I felt the wetness before I reached her pussy. She was soaked for me. I ran my hands along her seam and spread her juices up to her clit, rubbing small circles over the nub. She moaned and pushed her ass closer to me. I flicked her bra open and pulled the straps off her shoulder. My hands were drawn to her luscious breasts, my fingers brushing over her taut nipples.

I needed to be inside her now. I lined my cock up with her pussy and pulled her panties to the side. I rammed inside her, stopping when I was buried deep inside her. It was just as good as I remembered, hot, wet, and tight. I was going to take her all night long and work out all my frustrations on her delectable body.

CHAPTER 7

CECE

WITH MY ASS in the air and every crack of his palm against my skin, my center grew more wet. I'd never been so turned on by a man and he knew it based on the sounds coming from my mouth, but he wouldn't get his way the whole night. I wasn't into submission. I was into equal opportunity rough sex for both of us.

I bit my lip as he rammed inside me. His hard cock went so deep, every thrust felt like he was hitting my cervix. His hard breaths increased as his thrusts came harder and faster. I was so caught up in how good he was that I didn't realize I hadn't had my way with him yet. I was so lost in him, and that wasn't a good thing. I needed to keep my distance, but maybe after this orgasm. There would always be time for distance later.

My scalp burned as he yanked my hair back, holding my head up as he used my hair like reins on a horse. My orgasm rushed through me and my pussy clenched down on him, making his thrusts ragged. I barely heard him scream my name as he came inside me.

When he released my hair, I collapsed onto the mattress on my tummy, panting hard and barely able to move. He flopped down on the bed next to me and pulled me back against him. Umm. That was not happening. I didn't snuggle. I rolled away from him and put some space between us. His brows furrowed in question, but he didn't say anything. As my breathing calmed, I thought about just going home. I had been satisfied and I didn't need any more for the night, especially if he was going to try to cuddle with me. I didn't need that shit.

"You got a problem with lying next to me?"

"I don't cuddle. If you want to cuddle, get a teddy bear."

His eyes narrowed slightly, but he recovered quickly with a handsome smile. It was best to set boundaries now. I closed my eyes and relaxed into the covers.

"So, why are you staying in a hotel?"

"My house flooded."

I hid my smile and pretended to be totally clueless. "You don't live on the river. How did your house flood?"

"Apparently, I left the water on and the drain was covered. Funny thing is, I don't remember even turning on the water yesterday morning."

He was staring at the ceiling, running his hand over his chest. I watched his chest rise and fall with every breath, and my gaze skimmed over his beautiful body, taking in every mouth watering feature. He had some pretty impressive arms. If he were to wrap them around my neck, they would crush my windpipe in seconds.

"That sucks. How long will it take to clean up?"

"I don't know. They were working on getting all the water out yesterday and drying it out. Then they'll have to assess the damage." He huffed and ran a hand over his head. "It sucks because I built that house a few years ago when Ryan and I got the company off the ground. I designed it myself, so I'm not too happy about it being damaged."

I would be lying if I said I wasn't doing a happy dance inside. I had never been one to wish bad things on anyone, but knowing that I was getting my revenge, causing him water damage to a house that he loved so much, felt really good. Of course, he wouldn't know it was me yet. I still had plenty more in store for him. I did my best to school my features, not wanting to give away my joy at his predicament.

"So, I can find you here for the foreseeable future?"

He hesitated for a minute as if he wanted to consider something first. "What is this?"

"Umm, it's called sex, Logan. Surely, I don't need to explain that to you. You seem pretty well versed."

He turned to me, a sexy grin on his face. "I want to take you out sometime."

I shook my head, returning my own grin. "I don't date. The sex is great between us. Let's not complicate things."

"Usually that's my line."

"Then by all means, use it."

He smirked at me and I could tell he wanted to say more, but he let it go. My plan was going great. I had him buying my coffee, begging me for nights with him, and I even damaged his house. It wasn't bad work for the first week.

But I had to be careful now. I was so attracted to him that I was starting to crave him. The sex was unbelievable, and afterward, I started to see little pieces of the old Logan, the one that broke my heart. But every time he brushed his fingers over my skin, the anger inside me dulled, making me forget what I was doing. I had to keep in mind that the last time he was mine, he crushed me, and given the chance, he would do it again.

My plan when I showed up for the night was to draw him in, make him crave me more and more, but never really give myself over to him. It was a fine line that I was walking, but I was betting on the fact that he was a ladies' man and would get tired of me eventually. It would be just enough time to get my revenge before he got sick of me and left. But this time, I would be the one walking away happy.

I let my eyes slide shut and drifted off to sleep. I woke sometime later to the feeling of warmth all around me. I pried my eyes open to see the comforter over me and Logan's arm wrapped around me.

What the fuck? I told him I didn't snuggle. This shit didn't fly with me.

I threw the covers off and straddled his hips. I brought my hand back and laid a decent slap across his face. He startled awake, his eyes flying open.

"What the fuck did I say about cuddling?"

He looked confused as hell, and maybe even a little pissed. Good, because I was even more pissed. "Excuse me?"

"I woke up to your arm wrapped around me. Don't let it happen again."

His cock hardened under me and I moved my hips over his growing length. My moisture coated him, making it easier to grind against him. I moaned and closed my eyes, running my hands up under my hair and thrusting my breasts forward. Logan pushed his hips up, his cock centimeters from entering me. I sat up and angled myself over him, then sank down until he was buried inside me.

His hands cupped my breasts, pinching and pulling, causing my core to clench. My nipples started to burn with pain because of how rough he was being. I clenched tighter, strangling his cock with my pussy. A strangled noise tore from his throat.

"Fuck, you're gonna make me come if you keep doing that."

He sat up and carried me over to the desk, setting me down as he brushed stuff out of the way. Something sharp poked my ass and I reached behind me to find it was a letter opener. I grasped it in my hand and sliced down his bicep with it, drawing a thin line of blood.

He looked down at his arm, then glared at me as I smirked back.

"Watch yourself. You poked me in the ass with that."

"You give me a mark, I'll give you a mark. Only mine will be permanent. I'm gonna put my stamp on your ass, so every time I fuck you, I'll see you're mine."

"I'm not yours. I'm just here for a good time."

He thrust hard into me, wrapping his arms around my back, holding me to him. "Sweetheart, you may not know it, but you are mine and you always will be. I'm gonna fuck you so hard, you'll only remember my cock."

I panted with every thrust, digging my fingers into his back. I felt the blood under my fingers and I scratched him harder with every pound.

"Fuck, woman. You're gonna be the death of me."

"You have no idea."

He pushed me back on the desk and trailed his tongue down my body, biting my skin. Tiny little love bites covered my body, and I had no doubt there were teeth impressions on my skin. He paid extra attention to my breasts and nipples. It was almost painful, but for every bite, he stroked my clit, making me forget about everything else.

Within five minutes, we were both lying back on the bed, panting with exhaustion. I thought about getting up and going home, but I had to be up in four hours for work and I needed all the sleep I could get. I pulled the covers up over myself and rolled away from him, saying a half-hearted good night.

An alarm was going off somewhere, but my hands couldn't find it. I was knocking things over on my nightstand trying to find where the noise was coming from. Finally, I pried my eyes open to see that I wasn't in my room and there was no alarm on the nightstand. The noise cut off and I rolled over to see Logan's arm stretched over, resting on top of the alarm clock and his other hand thrown over his eyes. I took a minute to study his face in the early morning light. His features were harder now than they were ten years ago. His jaw was more defined and he had more scruff to his face.

"See something you like?"

"If I didn't, I wouldn't have come over last night."

I flung the covers off and walked over to the bathroom completely nude. I didn't care about modesty right now. I wanted him to get a good view of what I had to offer.

"I need a shower. Care to join me?"

He jumped out of bed and practically ran into the bathroom with me where he proceeded to maul me in the shower. Half an hour later, he left the shower and let me get cleaned up. I only had regular clothes with me, so I needed to go back to my apartment this morning. I'd brought some toiletries with me, so I was able to blow dry my hair and make it look acceptable for work. I put on my makeup and exited the bathroom in my towel. My bag was sitting on the bed and Logan was fully dressed in his suit for work.

"So, you never told me what you do, Logan," I said as I started pulling out clothes to get dressed.

"I own a construction company with a buddy of mine."

"Really? That doesn't look like construction attire."

"Construction is just one side to the business. I run the architectural and interior design divisions of the company. My buddy, Ryan, runs the construction side."

"Impressive."

"What is it you do?"

"I'm in marketing. I'm working over at JNP Marketing."

"So, you said you just moved here. Where are you originally from?"

Well, that was a tricky question because I was originally from around here, so I told him instead where I had been the last ten years.

"Philadelphia."

"Does all your family live there?"

"No."

"Any brothers or sisters?"

I zipped my bag and stared at him. "Are we really going to do this? Seriously? I already told you I don't date."

"I wasn't aware that getting to know someone required a date. We're sleeping together. I don't see the harm in learning a little about you."

"Fine. I have a brother and a sister. Both of my parents are alive and divorced. My favorite food is Italian and my favorite color is blue.

I love summer and hate winter. I like going out dancing with Vira, and I have little patience for relationships or anything resembling one. I like to fuck and I'm not ashamed of that. If you want something more, you're gonna have to find it somewhere else." I crossed my arms over my chest and glared at him. "Is that enough for now or would you also like my bra size?"

"34C."

I narrowed my eyes at him and scowled. He held up his hands in surrender and walked closer to me. He gave me a quick kiss and pulled back.

"Thank you. That wasn't so hard, was it?"

"Whatever. I have to get home and get dressed so I can go to work."

I grabbed my bag and slung it over my shoulder and headed for the door. As I opened the door, it was immediately shoved closed and two arms trapped me against the door. His hands slipped around my waist and trailed down to the waistline of my yoga pants. His fingers slipped inside my panties and two fingers pushed inside me. His other hand slid around my throat, squeezing slightly.

"As long as we're sleeping together, this pussy is mine. No one else gets access to this. Understand?"

"I expect the same from you." He loosened his grip and I spun around grabbing his cock slightly harder than was necessary. His eyes flashed, the only hint that my grip was too tight. "Same time tonight?"

He nodded and I released my death grip on him. Reaching behind me, I turned the knob and let myself out into the hallway. By the time I got home and ready for work, I was running behind. There would be no stopping at the coffee shop this morning, so I would have to have the office coffee.

The day went by quickly and I met Logan again at the hotel that night. I took everything he gave me and we had a great time, but I didn't stay the night even though he bitched about it for a good fifteen minutes. I couldn't get in the habit of sleeping with him. He asked to take me out this weekend, but I needed a break from him. He was invading my thoughts and if I wasn't careful, I would end up with stars in my eyes.

Vira and I took the weekend to hang out with each other around the apartment. She really wanted to go out, but I just couldn't bring myself to get all dressed up this weekend. Besides, I wasn't in the mood to find a new man. Sean stopped by on Saturday night and I discreetly excused myself to my bedroom so I didn't have to hear Sean and Vira fucking. Vira was loud and Sean was quite the dirty talker. Like, seriously dirty. I had never heard such filthy talk in all my life.

Unfortunately, being only a room away did nothing to dull the sound emanating from her room. I finally fell asleep around three in the morning and vowed to find a place of my own in the next six months. I'd never get any sleep if I had to listen to Vira fucking people all night long.

I was up early making coffee because Vira and Sean had woken me up an hour ago when they started going at it again. When it sounded like they had finished, I decided that since I wasn't getting back to sleep, I was going to need some coffee.

Sean walked out of the bedroom, handcuffs in one hand and his shoes in the other. I blushed when I remembered some of the things I'd heard him say to her last night.

"Aw, come on now, Cece. Don't be shy. Remember, I've seen what you do to Logan."

"That may be true, but you couldn't give me a play by play."

He laughed at me and then slid his shoes on. "I gotta get to work. Catch ya later, darlin'."

"I hope you wash those handcuffs before you use them at work," I called as he walked out the door.

CHAPTER 8

LOGAN

SHE WAS TAKING over every thought I had. I was always distracted no matter what I was doing, and it was really fucking with my day. I saw her every morning to get coffee, and I gladly paid her tab, hoping that the gesture would keep me in her good graces.

About mid-week, I couldn't take it anymore and stopped by her work to take her to lunch. Knocking on her door, I grinned when she glanced up from what she was working on. Her smile turned into a frown immediately. That wasn't a good sign for me.

"Hey, I'm off to lunch. I thought I'd see if you want to join me."

"Um...I'm kind of busy."

"Right, but you have to eat lunch, right?"

A few people were staring at her through the glass walls, probably gossiping about her and the man standing in her doorway. That's where I got her. She didn't want to make a scene. She stood from her desk, grabbed her purse and walked over to me, pasting a smile on her face. We took the elevator down to the first floor in silence, but the minute we were out of the building, she grabbed my arm and pulled me aside.

"Let's get one thing straight here. I'm not your girlfriend. I don't do dinners and lunches. The only reason I came with you is because people heard you asking and I didn't want to come off as a bitch in my workplace. You don't get to just show up where I work."

I smirked at her hostile reaction. "Yeah, I'm a real dick taking you out for lunch."

"Just don't get any ideas. We aren't a couple and we never will be."

I walked right up into her space and kissed her hard. "Just so long as you remember that your ass is mine. Until we're through, you belong to me."

She reared back and glared at me. "I belong to nobody. When I decide we're through, I will fuck whoever I want, whenever I want."

"You keep telling yourself that, sweetheart."

She turned and continued to walk down the street to the little Italian restaurant a block away. We walked in and were seated by the front window where we sat in silence looking over our menus.

"Cece?"

I looked up to see a well manicured man walk up to our table and pull Cece out of her chair. He was easily six feet tall and wore a spiffy suit with slicked back hair.

"Greg. Oh my gosh. It's so good to see you. What are you doing here?"

Her eyes lit up when she talked to this guy and I got the distinct feeling that he had an advantage here over me. I decided to sit back and let things play out. I had no clue who this guy was, but if I tried to stake a claim on Cece, it wouldn't work.

"I came in to interview at JNP."

"No way! I work there."

"I know. That's part of the reason I wanted to transfer."

His grin was playful and I couldn't tell if he was hitting on her or not. I couldn't figure out the dynamic of their relationship. Had they fucked? Were they just friends?

"Please sit down and eat lunch with me."

She just ignored me. She didn't even ask if I was okay with him joining us. What the fuck? He sat down and they faced each other, catching up on shit. She didn't even introduce me. I wasn't about to sit here and be the schmuck that sat by as another guy moved in on my girl.

"I'm Logan. Sam, was it? Cece's never mentioned you," I interrupted when Cece continued to ignore me.

"Greg. I know Cece from Philadelphia. How do you two know each other?"

"I'm fucking her."

Yeah, I was pissing all over her, marking my territory like a dog. Cece didn't seem happy about it, but I had a feeling it wasn't because I had told Greg we were fucking, but because I was blatantly trying to make this douchebag uncomfortable.

Instead, though, something passed between Greg and Cece, making me feel like I was intruding. He was looking at her with eyes that said he remembered every inch of her body. Cece had a wistful look on her face, so I decided I was going to need to remind her of who she was with. It looked like I was going to have to stake my claim after all.

"She's not available right now, so if that's what you're looking for, you need to move on."

"Excuse me, Logan, but I don't believe you speak for me." Cece glared at me, but I just smiled back.

"I seem to remember you calling my name when you came all over my face, so for now, I do speak for you."

I ran my hand up her thigh, under her dress that had ridden up her thigh, and slid my fingers under her panties causing her to gasp. Greg's eyes were narrowed in on my hand, and I didn't give a fuck if he saw what I was doing. He was going to get the full picture real quick.

I leaned in and kissed her neck as I worked my fingers along her slit, feeling how wet she was for me. Her eyes fluttered shut and I heard her whimper under my touch. Greg's eyes were shooting daggers at me, but I didn't give a shit. Right when Cece was well and truly worked up, I pulled my fingers out and brought them to my mouth, licking her cream from my fingers.

Her lips parted slightly and her eyes were bright with desire. She stood suddenly, grabbing my arm and pulling me through the restaurant and out the front door. I had no idea where she was taking me and I didn't ask. We walked a few blocks when she suddenly pulled me into a motel on the corner. It was run down and where I imagined hookers took their Johns.

She walked up to the desk and asked for a room, but I had my wallet out before she could pay. There was no way my girl was paying for this shitty room. In minutes, we were down the hall and in a crappy room that looked like something out of *The Shining*. She threw me down on the bed and climbed on top of me. I could hear the wood cracking from the bed frame as she started ripping the clothes from my body.

She pulled her dress up and sank down on my cock, riding me hard and fast. I peeled the top of her dress down and sat up so I could lick her tits. I didn't know how much of this I could take. I wanted her so badly, and I didn't mind her being in control some of the time, but right now I felt like staking my claim on her body. I wanted her to surrender to me.

I spun her around to her back and loomed over her. Her breathing was erratic as her breasts heaved from the exertion of riding my cock. I slammed into her over and over. The bed creaked one final time before I heard the wood splintering. The far side of the bed collapsed and we rolled across the mattress, falling to the ground and into the leg of the desk. My back slammed into the desk and I instinctively covered Cece as the desk collapsed on top of us.

When I lifted my head, my eyes locked with Cece. She was trying her best not to laugh at our predicament. I grew harder inside her, needing to finish what we started. I pushed the desk off of my back and then slammed into her again. Her laughing ceased as a moan tore from her throat. The sounds of our bodies slapping together filled the room until we both came, screaming our releases.

I collapsed on top of her, panting hard and seeing spots. Damn. This woman was going to kill me. I crawled off of her and surveyed the damage to the room. One of the legs on the bed had broken and the desk had collapsed on the floor with its contents scattered around the small space. I walked around to the other side of the bed and collected my clothes as Cece sat up and pulled herself together. There wasn't much I could do in the way of cleaning up, so I left everything for the motel to clean up.

"Don't ever try to stake your claim on me like that again."

"Sweetheart, there was no trying. That douchebag didn't have a chance against me. Just face it. You're mine, and that's the way it's staying."

"I'm not anybody's, and if that's the way you're going to act, we can end this right now. So you decide, are we ending things or are you going to back off?"

There was no way I was ending things with her. She had gotten under my skin and I couldn't walk away if I wanted. I walked up to her and pulled her against me. "I'm not walking away and neither are you. I can try to tone it down, but that's all I can promise. When I'm around you, I just want to throw you over my shoulder and carry you to the closest room to fuck you."

"Fucking isn't our problem. I have to get back to work. Don't show up there again. What we have doesn't bleed into my everyday life. Can you handle that?"

I nodded and she turned and walked out the door. Sighing, I made sure I had everything before going to the front desk and dropping a few hundred for repairs to the room. It was time to get back to work.

CHAPTER 9

CECE

I WAS STARTING to lose focus on what I was doing. I talked a good game with Logan, but he was wearing me down. As much as I hated him claiming me in public, I was so turned on by his actions. Dragging him to the motel and fucking him seemed like the best solution.

Now I was back at work and having a hard time concentrating on the simple marketing plan in front of me. All I could think about was going back to Logan's hotel room tonight and all the dirty things we could do. A knock at the door startled me from my thoughts.

"Can I come in?"

Greg was standing in the doorway, looking charming as ever. I had slept with him once and he was great in bed. I never repeated, so he never thought there would be more. Still, his comments at the restaurant led me to believe he still wanted more with me. I was going to have to take care of that right away.

"Hey, did you interview already?"

"Yeah, I just finished up. I think it went well. I should know in a week or two. They still have more interviews to do."

"Well, I hope you get what you want."

He smiled, then stepped further into the office. "Listen, I hope I didn't cause any problems between you and your boyfriend earlier. I wasn't trying to, but he was pushing my buttons, so I thought I'd push back."

"He's not my boyfriend. You know how I work." I gave him a knowing look to which he chuckled.

"Yeah, I'm aware. One of these days you'll settle down, though. I'm not saying it will be with me, but I wouldn't be opposed to it."

"Greg, you know…"

He held up both hands in surrender. "I'm just saying, when there's an opening, keep me in mind."

"I'll do that, but there won't be."

"I've gotta get back to Philadelphia. It was good seeing you again."

"It was. Maybe we'll be seeing you around here soon."

"Here's hoping."

He left and I finally buckled down and got to work. I couldn't spend all day daydreaming, or Greg would be taking my job.

Friday was here in the blink of an eye and I had never been happier. I had successfully avoided Logan the rest of the week, but now I felt like a junkie needing her next fix. I texted Vira, making plans to go out tonight, but she had to work. Not that it mattered. For my plan to work, all I needed was to contact Logan. Even though he hadn't reached out to me the rest of the week, I knew he still wanted me. That hadn't just gone away over night.

A knock at my door had me shaking off those thoughts. Mr. Johnson, my boss, was standing there with a sheepish look on his face.

"How are you, Cece? Enjoying the job?"

"I love it," I said honestly. "Everyone's great." The office slut walked past my office and glared at me, but I ignored her. I wasn't looking to fuck the boss.

"That's good," he nodded thoughtfully. "And the workload isn't too much?"

"No, I'm pretty much finished up with my projects. I'm just waiting for a few last minute changes from the design team, and then I can put these projects to bed until the meetings."

"Good, good." He turned to go, but stopped, his finger resting just above his lip. "I was wondering...I have this project that just came up. It's right in your wheelhouse, and I think you'd do great on it."

"Of course," I said enthusiastically.

"It's just...I need everything by Monday morning. It came up at the last minute," he said apologetically. "And you're the only one without little kids at home. I know that's a terrible—"

"It's fine," I reassured him. "I really don't mind."

"You're sure."

"I love a good challenge. Send everything my way and I'll get started on it immediately."

His shoulders sagged in relief. "You have no idea how happy that makes me. Thank you so much for doing this."

"No problem."

But when the project came through, I deflated quickly. This wasn't a quick project. I was going to be here all night preparing for this project, and I'd have to ask a few of the design team to come in tomorrow to work with me. I quickly got to work, spending the morning working with the design department to come up with some boards for the meeting on Monday.

After the mockups were done, I still had a ton of research to do on the marketing side. It would be rough, but that was expected on such a tight schedule. Still, I wanted it to be as accurate as possible. Normally, I had weeks to go over all the information that I now only had a few days to go over.

The rest of the day flew by with so much work that I didn't think I'd leave the office before ten. A huge part of me wanted to sneak out and see Logan, but if I didn't finish the project for Monday, I would be letting down my boss, and that wasn't the way I wanted to start at this company. Besides, I didn't want Logan thinking that I would be available to him whenever he wanted. I needed to maintain distance from him.

It was about eight o'clock when my phone pinged, signaling a text. It was from Logan.

Logan: When is your sexy ass getting here?
Me: Working late tonight. Not sure when I'll be done, but then I'm going home.
Logan: You know what they say about all work and no play.
Me: Yes, I know, but did Jack have deadlines to meet?

I didn't get another message so I continued on with my project. My stomach was cramping from not eating and I really wanted to go get something to eat, but the sooner I finished, the sooner I could go home for the night. Still, something from the vending machines would hold me over until I could leave. I went through the main office area where the cubicles were and made my way to the break room. It was a little creepy at night because they turned off the main lights and just left the night time lights on, which were scattered throughout the walkways.

Standing in front of the vending machines, I saw that there weren't a whole lot of options that would fill me up, but I decided on a couple of Snickers bars. As I was putting in my money, my stomach let out a loud growl, telling me the monster would soon jump out of my stomach and eat whatever was available.

"You shouldn't skip dinner to work late."

I practically banged my head against the vending machine from standing so fast. I spun around to see Logan standing in the doorway holding Chinese food from a local takeout place.

I was about to grin, but then I remembered how much I was supposed to hate him and decided reprimanding him would be best.

"I didn't invite you to my office. When I said I was working, I meant that I was working and I didn't have time for you."

"I'm aware, but you still need to eat. So, let's go sit down and eat and then you can get back to work."

I quirked an eyebrow, channeling Scarlett O'Hara, and stepped forward seductively and pulled the tie away from his shirt, running my fingers down the length of the silk.

"Mr. Walker, why don't you step into my office and we can review your request."

His eyebrows shot up and a slow grin spread across his face. I put a little extra sway in my hips on the way to my office. I sat down behind my desk, back straight with my chest pushed out. I crossed one leg over the other, letting my skirt pull up my thigh. I saw the moment his eyes trailed over my skin because it felt like heat was emanating from his very pores.

"Mr. Walker, as your boss, I'm sure you're aware of certain procedures we have in this office for working late nights. We wouldn't want anyone to get the idea I was sexually harassing you. As your boss, I require you to sign some paperwork that you have agreed to work late in the office with me."

Logan sat back, steepling his fingers in front of him. "And just what would this paperwork entail?"

"It's very basic. It says that you have to do whatever I say to get the job done in a timely manner. After all, you're getting paid to be here and service me in any way I need."

He stood and walked around the desk toward me. I indicated a blank piece of paper on the desk and handed him a pen.

"Just write as I speak." He took the pen and leaned over the desk giving me a nice view of his ass. I brushed my hand between his legs, feeling his balls heavy in his pants. "I, Logan, promise to throw Cece across this desk." I cupped his balls and gave a slight squeeze. The only noise he made was a slight intake of breath. "I promise to fuck her hard and make her beg for my cock." My fingers undid his zipper and I could feel his length hardening underneath. "I will be sure that she comes several times before I do to ensure my work is at its peak performance." I grabbed onto the length of him and started stroking him. He spun back around and hauled me to him, kissing me breathless. I was so lost in the moment that I forgot I was supposed to be the one in charge.

Pulling back, I slapped him across the face. "Do that again and I'll file a sexual harassment charge, Mr. Walker. Now, eat my pussy."

Logan swiped all the paperwork off my desk and pushed me back so I was lying across the desk. He pulled the side zipper down on my skirt and pulled it off me before spreading my legs and latching on to my panty covered mound. I felt his hot tongue through the thin fabric, my body quaking in need. He ripped the panties from my body and let his tongue work its magic on me. I barely had time to think about how wrong this was to do this in my office or that my office walls were made of glass and if someone came back here, I would be caught and probably fired. For some reason, that made this so much hotter.

"Is this your marketing strategy for this particular product, Mr. Walker?"

"Since the product is Chinese food, I would suggest we take a different approach. Allow me to demonstrate."

Logan took the first box of Chinese, pulling up my shirt, and setting the hot noodles on my tummy. The juices ran down the sides of my stomach and Logan's tongue lapped at the free running juices. He slurped one noodle into his mouth, it's sticky juice leaving a trail across my skin. I slid one finger through the sauce, trailing it up my belly and circling my nipple. His eyes darkened as he watched me, then he was wrapping a noodle around my nipple, his lips tilting playfully.

He sucked at my nipple, sucking the noodle into his mouth as he bit playfully at my tight bud. I groaned, my fingers running through my hair as I tried not to lose control. But he didn't stop there. He did the same with my other breast, his other hand slipping down to my pussy, slowly pushing a finger in and out.

Out of the corner of my eye, I saw him grab something as he leaned in and licked my ear. "I think this egg roll needs some dipping sauce," he whispered.

I felt it at my entrance, never actually seeing what he was doing. Spreading my legs wider, I opened for him, his eyes piercing mine as he just barely rubbed the egg roll at my entrance. He didn't need more than that. I was already soaked and leaking all over. The scratchy texture ran over my clit, sending sparks through my body, but then it was gone, leaving me craving more. He brought the roll to his mouth, taking a bit of it with a wicked grin on his face.

I sat up and took him by the tie, forcing him to switch places with me. I noticed the sweet and sour sauce on the desk. Two could play this game. I yanked his belt open and pulled his pants down, then popped the lid on the sauce. Tipping the container, I watched his cock harden as I dribbled the sauce over his cock. I knelt before him and took his hard length into my mouth, sucking and licking every inch of him. Then I took the container of sweet and sour sauce and dipped his balls in. A hiss slipped from his lips, probably because the sauce was still a little hot, but I replaced the cup with my tongue and licked all the sauce from him. My face was covered in sweet and sour sauce, and the taste of Logan's pre-cum.

The next thing I knew I was bent over the desk and he was pounding into me from behind. With every thrust, my hips slammed into the metal desk, no doubt leaving bruises. In my attempt to grab ahold of the other side of the desk, I sent my pen holder flying, pens scattering across the floor.

Logan put his hands on my hips and gripped tight as he continued his assault on my body. I could feel my walls tightening around his cock, and I couldn't hold back when his hips picked up the pace and he slammed deeper and harder into me. I came with a scream, and a few seconds later, felt him still behind me.

His heavy weight dropped down on top of me as I lay my head down on the desk and closed my eyes. It was hard to get my breathing under control with his giant frame on top of mine, but I relished in the warmth of his body. Soon, reality came crashing down and I remembered that I was not supposed to be basking in the afterglow with him. I pushed him off me and started gathering my clothes to put back on.

"Alright, I have to get back to work, and now that we've made a mess of my office, I have even more work to do, so you can leave."

Logan grabbed my chin and forced me to look at him. "I'll help you clean up, and the little bit that you managed to get in your mouth would not be considered dinner."

"Oh, Logan. I never thought I'd hear you describe yourself as little. Surely you deserve a slightly better accolade."

"Honey, I wasn't describing my cock, and we both know it would never be described as little."

His fingers brushed my sex and swirled the juices still lingering. His fingers pumped inside me, leaving me completely unable to resist him. My eyes closed as he continued his ministrations on my body. His thumb rubbed my clit faster and faster as his fingers started thrusting in and out of me. Despite the near state of exhaustion I had just been in, my body was a live wire now. My legs began to tremble and my breathing accelerated. Logan stepped closer and wrapped his arm around my back, holding me against the desk. Sparks flew as my orgasm tore through me and I pulsed against his fingers. My legs gave out, but Logan held me up, slowly rubbing his fingers over my still throbbing pussy.

"You can push me away all you want, sweetheart, but I'll still be here waiting for you," he whispered in my ear.

I swallowed hard, knowing it was true. It was getting more and more difficult to keep Logan at arm's length. I needed to finish what I started with him before I got in too deep, but for now, I pretended that we were just two people that were deeply attracted to one another.

Logan pulled back and wiped his fingers on some napkins. "How about we get dressed and clean up. Then we'll eat and you can get back to work."

I raised an eyebrow at him.

"Yes, we will actually eat the food."

We quickly dressed and sorted through all the papers that had been thrown to the floor. After everything was neatly back in place on my desk, we sat on the floor with the food spread out in front of us.

"So, tell me, Cece, where did you learn that tantalizing dance you did with Vira in the club?"

I blushed at his reminder of the first night we met. "Well, I met Vira a long time ago and she helped me to open myself up and explore my sexuality. She took me to a lot of clubs and helped me to loosen up and not be afraid to have fun."

"So, that whole dance between you two was just a routine? You've never..."

"Are you asking if Vira and I have ever gotten dirty?"

"Well, I would be lying if I said the thought repulsed me. I think it's every guy's fantasy to see two women kissing and running their hands over each other."

"Wouldn't you like to know."

"Oh, come on. If you tell me, I'll tell you something I've never told anyone else."

"How good is it?"

"Oh, it's good. You don't want to miss out on this story."

I thought about it and decided that no matter what his story turned out to be, there was no harm in letting him in on this secret.

"What Vira and I do stays strictly on the dance floor. Now, that's not to say that we haven't done some dirty stuff to each other to garner the attentions of the opposite sex, but we've never had anything more than that."

"What kind of dirty stuff?"

"In order to get the answer to that, you're gonna have to spill your secret."

He rolled his eyes, huffing in irritation. When I looked down, I could see his length growing through his pants. Apparently talking about girl on girl action was something that really got Logan wound up.

"Fine. When I was in college, I spread this rumor that this really hot girl and I had been fucking. The rumor was that we were doing really dirty stuff all around campus. I'll spare you the details, but this girl couldn't go anywhere without being harassed by guys looking for a fun time with her. After a while, I felt bad because that hadn't been my intention. I just wanted her to notice me, and that was my stupid way of getting her attention. One night, she approached me in the dorms and told me she wanted to fuck me against the wall where anyone could see us. I was like, hell yeah, this girl is more kinky than I thought. So I went along with it. Apparently, her friends were in on it and they had attached zip ties to some rings that were on a bulletin board. After she got me stripped naked, she said she wanted to blindfold me, and I went along with it. Then she put my hands in the zip ties, and I was thinking I was about to get real lucky. It got awfully quiet for a few minutes and I kept calling out to her. Then I heard all this running and girls laughing. She had left me naked and pinned to the wall for everyone to see. Fortunately, since no one saw my whole face, they couldn't be certain it was me, but I definitely learned my lesson after that."

"How did you get out of there?"

"Well, the bulletin board wasn't secured to the wall all that well, so I took it down and a buddy guided me to a room where he helped me get loose. I hid out in his room all night and waited for everyone to go back to their rooms before I snuck back to mine. People speculated, of course, but no one was certain it was me."

Interesting. So I wasn't the first person to get revenge on this man. "Well, it serves you right. Shows you not to mess with people."

"What made you decide to go into marketing?"

I picked at my food while we talked and I tried to keep the subjects light. I no longer felt the need to kick him out of my office, but I also didn't want to get in too deep with him. We talked for another half hour before I decided it was time to get back to work.

"Thanks for dinner, Logan, but I need to finish up my work for the night. I have to finish up all this stuff for Monday."

He leaned toward me and swiped his tongue across my lower lip. "You have sauce on you."

His tongue traced my lips and his breath fanned across my face. I wanted to push him off. I wanted to keep him at a distance, but Logan was pushing past my barriers and making it difficult to keep my wits about me. He kissed me deeply and started crawling over my body, pushing me down to the floor. His body hovered over mine as his hand cupped my jaw. His kisses forced me into submission as he hiked up my skirt and I heard his belt buckle come free.

As he slid inside me, something changed. This was slower, less intense, yet even more intense. We weren't going at each other with some crazy passion. He was making love to me. I tried to avoid his eyes, but he held my face and soon his eyes captivated me. His thrusts were slow and deep, every one pulling me in deeper. His eyes stayed on me the entire time, forcing me to accept what he was doing to me. I couldn't look away. I couldn't deny any longer that I wanted him. I couldn't deny that what was between us was special. I wanted to roll him over and do things my way, but my body betrayed me and kept me anchored to him.

My release came slowly, unfurling deep from within. He pushed deep inside, pressing kisses along my temple and down to my jaw before placing a sweet kiss on my lips. We stayed like that for a good minute, just staring into each other's eyes. The ding of the elevator pulled me from the moment and I quickly bucked him off me and pulled my skirt down, smoothing my hair the best I could. Logan worked just as quickly to adjust his pants and straighten his shirt. We kept up the appearance of a late night dinner just as my boss walked by, seeing my light on. He knocked on the glass and walked into my office.

"Late night dinner?"

"Yes, Mr. Johnson. This is my boyfriend, Logan. He brought me dinner since I was working on that campaign for Monday."

"Sorry about that. I didn't think you would be here that late."

"Well, there were a few changes I wanted to make, and I wanted it to be perfect. I should be done soon."

"Okay. Well, don't let me keep you. I just came to grab some paperwork I left behind. See you tomorrow. It was nice to meet you, Logan."

"You too."

Mr. Johnson walked off to his office and I blew out a breath. That could have ended very badly. Having sex in my office hadn't been part of the plan with Logan, and whatever just happened with us was definitely not something I wanted to repeat. That brought on feelings that I was trying to avoid.

"You'd better go. I have work to finish and then I need to get home to get some sleep before tomorrow."

"Alright." He came toward me and tried to kiss me, but I pulled away. "Don't do this. Not when we're finally taking this somewhere."

"I don't know what you're talking about, Logan. We're just having fun, and I have to work, so you need to leave."

He huffed out a laugh, but gathered up the leftovers and headed for the door. "See you around, Cece."

He was gone and I could finally breathe again. I finished up my work and was out the door an hour later. Office visits could not be repeated in the future.

CHAPTER 10

LOGAN

I WAS GOING INSANE. The whole week, I had been dying to see her, for her to call me and tell me she was coming over, but that never happened. So, I made the decision to go see her and demand her attention. I knew it was a stupid move based on her reaction the last time I showed up at her office, but she needed to eat, and I couldn't help myself.

From the moment I met her, I needed more of her. I couldn't figure out what it was about her, but I was drawn to her explosive personality. She was feisty and fun, but had these sweet moments that I knew she didn't want me to see— a small blush when I complimented her, the satisfied smile that she hid whenever we had sex...she didn't want me to see those moments, because it was like admitting that she enjoyed her time with me.

Breaking through her defenses was nearly impossible. Every time I got close, she pulled back and shut me down. For some reason, she didn't want to take a chance on me. That was usually my way of thinking. I'd never wanted a relationship until Cece came along. But when I made love to her last night, I saw in her eyes how much she wanted me. She was hesitant, though. She was scared to allow herself to be with me. I was going to have to change that and show her how great things could be between us if she only gave me a chance.

I couldn't sit on my hands and wait for her to come around. A woman like Cece needed to be pushed, but in a covert way. I needed her to see me as someone she enjoyed spending time with, but there had to be boundaries or she would get scared and run.

Sean was first on my list, as he could get Vira on board.

"You do know that it's my day off, don't you?" he grumbled as he answered the phone.

"I need you to get Vira to agree to go out for the day."

He sighed. "Seriously? It's...six o'clock in the morning."

"And we're burning daylight," I said irritatedly.

"Why do I need to get Vira to go out for the day?"

"Well, not just out. I need you to get her to go out with you. And me."

"You...is this a weird third wheel thing?"

I rolled my eyes. "Why does everyone assume that I'm doing something kinky? No, I want to take Cece paint balling, but I need Vira to agree to go along. She needs to be persuaded and Vira is just the woman for the job."

"Then why don't you just say that? This whole conversation could have gone a lot faster if you had just gotten to the point."

"Are you going to do this or not?"

He groaned. "I was going to sleep in today."

"Look, if you do this, you'll get sex at the end of the day."

"Yeah, but I could get that anyway."

"I'll pay for lunch for you."

"I could eat lunch here."

"You'll get to show Vira how strong and masculine you are while you're shooting people."

He sighed. "Don't you have any better reasons? These seriously suck."

"How about the fact that you wouldn't have met Vira if it wasn't for me? You know, you owe me. Cece told me what she had to listen to when you stayed over."

"Fine," he grumbled. "But you're buying me breakfast too. And none of that cheap fast-food shit. I want a real breakfast. A man's breakfast."

"Yeah, I got it. I'll take you for a man's breakfast."

He grunted and hung up the phone. Now I just needed to get a few more people on board. Calling Ryan, I dreaded what he would say.

"Fuck, there'd better be something seriously wrong at the office for you to call me at this time."

"I need you to go paintballing with me."

"Are you kidding me? You woke me up at the ass-crack of dawn to go paintballing? Fuck you."

He hung up, but I dialed him again. He picked up on the third ring. "What do you want now?"

"So, anyway, I need you to get all the guys together. And the girls. The more, the better."

He sighed heavily, mumbling something into his pillow. "Why? And it better be good."

Fuck, I hated this. "Alright, remember the woman from the club?"

"The one that you keep getting distracted over?"

"Well, I need to get her out of the sex zone."

"Hold on," he said. I heard shuffling in the background. "Okay, say that again."

"We're stuck in the sex zone. I need to get her *out* of that so I can persuade her to date me."

"You want to purposely take yourself out of the sex zone."

"I know how it sounds."

"It sounds like you've lost your damn mind. Why would you willingly take sex out of the equation?"

"If I play this right, we'll still have sex, but I'll also have the rest."

He groaned loudly. "Man, why? After all this time, why did you have to decide to do this today of all days?"

"Because...because I really like her," I admitted.

"And I really like my bed."

"No, I mean, I *like her* like her."

A heavy sigh filled the line, but I knew I had him. "You know I'm gonna get a lot of shit for waking everyone else up for this."

"I'll find a way to repay you."

"You'd better. I'm gonna call in a favor someday, and it's gonna be a big one. So fucking big that you'll regret asking a favor for this chick."

I grinned, because he didn't know how bad I had it for Cece. I was pretty sure I wouldn't be regretting anything about this.

"I appreciate it. Oh, and try to make me look good today."

He hung up. Bastard.

I got dressed and grabbed the clothes I'd gotten for Cece. I sent Sean a text that I would meet him at the restaurant after I got Cece. His response was a big fuck you. I headed over to Cece's dressed in camo from head to toe with paint all over my face. I was ready for battle with the bag in my hands. Cece was about to get a makeover. I knocked on the door and startled her with my appearance.

"Get Vira. We're going to have some fun."

"Um, excuse me, but I am not a dog. I don't just go wherever you tell me to."

"You have a choice. You can either get in the gear I got for you, or you can get fucked on your kitchen floor with Vira watching and then we'll leave. Which is it going to be?"

Vira walked out of her room, still looking sleepy. "What's this about going somewhere? Sean told me I had to convince Cece to go somewhere?"

"We're going paintballing," I said, shoving the bag at Cece.

She glared at me and grabbed the bag. "What is this?"

"Camo, so you can blend in."

She snorted as she pulled the outfit from the bag. "No, I'm not wearing that. I don't look good in that shade of green."

"It's not about looking good."

"Well, then why would I do it?"

"For fun."

"Fun? This is supposed to be fun? Running around throwing balls at people and scoring goals?"

"First, you don't throw the balls, you shoot them. Second, there are no goals."

"Then why would I play?"

"To win."

She shook her head, shoving the bag back at me. "No, I don't want to."

I smirked at her. "Why not? Are you scared you'll lose?"

Her eyes narrowed. "I never lose at anything."

"Then you can prove it today."

"I'll break a nail and get all dirty."

I slowly stepped forward, wrapping my arm around her waist as I whispered in her ear. "Sweetheart, there is nothing more that I'd like to do than get dirty with you." I nipped at her ear, then slapped her ass. "Now get your ass moving."

CHAPTER 11

CECE

SEAN EMERGED from Vira's room, zipping his fly. I hadn't even known that he was here, and based on the eye roll from Logan, he didn't know either.

"Did you bring my stuff also?"

"I brought it all. Everyone go get ready so we can get this show on the road."

Vira squealed in delight, and I narrowed my eyes at the traitorous bitch. This was not what I had in mind for today. Logan stood with his massive arms crossed in front of me, willing me to argue with him. Huffing, I turned and went to my room to get ready.

Fifteen minutes later, we all piled into several trucks and headed to the local diner.

"Can't we just get this over with?" I grumbled.

"No," Logan said, turning his head slightly. "I promised Sean a good breakfast."

"And why would you do that?"

The corner of his lip tipped up in amusement. "To persuade him to get Vira on my side."

I scoffed, irritated that my friend was so easily persuaded to work against me. We pulled into the diner and ate in record time, though I was mostly drinking coffee. It was way too early for actual food. When he showed up on my doorstep, I was sure that he was a figment of my imagination. No-one got up this early on a Sunday.

"So, who all is coming with us?" I asked Logan after we piled back into the truck.

"Sean and Vira, Jack, Luke and Anna, Ryan, Drew, and Sebastian."

"Okay, well I don't know most of them."

"You probably won't get to know most of them since we'll be covered in paint, except for those on our team."

"Are the teams already divided?"

"No, we'll do it when we get there."

I wasn't overly thrilled at being dragged out of my house at eight o'clock this morning, but if Vira was going, it wouldn't be so bad. We pulled up to a wooded area after a nice, scenic drive and Logan got me loaded up with face paint. I looked over to see all the others doing the same. My hair was pulled up in a tight bun and the rest of me was fully covered. I had to admit, I looked hot in camo. Even the boots were pretty kick ass. Vira, always going for fashion first, had tied her camo tee in a knot at her waist, showing off a good section of her toned stomach. She was a little irked when Sean made her put the coat back on.

We headed over to the entrance and were broken up into teams. Jack, Sean and Vira were on our team and Luke, Anna, Ryan, Drew, and Sebastian were on the other. We did quick introductions before breaking off and heading out into the woods. The first hour was a little boring. The guys were giving off hand signals and telling us to stay low and follow them.

Vira and I ended up falling behind because we were so bored.

"The shoes are cute at least. I think I look pretty bad ass," I said to Vira as we wandered around the woods.

"You definitely look hot. I was pissed when Sean made me put this coat on. It does nothing for my figure."

"Why are we out here anyway, and why did you so readily agree to come along?"

She shrugged. "It sounded like fun at the time. Now, we're just walking around while they play G.I. Joe."

I bent over to tie my shoelace when I felt something whiz past my head. I shrieked and dropped to the ground, covering my head. "What the fuck! Someone shot at me."

"Well, we are playing paintball," Vira said as she laid down beside me. We looked all around for anyone that could be aiming at us. That's when I saw it. Logan was standing next to Jack and Sean laughing at us. Those bastards.

"They're laughing at us. Come on. It's time for payback. We crawled over to a fallen log and hid behind it as we stripped our clothes off. Very slowly, we stood from our positions in only our bra and panties. I was wearing a cute pair of red, lacy bikinis with a matching bra, and Vira was wearing a black, lacy thong and matching bra. Both of us had taken our hair down and still had on our boots. We stepped out from our position and walked toward what we assumed was the center of the action with our guns slung over our shoulders.

"What the fuck?" It came off to our right, but I had no idea who said it. I heard a girly giggle, which could only be Anna, so that must be where the rest of that team was.

"Oh, shit. I didn't see this. Harper will kick my ass."

That must have been Jack, and he just gave away where Sean and Logan were standing. I pretended to see something interesting on the forest floor and bent over, giving one group a great view of my boobs and the other, my ass. I picked up a clump of squishy mud and spread it from my throat down to my belly.

Vira, never one to be outdone, undid her bra and let it slide to the ground before picking up some mud and rubbing it over her breasts. As we continued to put on a show for the guys, I couldn't help but wish that it was a little warmer outside. My nipples were painfully erect, and not because I was turned on.

As if being snapped out of a daydream, Sean and Logan finally ran forward, yelling at us.

"Goddamn, woman. Put your clothes on right fucking now," Logan roared at me.

"Vira, what the fuck do you think you're doing? You're showing your tits to everyone here. Put your clothes back on!" Sean yelled.

When they were a few steps from us, we swung our guns around and nailed each of them with several paintballs, eliciting more than a few swear words from them. Laughter from our right erupted and we swung our guns on them firing off several rounds, noting that Anna was also on our side, taking out her husband, Luke.

All of the guys were taken out by three little women. Not one of them stood a chance against us with their cocky attitudes. I hadn't initially wanted to come out here, but I had to say, this ended up being a very cathartic experience.

Logan stormed over to me and threw me over his shoulder, my ass swinging in the air for all to see. It didn't bother me. After all, I had just stripped down to my bra and panties and stood in front of all his friends. His friends hooted and hollered, and I heard similar sounds coming from Vira. I peeked back to see Vira getting much the same treatment as I was. He hauled me over into the dense growth of the trees, while branches pulled at my skin. I would have more than a few scratches by the time this day was done.

When we could no longer see any of his friends, he set me down on the ground and stepped back, his gaze roaming over my body. The mud had already started to dry and was now forming a hardened coat on my skin. His lips crashed down on mine while I was looking at my body and soon I felt his erection pressing against my stomach. He pushed me down to the ground, his body completely covering mine. Twigs dug into my back, but his kisses made me forget about the pain.

I grabbed his erection through his jeans and started stroking as I chased the orgasm that I could feel building inside. It didn't take much for Logan to get me where I needed to be. His mouth latched on to my nipples through the thin scrap of fabric, pulling and teasing me. I ripped his pants open and pushed them down, then spun him to his back and climbed on top of him. Sinking down hard, I took him all in me and rode him hard, coming just moments later. Logan lifted my hips and bucked up into me until he came a few thrusts later. We were both panting from the workout, but Logan wouldn't let up, kissing every inch of my skin. I watched his tongue move across my body, kissing all the scratches from the branches. It was only then that I realized how truly cold it was outside. My body started to shake and Logan grabbed his coat and wrapped it around me. My underwear was nowhere to be seen and I didn't even recall when they left my body.

As I stood, I almost fell back down. My body hurt everywhere and it suddenly occurred to me that having sex on branches was not necessarily the smartest idea.

"Easy there, Tiger. Let's get back and get the rest of your clothes before you freeze to death."

Luckily, I still had my shoes, so at least I didn't have to hitch a ride from Logan. That would have been embarrassing with my pussy hanging out. When we got back to the group, Sean and Vira were still missing, but the rest of them were all sitting around talking.

"Damn, girl. That must have been some wild sex. You blend into the forest with all those leaves and sticks in your hair," Sebastian said as his eyes roamed over my body appreciatively. Logan shot him a glare as my hands went to my hair and sure enough, there were knots with so many things from the forest floor that it would take a week to get untangled.

CHAPTER 12
LOGAN

MY WOMAN WAS sexy as fuck no matter what she was wearing, but coming out of the woods dressed in only my jacket and a pair of boots was sexy as hell. Even though I had just had her not ten minutes before, I needed to have her again. We found her clothes, and I helped block her so that she could get dressed.

"Seriously, Logan? I just stood out here in front of all of them in nothing but my bra and panties. I think the mystery is gone."

"I don't give a shit. They don't need a second showing."

Ahead of us, leaves and twigs started to crunch where Sean and Vira were making their way out. Apparently, Sean had much the same idea as I had. Vira looked no better than Cece did, but she had a big grin on her face. Sean looked like he would murder any of us if we even thought about making a comment.

"Vira, you're looking mighty…dirty," I said with a smirk. Sean glared at me, but I just laughed. "My wayward woman is just as bad, so don't think you can give me crap over this."

"Wayward woman?" Cece turned a glare on me. "First of all, I am not 'wayward' and second, I am not your woman. You're someone good to fuck. Let's just leave it at that."

"Cece, you can keep telling yourself whatever you want, but you were mine from the moment you walked into that club."

"I was never yours and I never will—"

I shut her up with a long, deep kiss. I didn't need to hear this shit over and over again. It was the same thing I'd heard since the moment we met, but that didn't mean I couldn't break her down. And I would.

"Now that you got your rocks off, can we head out?" Sebastian asked.

"Yeah, since the women kicked our asses, looks like we might as well head out," Ryan said.

We all grabbed our gear after the girls were finished dressing and headed for the trucks. I was starving by the time we were headed home. Something about having sex in the woods really geared up my appetite. Everyone else decided to head home, but Vira, Sean, Cece, and I stopped at a bar for some food. There were no restaurants for another thirty miles, and I didn't think I could wait that long. I needed food or I would pass out.

We walked in the bar and I immediately changed my mind. Bikers were everywhere in the bar. It was dark and smoky. Apparently, you could still smoke in this establishment.

"Sean, I think maybe we should head out. Doesn't look like someplace we'd be welcome."

"Copy that. Girls, let's find someplace else to eat."

"No. I'm hungry, and after the morning we've had, I need food now." Vira sashayed over to the bar and asked for a menu. The biker on the stool next to her grabbed her around the hips and pulled her in-between his legs.

"Hey, darling. What's a pretty thing like you doing in a place like this? You lookin' for someone to show you a good time?"

Vira, being the mouthy woman she was, didn't hold back at all. "Sugar, I got all the man I need right over there. I don't think trading in for a smaller model would be very smart, do you?"

The biker bristled and his cheeks flushed red. "You better watch that mouth darlin', or you're gonna trip and fall with that pretty little mouth landing on my cock."

"If only someone could find it," she shot back.

The biker grabbed tightly to her arm, but Sean stepped forward with the most menacing look I'd ever seen. I pulled Cece in close to me, protecting her from any other assholes who thought she was fair game.

"Get your hands off her. Now."

Sean's eyes were black as night. There were only a few times I had seen so much rage emanating off this man.

"I don't think so, Ranger Rick. I think I'll keep her right where she is."

"He's not a ranger. He's a cop." It was out of Cece's mouth before I could stop her. I rolled my eyes to the heavens and prayed we'd get out alive. Sean, to his credit, didn't even flinch at the menacing glare he received from every biker in the bar.

"A copper, huh? I don't believe your kind is allowed in here. This is a biker bar, so why don't you leave me here with this sweet piece of ass and be on your way."

"Take your hands off her now."

"Or what?"

In a flash, Sean grabbed Vira and yanked her down, while shoving his elbow into the loud mouth's face. He fell backward off his stool into the next guy, who caught him before they both fell to the ground. Sean grabbed Vira's hand and headed for the exit, but a line of bikers blocked the door.

"You just fucked with the wrong bikers, asshole."

"Get out of my way. We're leaving." Sean growled, refusing to back down.

"Oh, you're leaving alright, but it'll be in a body bag."

I had no problem fighting these guys, but we were sorely outnumbered, and we had the girls with us. There was no way I could allow them to get hurt. I stepped forward, trying to be the voice of reason.

"Look, we'll be on our way and you won't ever see us again. Just move away from the door."

"Right." The biker laughed maniacally. The hairs on the back of my neck stood up. Shit was about to get ugly. The guy's fist flew forward just as Sean pushed Vira out of the way. He landed one shot to Sean's face before Sean fought back, beating the crap out of the biker. I shoved Cece towards Vira and got a few punches in at the wall of bikers standing before us. They kept coming at us, harder and faster. The next guy I turned to had Cece in front of him, one arm wrapped around her throat. Anger bubbled up inside me, but Cece just smirked at me.

She swung her elbow back and nailed the guy in the solar plexus, then stomped down on his foot. He bent over and she swung her elbow back into the guy's nose, then slammed her fist down into his nuts.

"As my girl, Sandy, always says, 'Just remember to SING'." She said it as if she hadn't just had some guy's arm around her throat. The guy stood up behind her and I pushed her aside, knocking him out in one punch. I noticed that a lot of the bikers were happily sitting watching the fight with amusement. They'd probably already had a few, which would only work to our advantage.

Some guy was going after Vira, and I was about to step forward when she reached behind the bar and grabbed a bottle of vodka, swinging out and smashing it against his head. Sean was still fighting off several bikers, so I stepped up and took care of a few that were ganging up on him. I took several shots to the face and kidneys before we broke free from that group. Most were now down on the floor moaning or knocked out.

Heaving from the exertion, I looked up to see Vira and Cece surrounded by bikers, but they didn't look scared at all. Cece picked up a chair and swung it through the air, smashing one biker in the face, his teeth flying from his mouth. Then she ducked down and slammed her fist into another guy's junk. Damn, these women fought dirty. Vira swung her chair at another guy, hitting him in the back and sending him into a crowd of guys sitting down.

We had cleared out the bikers who were standing in front of the door, but as exciting as it was to watch Vira and Cece kicking their asses, it was time to go. Sean whistled and they both looked up. He jerked his head and they immediately dropped their chairs and came running. We ran out to the trucks and spun out of the lot in seconds. I kept my eyes on the rearview mirror, but luckily nobody followed. They were probably too drunk.

CHAPTER 13

CECE

"WHAT THE FUCK were you thinking back there?"

We were on our way back to his house after screeching out of the bar's parking lot. He was growlier than a mother bear and taking it out on me.

"Excuse me? What was I thinking? I didn't do a damn thing wrong."

"You should have gotten out of the way and stayed down. Do you realize how much you could have been hurt? Any one of those bikers would have loved to have grabbed you and made you their whore. You're just lucky that Sean and I got you both out of there."

"If I remember correctly, Vira and I did quite a bit of damage on our own. Besides, I knew you were there and would take care of it. Did you see Sean's face in there? I've never seen anyone so lethal in all my life. He was amazing, the way he took on those bikers. I always thought Sean was this big teddy bear, but man, get him riled up and he can really do some damage." I blew out a breath and fanned my face. "I think my panties got a little wet back there."

A growl escaped from Logan's lips and when I looked over, his knuckles were white against the steering wheel. "Great. I got it. Sean really did it for you back there."

"Oh, is someone feeling inadequate?" I reached over and pet his cheeks. "Don't worry, sweetie. You were amazing too. I saw you take down those guys. None of them stood a chance against you."

"Yeah, well next time start with that."

He huffed in annoyance and continued to glare out the windshield. This was going to take some great acting on my part when we got home. I was going to need to build up his confidence or he would be brooding all night long. On the ride home, I drifted in and out of sleep against the window and only realized we were back to his place when he turned off the engine. Now that I had been sitting a while, I noticed my body was sore in a few places. Well, no time like the present to really play it up.

I pushed my head away from the window and let out a hiss. "Ow."

"What's wrong? Are you okay?"

"Yeah, I'm just a little sore."

"Stay there. I'll help you out."

I rolled my eyes and waited for him to come around. I was perfectly capable of getting out of the truck on my own, but if it made him feel better, I'd gladly pretend. He opened the door and eased me down to the ground. No joke, my legs almost collapsed from underneath me. I guess I was more worn out than I thought. Logan scooped me up in his arms and carried me inside. He took me upstairs to his bathroom and set me on the toilet while he started the tub. He had one of those large garden tubs, and it was calling my name.

Logan started stripping me of my clothes and I saw right away why I was so sore. I had several bruises on my back from when we were in the bar. I hadn't realized that anyone had even hit me, but there was a lot of shoving and it could have happened at any time.

He took his time picking leaves and twigs out of my hair, running his fingers through the strands for tiny pieces. When he was done, he picked me up and set me in the steaming water. At first, the heat stung against my cuts, but after a minute I relaxed back into the warmth. I closed my eyes and was surprised when Logan pushed me forward and climbed in behind me.

Picking up some body wash, he poured some in a washcloth and rubbed it together before gently washing my body. His hands glided across my skin, caressing every inch of me.

"You've got quite a few scratches on you. Maybe the woods wasn't the best place to work out my frustrations on you."

"You didn't hear me complaining."

"Still, I don't like to see your beautiful skin all torn up."

"It's fine, but thank you for taking care of me."

His mood seemed a little lighter after that, and I was glad my plan had worked. The last thing I needed was Logan feeling like he wasn't as good as Sean. Then I wondered why I cared that much when I was still planning my revenge against him.

Over the next week I rarely saw Logan. I was busy at work with multiple projects that needed to be finished up, and at the end of the day, I was just too tired to head over to see him. He stopped by Wednesday night and stayed over, even though I protested.

"Logan, don't get any ideas. Just because you stop by for a quick fuck doesn't mean you get to stay the night."

"Seriously, Cece? Stop being a bitch and let's go to sleep. I'm tired."

"Fine, but you stay on your side of the bed."

The next morning I woke to Logan wrapped around me. I was content for all of two point five seconds, until I remembered my vow of revenge. I flung the covers off and stalked to the kitchen where I got a cold cup of water. Stomping back to my room, I threw back the covers and emptied the cup right on his dick.

"What the fuck!"

I heard the door to Vira's room open and footsteps head my way, but that didn't stop me.

"I told you not to fucking snuggle with me. Now get out before I do something worse than pour cold water on your dick."

"Christ, Cece. I was asleep. I didn't know that I did that. Geez, you'd think I groped you in your sleep or something."

"That would have been preferable." I crossed my arms over my chest and tapped my foot on the floor in impatience.

"Alright, fine. I'm going."

He grabbed his clothes off the floor and walked into the living room where Sean was smirking at him.

"Kicked out before breakfast, huh?"

"Shut up, fucker."

"Don't get too smug, Sean. You're leaving too." Vira crossed her arms over her chest and gave him a pointed look.

"What the fuck did I do?"

"You should be happy you got more than one night with me. I don't do sleepovers or breakfast."

"Well, that's just not true, because I've slept here multiple times and have plenty of breakfasts with you."

She tossed his clothes at him, his belt buckle hitting him in the face.

"Right. So be glad with what you got."

I walked over to the door and held it open as both men grabbed their clothes and left the apartment none too happy. Through the door, Vira and I could hear them in the hallway getting dressed.

"Thanks a lot fucker. I usually get breakfast."

"It's not my fault you opened your big mouth."

"This is all because you couldn't stay on your side of the bed. If she doesn't want to snuggle, don't snuggle, you stupid fucker."

The conversation continued as they walked down the hall, and Vira and I stood inside laughing. Fucking with them was just too fun.

I didn't let Logan stay over the next night and I refused to answer any of his calls. Friday couldn't come fast enough. I had fun plans with Vira, and nothing was going to stand in my way. I stopped by the cafe for my usual flirtation with Logan before heading off to work, but when I got to the office, I was hit with a massive workload. Apparently, Mr. Johnson was so thrilled with my work on the last project that he gave me another that would also have a Saturday morning meeting.

I called Vira to let her know of my change, which was fine with her because she also had to work. I got back to work and hoped that I could get enough done that I didn't have to work too late tonight.

Once again, the day got away from me and I was left begging the snack machine gods to send me something good. Alas, they didn't listen, and I was stuck with Snickers bars for dinner once again.

"You must be doing the same thing I am."

I practically jumped out of my skin when I heard the voice behind me. I had been bent over retrieving my food, so whoever was behind me got a nice view of my ass. Perfect. I turned around to see a handsome man standing behind me. I had never met him, but he must work here if he was here this late at night.

"I'm sorry, I don't think we've met. I'm Cece."

I stuck out my hand and he wrapped his large hand around mine, rubbing his thumb over my hand. It was a little too familiar and I quickly snatched my hand back.

"It's nice to meet you. What are you doing up here so late?"

"Oh, you know. Work never stops. I didn't catch your name."

"I didn't give it."

Well, that was a little disturbing. This guy must think he was being mysterious, but really, he was creeping me out. Time to get back to work.

"Alright, well I have a lot to do, so if you'll excuse me."

I went to step around him, but he stepped in front of me. Seriously? I pulled my shoulders back and plastered on a fake smile.

"I need you to move. I have work to do."

"Work is boring. I have something we could do that's more fun."

"Thanks for the offer, but I don't have time to have fun right now. I need to get back to work."

His soulless eyes looked over my body, giving me the chills. His hand went to my shoulder and skated down my arm and over my waist. Some men didn't know when a girl was shutting down their advances, so it looked like I was going to have to be a bitch to him.

"Look, jackass. I didn't say you could touch me. Get your filthy hands off me and get out of my way. I was trying to be nice, but you're not understanding. I'm not interested, so back off."

His eyes darkened and he gripped my hair roughly. Apparently, all I did was poke the bear. This guy was dangerous. I didn't know why I hadn't seen it before. False bravado? I guess I thought I could tell him to leave me alone and he would, but now I had stupidly mouthed off to him and he got angry. I was cornered in the break room with a guy who didn't take no for an answer.

I looked up into his eyes as he moved in closer. When I felt his chest brush mine, I rammed my knee into his crotch. He instantly released me, falling to the floor and holding his crotch. I ran around him back to my office. Screw working late, I was getting out of here. I grabbed my purse and headed for the door. I briefly thought of locking myself in my office and calling the police, but this guy wouldn't be stopped by a locked door. Besides, the walls were glass and he could easily break the glass if he really wanted me.

I quickly grabbed my purse and took the long way to the elevator to avoid passing the break room, which may have been a stupid idea when I realized that this area was completely dark. Adrenaline was keeping the panic at bay for now. My only thought was getting out of this building. I half ran down the hall to the elevator. I wanted to run faster, but it was so dark, I could hardly see where I was going. On top of that, I was trying not to make any noise. I saw the red glow from the exit sign further ahead. It was already too late when I saw the large figure coming at me. His body hit me with such force that I was thrown against the glass, my head bouncing against the wall.

It took me a second to regain my wits as spots floated in front of my eyes. When I did, I felt his hands on me, pinning me to the floor. His minty breath misting over my face.

"I just wanted to talk. You didn't have to be such a bitch."

"I told you I had work to do," I spat, struggling to break free from him. "What was I supposed to think when you wouldn't let me leave? Get off of me."

He pushed himself further onto my body and I felt his erection rubbing against me. A whimper escaped my lips as one hand pushed down my pants. When it finally kicked in what was about to happen, I bucked my hips and tried to pry my wrists free of his grasp. His grip tightened painfully and I started yelling. I knew it was pointless. We were the only ones here. There was no one to help me.

"Shut up, bitch. You know you want it. I see the way you flaunt your body around the office, wearing your tight skirts. You're asking for it from every guy around here. We all want you, and we know you want us too. Now I'm taking what's mine."

He settled his body back on top of mine to keep me still, keeping one hand around my wrists and the other snaked up my shirt to fondle my breasts. Bile rose in my throat, and with every touch, every pinch from his fingers, the nausea grew until I couldn't hold it back. I barely had time to turn my head to the side before violently vomiting. He pulled back slightly, a look of disgust on his face.

With the added distance, I used my knee to try and get him off me as I screamed like my life depended on it. But I couldn't reach my intended target, and my scream was instantly cut off when he reared back and punched me in the face. Dazed, I lost my ability to fight. I felt a shoe to my side that knocked the wind out of me, and then my attacker was gone. Someone had tackled him off me, and it must have been him that kicked me in the process. I didn't care. I pulled my pants back up and scooted into a darkened corner, watching the two of them fight. Punches were thrown and I heard grunting, but I couldn't tell who was winning. I closed my eyes, covering my ears as I waited for it all to end. I felt a swoosh of air as someone ran past me and I prayed it was my attacker leaving.

"Hey, are you okay?"

Though muddled by my hands, I recognized the voice instantly. My eyes flew open, and relief flooded me when I saw Logan standing in front of me, panting as his eyes roamed over me in concern. I flung myself at him, wrapping my arms tightly around his neck.

"How are you here?" I whispered.

"I talked to Vira and she said you had to work late. I came to bring you dinner."

My whole body was shaking, the feel of his hands still on me. I wanted the memories gone. I wanted to wind back the clock and leave the office early. But I couldn't do that. "Is he gone?"

"Yeah, he landed a well placed punch and ran off. I'm sorry I didn't catch him."

"I'm just glad he's gone."

I sagged into his body, the adrenaline wearing off and the shakes setting in even harder than the moment before. He gripped me closer to him, rubbing my back and trying to ease my body. He settled us on the ground with me in his lap. I had never in the last ten years figured that I would be attacked for the way I dressed. I wore sexy clothes, but never trashy clothes. I always dressed more professional than sexy in the work place, but that didn't mean I had to look like an old woman. Now, I was regretting every single outfit I had ever worn, knowing that each piece could have resulted in something much worse.

I barely registered that Logan was talking to someone on the phone, but my brain was going fuzzy and I could only stare off into space. I don't know how long we stayed like that, but I tensed in his arms when I heard the elevator doors open. Had he come back? We should have moved. He could easily find me over here. I pushed away from Logan, but he held me tight.

"It's okay. I called Sean. He's a police officer, remember?"

"I don't want to report this. The whole office will know about it. I don't want everyone looking at me like that."

His eyes softened as his hand came up to cup my cheek. "Sweetheart, your bosses need to know. They need extra security if people are going to be here at night, and they can't have a rapist walking around the building. Besides, someone will look at the camera feed tomorrow when they notice this crack in the wall."

Sean walked up to us slowly and kneeled down in front of me. My cheeks burned red as embarrassment settled in.

"Hey, Cece. Are you okay?"

Sean's voice was very gentle, but I didn't see pity in his eyes, only concern.

My head nodded with a jerk up and down.

"Okay. I want to take you to the hospital to get checked out. Do you want to take an ambulance?"

"I don't need to go. I'm fine."

"You could have your attacker's DNA on you, under your fingernails. We need to take you in to be checked over and get samples."

Shit. I hadn't thought of that. I really didn't want to go to the hospital. I just wanted my bed, but would I be safe if they didn't catch him? He knew who I was, but I had no idea who he was.

As if Sean read my mind, he asked, "Do you know who attacked you?"

I shook my head slightly, remembering the man's voice as he walked up behind me in the lounge. Closing my eyes, I took a deep breath, trying to quell my nerves. "No. I've never seen him before, but he works here."

"Okay. How do you know that?"

"He said that I walk around the office tempting all the guys with the way I dress."

I felt Logan tense around me. I didn't really want to talk about this in front of Logan. I needed distance from him.

"Can we talk about this in private?"

Sean nodded, but Logan protested. "No, I want to be there when you talk to him."

I pushed out of his arms and stood up, giving myself space. "But I don't want you there."

I couldn't look at him as I said it. I needed space from him. What happened was intimate, but not in a good way. I didn't want him getting close to me and comforting me. I was supposed to be getting my revenge, not falling into his arms for comfort. I couldn't risk being drawn closer to him, sharing this with him. It was too personal.

The other part of me was ashamed to admit that I didn't want him to hear the details because he might look at me differently. I was very sexual and confident, but now, I didn't know what I was. He would know that and he would be gentle with me. I didn't think I could take that. I didn't want sex right now, but I didn't want to be handled with kid gloves either. It would just make me feel worse about myself.

"How about we go to the hospital and have them look you over and Logan can stay in the waiting room. When the nurses are done with you, I'll take your statement. If you want me to give you a ride home, I can. Otherwise, Logan will be there waiting for you."

I agreed and we went to the hospital where I was checked out. I was fine other than a bump on the head that was causing a slight headache, and a swollen cheek. I didn't have a concussion though, so that was a relief. The staff called in a SANE nurse, but I didn't think it would be any use. I didn't scratch him and I didn't remember him spitting on me or anything. Logan had interrupted before things were taken that far. I was photographed where I had minor bruising and my nails were scraped. The nurses took my clothes for evidence and I was given scrubs to change into. Then Sean came in and took my statement. I felt numb as I relived the events of the night. When we were all done, Sean walked me out into the waiting room where Logan was waiting. Part of me was surprised he was there. I knew that he was a caring person, he always had been. Still, some part of me expected that he would say I wasn't worth the hassle.

Sean told me that he could drop me at my apartment, but that was the last place I wanted to be. I loved Vira, but the thought of explaining what happened to one more person tonight was daunting. Logan pushed for me to go back to his house, and I finally relented, just wanting to take a shower and go to sleep.

CHAPTER 14

LOGAN

I COULD TELL that Cece was doing her best to hold it together. She basically stared into space the whole drive back to his house. I was pissed when she didn't want me there with her when she gave her statement. She wouldn't let me in. It was like she expected me to walk away at any moment. She had all her defenses up before, but now it was even worse. She wouldn't even look at me.

She had texted me earlier to say she would be working late again. I had thoughts of the last time we had dinner at her work. That night had turned out very differently than tonight.

I thought if I kept pushing, kept bringing her dinner when she didn't expect it, we could just sit and have a conversation, behave like normal people that were dating. I just wanted to get to know her better. So, I went against my instincts to step back, and I brought her dinner again.

I was stepping off the elevator when I heard her screams. I dropped the food and ran, but I had no idea where to go. The whole floor was a maze of hallways and cubicles. I almost missed her because it was so dark where she was, but then I heard her scream again, and anger filled me with what I saw as I got closer. I attacked the guy on top of her and I thought I had him down, but then I got distracted looking for Cece and he got in a good punch to my eye. His punch was like a hammer and momentarily stunned me. It was enough time for him to run off. I could have chased him, but I was more concerned about Cece. My priority was making sure she was okay.

When we reached my house, I hurried to her side to help her out. Her body had to be sore after fighting that guy off. I wanted to carry her up, but I wasn't sure she would allow that, especially in such a public place. Besides, maybe she wouldn't be comfortable with my arms around her. Maybe she needed space. But I took the chance that she would let me hold her hand, and when she didn't pull away, I figured she was pretty out of it. We made it to the room and she walked in, staring at a spot on the floor. It was like the lights had shut off in her mind for the night.

"Do you want a shower or bed?"

When she didn't respond, I moved closer and put my hand on her shoulder.

"Sweetheart."

She finally looked up at me and I could see that she hadn't heard me speaking.

"Sorry, what did you say?"

"Do you want a shower or bed?"

She looked over at the bed and then down at herself. After a moment she headed towards the bathroom without another word. She shut the door, and after a few minutes, I heard the shower turn on. I took the opportunity to call Sean and find out what had happened.

"Hey, Logan. How's Cece?"

"She's...I don't really know. She was quiet the whole way home. She's in the shower now."

Sean blew out a breath. "Well, there wasn't much to get from the scene, but we did contact security to get the video feed of the hallway. I have a feeling it's not going to show much. It was too dark in the building to get an accurate picture."

"I need you to tell me about her statement."

"Logan, if she doesn't want you to know..."

"I just need to know if she was raped. She's staying with me and I need to know so that I don't do something to scare her."

"She wasn't raped. He grabbed her, but he didn't get any further. Everything else, she's going to have to tell you."

"Alright. Thanks for letting me know."

"Call me if you need anything. Maybe stick close to her until this guy is found."

"Already on it."

I hung up with him and sat down in the armchair, thanking God that it hadn't been worse. After twenty minutes, she still wasn't out of the shower and I was starting to get worried about her, but just as I was about to walk in, the shower shut off. Remembering that she had gone in there without a change of clothes, I grabbed a t-shirt and boxers from my bag and knocked on the door.

"Cece, I have a shirt and shorts you can wear to bed."

The door opened slightly and her arm poked out to grab the clothes. She shut the door and a few minutes later came out. She was pulling at the t-shirt, like she could make it longer. She looked so vulnerable standing there, so I walked over to her and wrapped my hand around hers. Her gaze jerked to mine and I could see her mind spinning, trying to decide if she should accept my comfort or not.

"How about we go in the bathroom and I'll dry your hair?"

"Okay." I barely heard it, but at least she had spoken.

"Are you hungry? I could order some take out."

"No. I just want to go to bed."

I walked behind her into the bathroom and brought the hair dryer over to where she sat on the toilet. Her hair had a few knots, but I did my best to finger comb her hair as I dried it. It took a while to dry her hair because it was so long, but she didn't seem to mind. Her eyes were closed and I half wondered if she was sleeping. When I finished, she opened her eyes and stared at me for a minute.

"Will you stay with me in bed?"

"Of course. Go get in and I'll be there in a minute."

She walked out of the bathroom and I got cleaned up for the night. I made sure to dress in boxers and a t-shirt. She didn't need a naked man in bed with her tonight. I turned off the lights and was about to climb into bed when I heard her breathing accelerate.

"Logan, can you...I need...turn on..."

I could hear the panic in her voice, but I didn't know what was wrong.

"Turn on the lights!" She yelled, and I immediately turned on the lamp on the nightstand. Then I went over to the corner of the room where the floor lamp was and turned that on low. When I looked back at her, her chest was rising rapidly and there were tears in her eyes.

"I'm sorry. I wasn't thinking."

She shook her head. "It's not you. I just need to adjust."

I heard her sniff, and then the tears started streaming down her face as she attempted not to cry. Her throat was working overtime as she tried to gain control of her emotions, but she was failing miserably. I climbed onto the bed and pulled her into my chest where I let her cry. Running my hand up and down her back, I did everything I could to soothe her. After about ten minutes, she seemed to be all cried out. I had no idea what to say to her or what to do, so I grabbed the remote and turned on the TV. When I couldn't sleep, I always needed a distraction, so I hoped this helped. I kept the volume low as we watched *While You Were Sleeping*.

After five minutes, she relaxed in my arms, and ten minutes after that she was asleep. I pulled her down into the bed with me further and continued to watch the movie. I couldn't shut my mind off, and I kept replaying what had happened, what would have happened had I not shown up when I did. The chances of catching this guy weren't that good based on the video footage, so I hoped that she could identify him by company photos.

I watched TV for a few more hours before I finally fell asleep. When I woke the next morning, the TV was still on and I had only slept a few hours. I pried her from my arms and got up to shut the curtains. I wanted her to sleep as long as possible today. She didn't need to go anywhere first thing this morning, so it would be best if she rested. I went to the bathroom, then made some breakfast. I wanted something for her to eat as soon as she got up, so I made some biscuits and poured some orange juice. I could make a bigger breakfast later, but I was sure she would be hungry right away.

I wasn't particularly hungry yet, so I climbed back in bed and went back to sleep while holding her. I didn't want her waking up and panicking because she was in my arms, but she had fallen asleep that way, so I wrapped my arms around her again.

The next time I woke up, the bed was empty next to me. I sat up, panicked that she had left me. That hurt more than it should. She probably needed space, but I couldn't stand the thought of her not wanting to stay with me. I needed her near me right now and to know that she was okay, but the thought of her not needing me or wanting me tore me up inside.

As I was beating myself up with these thoughts, the bathroom door opened and Cece stepped out. Relief flooded through me at the sight of her. She stopped when she saw I was awake and started fidgeting with her hands. Then she walked over to the nightstand where the tray of food sat. She poured two glasses of orange juice and handed one over. She sat down on the bed and snuggled under the covers again, then tore pieces off her croissant.

"Thank you for last night."

"Anytime, sweetheart. Do you want to talk about it?"

"No."

We sat in companionable silence while we finished our breakfast, then Cece set her plate on the nightstand and laid down again. She stared at the ceiling and I sat there watching her without a clue as to what to do or say. I didn't know what she needed, and she wasn't being very forthcoming with that information. After a few minutes, she closed her eyes and went back to sleep. I turned on the TV, keeping the volume down, and channel surfed for a while. A buzzing phone pulled my attention from the TV and I rushed to find it before it woke Cece. The noise was coming from her purse, and while I didn't want to snoop, I didn't think checking the caller ID would hurt. When I saw it was Vira, I thought it best to answer.

"Cece, where the fuck are you? Sean told me what happened and you'd better start talking."

"This is Logan, and Cece is fine. She's sleeping."

"Logan? She's with you?"

Surprise was evident in her voice and that made me wonder why that was surprising. Surely, Vira knew that we were seeing each other, so why was it such a shock?

"She didn't want to go home last night and explain everything. It was a pretty rough night for her and she just wanted to go to sleep. We're at my house."

"I can't believe she didn't come to me. I could have been there for her."

"She didn't want to talk about it. She still doesn't. However, maybe you could do her a favor and bring over some stuff for her. She didn't have anything with her last night and I'm sure she would appreciate a change of clothes and toiletries."

"Of course, I'll bring that over, and when I get there, you're going to open the door and let me talk to her."

"I wouldn't have it any other way. Just give her a few more hours. She's pretty wiped out."

"Yeah, I'll come by around eleven."

"See ya then."

I walked back over to the bed, my stomach growling. I hadn't eaten dinner last night and now I was starving. Waiting for Cece could take a long time, so I headed downstairs and cooked anything edible. I hopped in the shower and quickly soaped off the grime from yesterday. Drying off, I looked at my face in the mirror and saw a pretty shiner staring back at me. I should have put ice on it last night, but it was the last thing on my mind.

I headed back downstairs and filled a plate to eat. Now that I was clean, I was ready to dig in.

"Is there any left for me?"

I spun around in my chair, happy to see that Cece looked a lot better after some more rest. "Of course. I made pretty much everything in the house because I was so hungry. Come grab a plate."

She walked over to the table and made herself a plate, piling it high with eggs, bacon, and french toast. Then she walked over to the other side of the table and sat down with me.

"I'm starving. I didn't have a very big lunch yesterday. My boss wanted me to finish a project before the weekend, so I just grabbed a quick sandwich." She stared at her food a minute before rubbing her forehead. "Shit. I didn't finish the project."

"I'm sure, given the circumstances, he'll give you a break."

"I know, but I'm still trying to prove myself at the company, and I want to make a good impression."

"I don't know if they'll even allow you up there yet. It could still be considered a crime scene, but if you really want to get up there, I'll go with you."

"That's really not necessary. I can go into work without a bodyguard."

"That guy is still out there, and if he works in your building, no one will think twice about letting him up there. You really shouldn't go anywhere alone until he's caught. In fact, we could call Sean and see if he has the employee photos yet. Then you could go to the station and identify the asshole. No faster way to get your life back."

She poured herself a cup of coffee and added cream and sugar. "Go ahead and call him. The sooner we get this over with, the better."

After talking to Sean, we agreed to head to the station this afternoon. The HR department was getting together photos, and security had contacted the building manager to get photos of all building staff. Cece was taking a shower when Vira arrived.

"Where is that bitch? Let me see her."

I opened the door for her and she came storming into the living room.

"Good morning to you too. Yes, I'm fine. Thank you for asking."

She spun around and glared at me. "Were you attacked by some pervert last night?"

"Actually, I was," I said as I pointed to my face, "but I get what you're saying. She's in the shower right now."

Vira tossed the bag for Cece on the floor and ran up the steps. I could hear her pounding on the bathroom door from where I stood. I walked halfway up the stairs, just enough to hear their conversation.

"Bitch, why the fuck didn't you call me yesterday? Do I need to start going everywhere with you now so you don't get yourself killed?"

"Hey, hoochie, I'm perfectly capable of taking care of myself. I had him right where I wanted him when Logan came running in and got himself punched."

I rolled my eyes. These two were nuts. I ignored their banter and looked through my emails on my computer while I waited. Twenty minutes later, Cece came downstairs looking totally refreshed.

"So what did you bring me to wear?"

"Don't worry. I only packed the best for you."

Vira reached into the bag and pulled out skinny jeans and a black top. She went into the downstairs bathroom to change, and when she came back out, I couldn't help but notice how hot she looked. The top was low cut and showed a respectable amount of cleavage. This was something Cece would wear without any qualms before, but I could see the uncertainty in her eyes. Her attacker said that she dressed to get men's attention and now that comment was causing her to rethink what she wore. Cece didn't dress slutty. She was an attractive woman and she dressed to impress, but I never thought that her clothes were leading men on. No rational man would think that.

"We have to get to the station, so Vira, could you excuse us so that we can finish getting ready and head out?"

I posed it as a question, but the look I gave her left no room for her to say no. I knew that was exactly what she wanted to do, but I gave her a slight shake of my head. She took the hint and gave Cece a hug.

"I have to work later today, but call me if you need me."

"Thanks for the clothes, Vira."

Cece rummaged through the bag, looking for something and I watched her for a minute before walking over.

"Cece, look at me."

She continued to look in her bag, so I placed my hand on top of hers, stopping her search.

"Look at me."

She looked up and I saw defiance, but I also saw that she was trying to hide the tears that were threatening to spill over.

"You look great. You weren't attacked because of the way you dress. If that asshole took it as an invitation, then he's fucked up. There is nothing wrong with the way you dress and you can't let him change who you are."

A tear leaked down her face, but she quickly wiped it away and swallowed thickly. "I know it's not my fault, but it makes me wonder about how I've dressed all these years and how every day could have ended differently. Come on. Just think of how we met. I wasn't exactly dressed like a good girl."

"No, you weren't. You looked fucking hot and we both know what that did to me, but Cece, a real man doesn't take what he wants just because you're dressed sexy."

After a few minutes, she nodded and she pulled herself together, slipping on her black heels and grabbing her purse. We headed down to the station and Cece walked in there with her head held high. I could tell she was trying her hardest to appear confident. No woman wanted to be seen as a victim and this woman was definitely too strong to let her guard down in front of others.

Sean met us and took us back to a conference room to go over photos. Cece spent a good hour going over all the photos, but none of them matched her attacker. Next she went through photos of building employees, but she had no luck with those either.

"Okay, well our next move is to look at employees from other companies in the building. That may take some time to get. Give us a few days and we'll have you come back in when we get the rest of the photos. In the meantime, maybe you should stay with someone since you and Vira work opposite schedules."

She nodded, but didn't say anything.

"We need you to sit with a sketch artist also. Since we can't easily find this guy, we need something to go off of. Then I can take the sketch to your apartment building and ask around."

Cece's head jerked up. "What do you mean? Why would you need to go to my apartment building?"

Sean scratched his beard and didn't look at her right away. He looked a little uncomfortable with what he needed to say. "We have to consider the possibility that this guy has been following you. He didn't work for your company, but he followed you into your place of work. We don't even know if this guy works in the building. His comments about watching you and how you dress for men leads me to believe that he may have been watching you for a while, waiting to get you alone. He could be someone that passed you on the street and became obsessed with you, but either way, we need to expand our search for him. Unfortunately, if we don't have any luck at your apartment building, there won't be much we can do other than pass his sketch around."

"What about the evidence you collected from her? Anything there?" I asked.

"No. There was nothing. I'm sorry, Cece, but this may end up going nowhere. Please be careful and look out for anyone suspicious. We'll keep working our end and hopefully we'll come up with something."

Cece nodded and we set up a time for her to sit with a sketch artist, then we walked out of the building to the parking lot. Cece held her head high as we left the police station, but I knew that had been a blow for her. I'd just have to be her shadow for a while, something I would willingly do. Now I just had to convince Cece that it was for the best.

CHAPTER 15

CECE

HE WAS STILL OUT THERE, and they didn't know if they would be able to find him. I didn't know quite how to take that news. It was very possible that the man that attacked me had never seen me before in his life. However, that didn't match up to what he had said to me. But the things he spewed, it was like he had noticed a while ago. And how could he have not, when he knew that I would be in the office after hours?

Now, as I left the police station, I felt the confidence that I had grown accustomed to slipping from my grasp. I felt hunted, threatened. Staring out the window, I wondered if every man that passed was him. If I kept going this way, I would go crazy. I couldn't allow this man to steal my life from me.

Before I realized what was happening, Logan had taken me back to his house and ushered me inside. I was so lost in my thoughts that I hadn't realized where we were going. Now I wasn't sure what to do. Logan had been great with me, comforting me when I needed it, and taking care of me in every way. He'd always been great like that... until he wasn't. I didn't know if I could trust him. What if I did something he didn't like? Would he walk away like he did last time? Or what if he decided I was too damaged now...dirty...could I chance letting him in only to be crushed again? I had to find a way to take control.

As we walked into his house, I decided the only way to solve my problem with Logan and get rid of the feel of that man's hands on me, was to have sex with Logan. I wasn't so traumatized that I couldn't enjoy sex with a man that I actually wanted to have sex with. And I needed this. Logan had made everything right so far. I knew he wouldn't let me down now. And if he didn't, I would go home.

"Do you want to order some dinner or go out to eat?" He picked up some take out menus and started flipping through them.

"I want something to eat, but it has nothing to do with food."

Logan stopped his perusal and looked up at me uncomfortably.

"Yeah, I'm not in the mood right now. I'm kinda beat. I think I just want to eat dinner and go to sleep."

I called bullshit. I walked up to him and grabbed his cock and started stroking him. He hardened instantly under my touch, and I knew what this was about.

"Hmm." I tilted my head, giving him a saucy smile. "Either you're lying to me because you think it's too soon for me to want sex, or you don't want me because you think I'm damaged goods. Based on the size of your cock right now, I would say it's the first one."

He gulped and closed his eyes for a second before pulling my hand away from him. "Look, I get that you want to feel normal, but this isn't the way."

"I didn't ask you for your opinion," I snapped. "I want to fuck, so either give me that or I'll go find someone else that will give me what I need."

He stared at me, his eyes turning cold. Obviously, he didn't like my demands, but I didn't give a shit at the moment. I knew what I needed, and nobody was going to tell me differently.

"I'm not gonna fuck you right now. You were attacked last night, and you may not see it, but fucking me is not going to help you feel better about yourself."

Grabbing my belongings, I turned and walked out his front door, not looking back. If he wouldn't fuck me, I'd find somebody else that was willing. Right now, all I wanted was someone's hands on me that would erase the memory of the creep from last night. I hoped that when I got to the door he would stop me. I thought maybe he would change his mind, knowing that I would do just as I promised, but when I opened the door, he didn't move at all. Swallowing hard, I walked to my car and vowed I wouldn't look back. I'd never needed a man before, and I wasn't about to start with a man that so callously tossed me aside years ago.

Sean had brought my car here, so I got in and headed back to my apartment. Vira wasn't home, so I would be going out alone tonight. It didn't bother me, I used to do it all the time in Philadelphia. I had a few girlfriends, but no one understood me like Vira. I picked up some Mexican on the way home and sat in front of the TV while I ate. I had a few hours before I would head out, so I took a shower and gave myself a manicure and pedicure. I took extra time to do my hair and makeup. I needed to look spectacular tonight. Not just any guy would do tonight. I needed the best of the best and getting the best required looking your best.

As I looked at myself in the mirror, I pretended I was dressing for Logan, that he would join me at the club, but I knew he wouldn't. I shook him from my mind. He wasn't important anymore. To hell with my plans for him. I got my revenge on him. Anything else would have to be on the back burner for now.

I got into the club with no problems when the bouncer recognized me. He gave me an appreciative look that normally gave me a confidence boost, but tonight made me self-conscious.

Shoving those feelings to the side, I strutted to the bar and ordered an amaretto stone sour. I didn't need to be drunk tonight, but I wanted to let loose more than what I was currently feeling. As I drank, I scoped out the tables, looking for a guy to take home. A table in the corner had five guys drinking beer and laughing. A few of them were pretty good prospects, but I wouldn't know for sure until I got closer.

I swayed my hips as I walked over to their table and immediately caught their attention. Three were particularly interested, which I assumed meant that the other two were already taken. One was extremely good looking, but the other two were also hot. I would be lucky to go home with any of them tonight. I felt like myself again as their eyes roamed over my body. I was wearing skin tight jeans, a halter that had a deep v down to my belly button with a strand of beads holding the two sides together, and black stilettos.

"Hey, boys. I'm looking for someone to have fun with tonight." I raised one eyebrow and gave a saucy smile. "Anyone game?"

I turned on my heel and strutted my stuff over to the dance floor. I started dancing and felt two arms wrap around my waist, but was slightly surprised when one of the other guys appeared in front of me. I didn't normally dance with more than one guy at a time, but tonight I wanted to let loose and feel like me again. It may be slightly reckless, but my body was telling me to go with it. The three of us spent the next hour grinding on the dance floor, our sweaty bodies rubbing against one another. It was erotic and exactly what I needed.

I was ready to get out of there, so I turned to them and gave a wicked grin.

"I'll be heading back to a my place. Care to join me?"

I hadn't even gotten their names and I didn't need to. They were fun for the night and nothing more. One looked at the other, almost like they had to decide if they were willing to do this, but it was only seconds later they were following me out the door. I told them to follow me home and got in my car, excitement running through my veins. When we walked into my building, the stairs sounded like a good idea. No better way to get in the mood than by having them stare at my ass for a few flights.

When I rounded the corner to my apartment though, my smile faltered. Logan was standing outside my door and he clocked me as soon as I rounded the corner. There was no mistaking what was going on here. I had two men that were following me back to my apartment. I felt bad for all of two seconds before I remembered that he hadn't been willing to help me when I needed it. He'd allowed me to walk out the door, and now he had to deal with the consequences.

It wasn't until I walked closer that I realized this may be the best form of revenge I could take on him. Though, I wasn't sure if this was revenge for our past, or for him letting me down when I needed him tonight. He had screwed me over one too many times, and I was tired of men taking all the control. I'd done my own thing for years now, and just because Logan had returned to my life didn't mean I would stop just for him.

His eyes followed me as I sauntered up to my door with two men following. The hatred in his eyes had me smirking at him. He knew exactly what was going on here, and now he was witnessing what he was missing out on.

"You'll fucking leave if you know what's good for you," he snarled.

"I didn't know we were expecting a third guy. No offense, man, but I'm not really cool with that. I don't know you," handsome man number one said.

I turned away from Logan and opened my door. "You weren't invited to the party, Logan. Boys, why don't you go ahead and make yourselves comfortable. I'll be right in."

They walked through the door and I caught a glimpse of one taking off his shirt. He had a nice body that I couldn't help but stare at. Logan grabbed my arm and spun me against the wall. Anger poured off him and his eyes pierced through to my heart. He was begging me not to do this, but I had already made up my mind, and I wouldn't back down.

"Don't do this, Cece. This isn't going to help. Please. You're only going to regret this."

I stared straight into his eyes, giving him my best bitch face. "Logan, for some reason, you seem to think your opinion would matter to me. We fucked and that's it. Don't go making it out to be more than that. Besides, I already offered myself to you, and you turned me down. What I do in my spare time is no longer your concern."

He pulled back sharply. I could see that my words stung and that's precisely what I was going for. It wasn't exactly the way I had planned my revenge, but it worked nonetheless. My chest felt like it was going to cave in at the look on his face. I got my revenge, but it didn't feel as good as I thought it would.

He stepped back further, shoving his hands in his pockets, then turned and walked away. I almost called after him, but then I remembered why I needed this. There was no room for Logan in my mind.

Shaking off his look, I stepped into my apartment and faced two gorgeously naked men. They each still had their boxers on. It probably would have been uncomfortable for them to both be standing around with their junk hanging out.

I had never done this before, so I didn't really know where to start. Luckily, hot guy number one walked over to me and pulled me in for a scorching kiss. I felt his hands grip my ass, but then there was a body behind me. Warm lips caressed my neck at the same time that another set of lips took my mouth. There were so many sensations running through my body. My nipples tightened, my pussy clenched with need, and my heart hammered in my chest. Hands roamed over my ass and my breasts. Erections pressed at me from both sides.

Fingers untied my halter and pulled my top over my head, exposing my breasts to the man before me. His mouth covered my nipples and sucked them playfully. The man behind skimmed his hands down my sides and removed my shoes. His hands ran across my pussy as he reached up and unzipped my jeans, dragging them down my legs. I was losing track of who was touching me where. When I felt fingers pressing at my wet folds at the same time my nipples were being pulled, I shot off like a rocket, moaning and screaming in ecstasy. I practically collapsed and one of them caught me and carried me over to my bedroom. He placed me on the bed and told me to get on my knees, my body willingly following his command.

Over the next hour, I was fucked in every hole possible. My body was used and sore, and even if I wanted to, I couldn't take any more tonight. Luckily, I didn't need to ask them to leave because when they caught their breath, they started getting dressed. I thanked them for the fun time and walked them to the front door. One of them asked for my number, but I wasn't interested in repeating. I hardly ever did, except with Logan, but that was different. I let the guys out and watched them walk down the hall. I was just about to close the door when I heard his voice.

"I guess I don't have to ask how it went."

I turned to see Logan walking towards me from the other end of the hall. I couldn't read his face. Normally, I could tell what he was thinking, but he was closed off now. I wondered if he thought I was a slut or if he pitied me. The anger of his rejection still coursed through me, and I had a hard time feeling bad at the moment. I crossed my arms over my chest and leaned against the doorframe.

"Spying on me? Trying to see if I moaned louder for them than I did for you?"

He looked down and let out a small chuckle. The thing was, that chuckle sounded so sad, and that made me feel like shit. I wasn't sure why. I had offered myself to him, and he didn't want me. When he looked back up at me, he almost looked like I had hurt him, but that couldn't be possible. Logan only cared while it was good for him.

He sighed heavily, his head hanging to the ground as he let out a humorless chuckle. "I was worried that you might freak out, so I stuck around."

"Well, as you can see, I'm perfectly fine, and I'm sure you heard how much I enjoyed it."

He stared at me in concern, his eyes studying my face for any sign I wasn't okay. Then he wiped all emotion from his face. "I just wanted to make sure you were alright."

He turned and walked down the hall before I could say anything else. I was a little stunned. I really thought he didn't care. All those attempts to get more from me, he was just using me until he was ready to toss me away. Even if I had stayed with him tonight, how much longer would it have been until he walked away for good and I ended up with a broken heart again? But none of those thoughts jived with the man that just walked away from me.

I shut the door as he disappeared and looked at my apartment, my clothes strewn on the floor. I got what I needed tonight. Those men erased the feel of strange hands on me. I thoroughly enjoyed myself, but for some reason, I wanted to cry. My chest started to hurt and I felt tears prick my eyes. I swiped at my face, angry at myself, because I knew deep down the reason I was so upset was because I hurt Logan. I could see it in his eyes as I baited him. He had wanted to help me and I tossed him aside. He stuck around to see if I was alright and had heard everything that was going on in my apartment. That was cruel and unusual punishment to put himself through, and he had done it for me, to make sure I didn't get hurt.

A cry tore out of my mouth and I sank to the floor. I had meant to get my revenge on him, but I never knew it would hurt so much. I had slept with many guys over the years, but they always knew there would never be more. I had told that to Logan also, but he didn't let me push him away, and when I was hurting, he was there for me. Revenge had been sweet, but the aftermath was excruciatingly painful.

CHAPTER 16

LOGAN

IF YOU LOOKED up self-inflicted torture online, there would be a picture of me sitting outside Cece's apartment. When she stepped off the elevator with two guys, my stomach about bottomed out. I didn't want to take advantage of her vulnerability and sleep with her, and I stupidly didn't believe her when she told me she would find someone else.

I headed over to Ryan's house, needing to get drunk. I couldn't eliminate the image of those men walking out of her apartment, but worse, I heard her moans of pleasure on repeat in my head. It was torture, and apparently, I was great at torturing myself.

When I pulled up to Ryan's house, I realized it was poker night. All the guys were here. Fuck, I really didn't need everyone looking at me with pity, or worse, disgust. They'd say I deserved it, that it was payback for the years I had screwed around with women. But I couldn't drive away either. I needed someone right now, and I needed something hard to drink.

I knocked on his door, not at all surprised when he answered with a grin. "Man, you're late. We're almost done."

I must have looked like shit, because the smile fell from his face and he actually looked a little worried. "What's going on?"

"I, uh...I just came from Cece's."

He nodded. "Sean told us what happened. I just didn't think things were actually that serious between you two."

I frowned. "I took her paintballing with us."

He shrugged. "Yeah, but I figured you were just chasing the unattainable."

"Still, she was attacked," I said, a little pissed that he was brushing it off.

He waved me in. "Look, I'm not trying to make it sound like what happened to her wasn't bad. I just didn't realize that things were that serious between you two."

We headed downstairs where the rest of the guys were. Sean caught my eye immediately, a frown marring his face as he studied me. "What's going on?"

Sighing, I figured that I might as well lay it all out in all my stupid glory. "My...sort of girlfriend almost got raped. She pushed me away when I wouldn't sleep with her right after, and then she went and picked up two guys at a club."

"Ouch," Sebastian said, taking a sip of his beer.

Drew pushed a bottle of beer to me. "I think you need this."

"That's not the worst," I chuckled. "Stupid me, I wanted to make sure she was okay, so I stuck around in the hallway of her apartment building, waiting for her to get back."

"Why?" Jack asked incredulously. "Were you hoping for a kick to the nuts?"

"I would have at least seen that coming," I muttered. "She walked right past me, let the guys into her apartment, and basically told me that since I wouldn't give her what she needed, she found it somewhere else."

"With two guys?" Cole said, his eyebrows shooting up.

"How do you compete with two guys?" Drew muttered.

"I don't," I said bluntly.

"So...what happened?" Sean asked. "Did they stick around?"

I nodded. "And so did I."

"You...you sat out in the hallway and listened?" Ryan asked.

"I was worried."

"Why?"

I glared at him. "Because I'm a dumb fuck. I thought she would freak out. I thought she would have a panic attack or something, and I wanted to be there for her."

The guys winced.

"Yep, I heard the whole damn thing, just sat out there like a schmuck, listening to her screw two men."

"Maybe they were pretending," Sebastian offered. "Maybe she didn't actually screw them, just wanted you to think that she was."

I shook my head. "I'd recognize those sounds anywhere."

"Man, you must have the worst timing ever," Jack said. "I mean, you screw women all the time, and when you finally find someone you like, she fucks two guys while you're outside the room listening."

I glared at him, throwing my bottle cap at him. "Thanks for the recap. It's not like it's on replay in my head or anything."

"So, what are you going to do?" Sean asked.

"You mean, am I going to stick around?"

He leaned forward on the table. "Look, I get that it fucking hurts, but you can't blame her for what she did. She's freaking out. I've seen it before. They all have different reactions to something like that."

"He's right," Sebastian said. "I'm not saying what she did was right, but she was obviously pushing you away because she didn't know how to deal with what happened."

"Don't you think I know that? That's why I hung around. But you should have seen her face. When she opened the door and let them out, there was no regret on her face, only satisfaction."

"Are you gonna see her again?" Ryan asked.

I shook my head. "I can't. I just...I thought maybe she was the one."

The room turned silent and I couldn't look at any of them. Yeah, it was pretty fucking clear that none of them thought I was capable of having an actual relationship with a woman. But Cece was different. I saw something in her that I had never seen in another woman. Now that was all over. I could never sleep with her again. Even if she was hurting, she slept with them on purpose. She was trying to hurt me.

I let out a humorless laugh. "You know, the ironic part is that I sleep with women all the time, not caring about their feelings or what they want or need. Now the same thing happened to me, and it's my heart that's broken. If I sleep with her again..." I shook my head. "I don't think I could do it."

Ryan sighed. "Fuck, I think we need the hard stuff."

CHAPTER 17

CECE

THE NEXT MORNING, I woke to the smell of coffee, which was unusual because Vira never willingly got out of bed in the morning on a weekend. I climbed out of bed and went to the kitchen where Vira sat on a stool. Her look said that I was in big trouble. I needed coffee to deal with her this morning, so I grabbed my cup and doctored it up before sitting down with her.

"Okay, lay it on me."

"Would you like to tell me why Sean texted me that I needed to keep an eye on you because Logan would no longer be around? I thought that was the plan, but you didn't tell me you were that far along."

She eyed me skeptically and I knew I was busted. She could always tell when I was trying to hide stuff from her. Better to tell her now and move on with my day.

"Let's just say the plan moved forward unexpectedly."

"Meaning what?"

I explained to her what happened at the police station and a look of sympathy crossed her face, then rage.

"You mean to tell me that he wasn't gonna stick around because that asshole's on the loose?"

"No. He was perfectly willing to stick around, but when we got back to the hotel, I asked him to fuck me and he wouldn't. He said it wouldn't help me and I would only be hurting myself. So, I walked out the door and then went to the club and picked up someone...someones." I turned my head away and blushed. I normally wasn't a prude, but this was a lot, even for me.

"You picked up two guys? Nice. Were they good in bed?"

The grin on Vira's face should make me feel better. This was normal for us, this total lack of judgment over our sexuality, but I wasn't quite as sexual as Vira, and last night was not my finest moment, not that she would see it that way.

"That part was great. They were exactly what I needed. I just wanted to get out of my head and not feel, but Logan seemed to think it was moving too fast after the attack. He just didn't get that it was what I needed."

"Honey, there's nothing wrong with what you did. Not everyone is going to feel the same way in that situation. You did what you had to do, and screw him if he doesn't understand."

This was what I loved about Vira, unconditional support. She never judged me, probably because I learned from her, but she always knew what I needed.

"Well, it was all good until we got back here and Logan was waiting in the hallway. I basically told him that since he wouldn't give me what I needed, I found it somewhere else. Honestly, my first thought was that it was the ultimate revenge."

"I'd say. Waving two guys in his face had to be a shot to the nuts."

"Well, like I said, they were great in bed and I was very satisfied, until they left and Logan was still in the hallway." I lifted my eyes to meet hers. "He waited around to make sure I didn't freak out, and he heard everything. I wish I could say that it made me feel good, but when I realized how sincere he was being, I felt like a total shit bag. I got my revenge, but I totally hurt him."

"That's what you wanted, though. You can't tell me that you honestly didn't think he would be hurt by the time you were done with him?"

"It's not that." I fiddled with my coffee mug as I tried to think about what exactly I was trying to say. "No one ever tells you how horrible you'll feel when you hurt someone else like that. I only thought about how I felt after he left me ten years ago. I thought revenge would feel great, but the look on his face...it wasn't worth it. I don't feel vindicated. I feel like I'm lower than him. He doesn't even know who I really am. I manipulated him."

"And you're trying to tell me that he didn't totally ruin you ten years ago? You changed everything about yourself to the point that he doesn't even recognize you."

I was ashamed now and I couldn't look at her. My voice was quiet as I finally came out and said the truth of the matter. "Come on, Vira. It was ten years ago. We were both young and stupid. How many guys do you know that wouldn't run when a girl clings to him and tells him she loves him at that age? I'm not saying it was right, but we were so young. I'm older now and I know better than to play with someone's heart like that. I know the damage it causes." Tears filled my eyes as shame took over my body. "He said horrible things to me, but I let two guys into my apartment, ready to fuck them, while knowing that he knew exactly what was going on inside. He may have been an asshole, but I'm scum for what I did. Even if I wanted a chance with him, I could never get it now."

"Is that what you want? A chance?"

"I don't know, and I guess now I'll never have the opportunity to find out. He was starting to wear me down, and I wonder now how much longer I would have lasted before I started to fall again."

"You know, if you want a chance with him, there are two little words that can go a long way to helping you."

"Fuck you?" I said as I threw a pillow at her. No one liked being told they needed to apologize to someone else, but she was right. Even if nothing came of it, I owed him an apology for my behavior.

I basically spent the rest of Sunday drowning in my own sorrow and sleeping. I contacted my boss and told him I needed to stop at the police station tomorrow to meet with a sketch artist. He was very understanding and apologized profusely for what happened. He said he'd taken security measures to ensure staff safety. I hoped he was right, because right now, I was not feeling like walking back into that building. I wanted to ask to work from home, but if I got stuck in that way of life, I might become a hermit.

Monday morning, I walked into the police station at eight-thirty. My palms were sweaty and I felt like my heart would leap out of my chest at any moment. Could people see it pounding through my blouse? I looked down, relieved to see that it wasn't that noticeable.

Sean came out when the receptionist called him, and he led me back to a room where I could work with the sketch artist. He couldn't stick around because he had a case he had to follow up on. It took about an hour to finish the sketch and by the time I was done, I was a wreck. I didn't understand it. I had been attacked by a man, yet I went out the next night and picked up two guys, but today, giving a description made me sick to my stomach.

When I left the room, Sean was trying to ask me how it went, but my only thought was getting away from here as fast as possible. The room kept spinning and everything seemed to be moving on fast forward. As I looked at Sean, his face was moving in yawning motions and the sound coming out of his mouth came at me from a distance. Air. I needed air. I staggered to the door and stumbled down the sidewalk. I knew that I couldn't drive right now, but I needed to get home. There was no way I could work like this. I knew I couldn't pull it together and walk into that building. If I couldn't finish the sketch without losing it, there was no way I could go up into the building where it had happened.

Cars blurred past me as I made my way down the sidewalk, tripping over my feet in my desperate attempt to get home. I looked around the street, trying to figure out if I was even headed in the right direction, but I couldn't see through my blurred vision. I barely made out a sign across the street that seemed familiar and stepped off the sidewalk to head toward it. Horns blared and I felt myself being pulled back onto the sidewalk. In my confusion, I was sure that my attacker had found me and screamed like I was being murdered.

"Calm down. Let's go to that bench and sit down."

In my haze, I recognized Logan's voice and somehow that helped me to keep the panic at bay for a little bit longer. When I got to the bench, he pushed me into a seated position, then pushed my head down between my knees.

"Take deep breaths, sweetheart." He began rubbing up and down the length of my back and after about five minutes, my breathing returned to a more normal pace. The world stopped moving so fast and I no longer felt like I was on a rocking ship. Logan handed me a tissue and that's when I realized that I had been crying. I dabbed at my cheeks and blew my nose, now thoroughly embarrassed for my freak out.

"How about we get you home?"

I nodded, not knowing what else to say. He led me over to his truck and I climbed inside and buckled in.

"I knew you had your appointment this morning, so I came to see how you were doing. I was close by when Sean called and said you ran out and looked like you were gonna pass out. I just happened to see you on the sidewalk when I pulled up. You scared the shit out of me. You almost walked right into traffic."

"I wasn't...my mind..." I had to stop. I didn't know how to be vulnerable around this man. I had hurt him and he came back to check on me, again. "The world was spinning. I wasn't trying to walk into traffic, I just didn't really know where I was walking. Thank you for calming me down."

We were quiet the rest of the way to my apartment and he walked me upstairs to check it out and make sure it was safe. Vira was still home, so I wasn't worried about anything, but it was comforting to have him looking out for me. We must have woken her up because Vira came out of her bedroom looking very tired, but she perked up when she saw Logan.

"Did we wake you, Vira?"

"No. I'm actually working a double today, so I have to leave in an hour."

That bitch. She had told me her schedule yesterday, and she never worked a double. She was trying to get Logan to stay so I could talk to him. I wasn't sure I was ready for that, but Vira always meddled if she thought it was for my own good.

"Why are you back home?"

"I kind of freaked out at the station. I don't think I'm ready to go back to work yet." Tears threatened to emerge again, but I was no whiner, so I blinked them back and walked over to the couch.

"Shit. Honey, I can't stay. Logan, do you think you could stay with her? I don't want her to be alone."

I couldn't look over at him. What he must think of me, and now Vira was asking him to stay. He would probably rather be at a knitting group than sitting here with me.

"I have to call and move a few things around, but I think I can work it out."

Logan pulled out his phone and stayed in the kitchen to make his calls. Vira came over to the couch and I glared at her.

"You don't have to work, bitch."

She raised an eyebrow at me. "I don't know what you're talking about. Now, if you'll excuse me, I need to get ready for work."

She got up from the couch and went to her bedroom, shutting the door behind her. Staying in my work clothes was definitely not something I was interested in. I needed comfy clothes now. I went to my room and put on a pair of sweats and a sweatshirt that was still soft on the inside. Then I grabbed a pair of socks and a ponytail holder. I took it one step further and washed all the makeup off my face. I was slightly worried that without the makeup, Logan would recognize me, but honestly, at this point, I almost wished he knew who I was. It would be so much easier. I curled up on my bed and stared out the window, thinking how my life had taken a drastic turn in a short period of time. I could hear Logan on the phone, telling someone that I wasn't up to working yet and we'd have to see how tomorrow was. He walked into my bedroom, looking unsure of what to do. It was time to apologize.

CHAPTER 18

LOGAN

I REMEMBERED Monday morning that Cece had an appointment at the police station. I tried to forget about it and went to work, but I couldn't concentrate. I kept wondering if she was okay as she described her attacker. I must have been a glutton for punishment, because I grabbed my keys and headed to the station. When Sean called and said Cece had walked out and wasn't holding it together, I was glad I had come. When I parked in front of the station, I searched for her car, but she wasn't by it. My eyes scanned the sidewalk and I ran to her, just catching her before she stumbled into the street. She was a wreck. Her breathing was ragged and she couldn't seem to focus.

I took her back to her place so her co-workers wouldn't see her like that. There was no way she would want anyone to see her that freaked out. I called her boss and let him know she was in no condition to go in after the stress of giving her assailants description. He was very understanding and told me to have her let him know when she was ready to go back.

The next call wouldn't be so easy. I dialed Ryan's number,

waiting for him to pick up. "Where are you?" he hissed into the phone.

"I'm with Cece."

"Are you serious? We have a meeting this morning. You were supposed to be here ten minutes ago."

Fuck, I forgot about that. "Look, I'm really sorry, but I can't leave her right now. She freaked out after going to the police station. She's barely functioning."

He snorted. "After what she did to you, you're still hanging on her every word."

"Look, I don't expect you to get it, but I can't leave her. If you saw her..." I swallowed down my emotions, shaking my head. "I just can't do it."

"Fine, but you'd better be in tomorrow. I can't run this place by myself."

"I know. I promise. I'll be in tomorrow."

After a heavy sigh, he finally agreed. "I'll see you tomorrow."

I went in search of Cece and found her snuggled up on her bed, staring out the window. She looked so vulnerable sitting there in her sweats, with her makeup removed and her hair down. She appeared younger and more innocent that way. Something nagged at me, but I couldn't figure out what it was. I stared at her a minute, trying to figure it out, but I couldn't make the connection in my brain.

She turned her gaze to me and regret showed in her eyes. I didn't know what to say to her. I wished I could turn back the clock, but that wasn't possible. I was man enough to admit that I was hurt by what went down the other night, but for now, I would help her through today and then move on.

"Logan, can we talk for a minute?"

"Sure." I walked toward her and sat down on the edge of the bed. It was too close to her and felt too intimate, but before I got a chance to move, she started talking.

"I'm sorry for what happened Saturday night. The things I said were cruel, and if I could take them back, I would. You didn't deserve that from me after everything you did for me."

I nodded. "I'm sorry I tried to tell you how to deal with what happened. Obviously, you knew what you needed more than I did." I couldn't help the bite that came out in those words and I saw her flinch back slightly. God, I was being an ass. "Let's forget about it. What's done is done. Time to move on."

She looked down and fidgeted some more. The tension was thick in the room, as neither of us knew how to move on. An apology was nice, but it didn't change the way things were between us.

"What would you like to do today?"

Tears welled in her eyes as she looked at me. She was trying to hide the hurt I had inflicted, but she was doing a shitty job. I hadn't meant to get any digs in. She'd had a rough enough day, but the damage from Saturday was still raw and I didn't feel totally in control right now. I had too many emotions swirling to fully control them. Staying here with her might not have been such a great idea, but it was too late to back out now.

She swiped at her face and shrugged. "Honestly, I just want to lounge around all day. I think I'm gonna sleep, so you should probably just go and do something productive with your day."

There was no bite to her tone, just finality. She was dismissing me and ending this awkward tension. I should take the out and leave. I should, but I promised Vira that I would make sure she was okay, and I hadn't even been here a half hour yet.

"How about you get some sleep and I'll just hang out in the living room for a little bit."

"That's really not necessary. I'm a big girl and I'll be fine on my own."

"Humor me."

She turned away from me and laid down in the bed, effectively shutting me out. I closed her door and went out into the living room to watch some TV. Normally, I would get some work done if I was at home for the day with nothing to do, but I didn't have any of my stuff with me.

About an hour later, I went to check on Cece. She was sleeping, but it didn't look peaceful. She was frowning in her sleep and she kept shifting. I thought about waking her up, but if she was fine, I would feel like an ass. This morning must have taken it out of her because she slept well into the afternoon. I had put together some dinner for her and was just sticking it in the oven when she came out of her room. If anything, she looked worse now than before she went to sleep. She had dark circles under her eyes and she still looked exhausted.

"Maybe you should take another day off of work. You look like you're still pretty tired."

"I'm fine. I'm just a little hungry."

"Well, I put together a casserole for you. It'll be ready in forty-five minutes."

"Thank you. That was very nice of you."

Silence stretched between us, making us both very uncomfortable. I was ready to leave. I'd had enough of babysitting for one day. If things hadn't gone down the way they had, I'd have stayed with her as long as she needed and probably would have insisted on sticking around longer. But things had ended badly and while I didn't wish her ill will, I had no desire to stick around someone that could treat me like crap when I was trying to help. I understood why she did what she did, but that didn't make it alright in my book.

"I'm gonna head home. Will you be alright here?"

"Yeah, I'm fine. Are you sure you don't want to stick around for dinner? I mean, you made it."

"No, that's okay." I picked up my jacket and headed for the door. "I have stuff to do. Don't forget to lock the door when I leave."

I opened the door and walked out, waiting until I heard the lock click in place before heading down the hall. When I got in the truck, I called Sean for an update.

"Sean, give me some good news. Tell me you have a lead on this guy."

"Sorry. We've got nothing. We ran his sketch through the database, but we haven't gotten any hits yet. We sent out an APB, but we haven't heard anything yet. How's Cece holding up?"

"She slept all day. You should have seen her when I found her. She was practically in the street hyperventilating. I don't know how she's gonna make it back into the office."

"You're making it sound like the two of you are back together."

"I didn't say we were."

"You didn't say you weren't either."

"Yep. I'm aware."

"But you aren't going to tell me."

I sighed into the phone. "What's done is done and nothing's gonna change that. Just keep me posted on what's going on with the case."

"If you two are done, then why do you care?"

"Because I'm not an asshole."

I hung up the phone before he could say anything else. I didn't need my friends asking a lot of questions. In their eyes, I was already a screw up. I'd had the hottest fucking girl in the world and I had screwed it up big time. I wasn't the only one to blame, but I put the wheels in motion. A huge part of me wanted to run back to her and make everything better for her, but I wouldn't be the idiot that pined away after a girl that had no interest in me other than sex.

I threw myself into work throughout the week. I tried my best to not think about Cece and wonder what she was up to. That was difficult to achieve considering that I called Sean every day to find out if there was anything new on the case. He'd taken the police sketch to her workplace and showed it around the building, but nobody recognized the guy. Then, he went by her apartment and showed it to the building manager and they'd agreed to hang the sketch in the lobby along with a notice to call the police if he was seen.

Still, none of this made Cece any safer, and I didn't think I would be able to sleep well at night until this guy was caught. As much as I tried not to care, she had gotten under my skin and I was hooked. I wasn't sure what I was going to do about that fact. Unfortunately, Sean knew my secret. Despite telling the guys about how Cece treated me, Sean was fully aware of the fact that I was falling for her.

Sean called me on Friday while I was at the office. I was in a meeting, and it bugged the shit out of me that I couldn't get up and leave to call him back. If he was calling, it meant he had something, and I was dying to know what that was. As soon as I left, I went to my office and called him.

"Sean, tell me you have good news."

"I don't have good news per se, but I do have a possible lead. I showed the sketch down at the club and the bartender said that he's usually there on Friday and Saturday nights. He didn't have a name, so I have nothing to go on, but I was thinking that if this guy really wants Cece, maybe we could draw him out."

"You want to use Cece as bait? Are fucking kidding me? No. No way. There's no way she'll be able to go to that club knowing that he could be there."

"She'd be okay if you were there with her. I already got approval to take a few officers to the club on Friday and Saturday to be there, *if* Cece is willing to work with us. This is our best shot at catching this guy."

"Don't they have video feed at the bar? We could find him on video and track his credit cards..."

"He always pays in cash. Logan, we have no other way to track him."

I was quiet as I thought about it. I didn't want to put Cece in any danger, but it might be more dangerous to leave this psycho on the loose. Even if he never came after Cece again, she would always wonder if he was watching her, and as long as he was free, he could do the same or worse to other women.

"Alright, I'll talk to Cece about it, but if she doesn't want to do it, I'm not going to try to persuade her otherwise."

"That's all I'm asking. Let me know what she says. We could go tonight if it works for her."

"Yeah. I'll call you later."

I hung up, then made my way over to the firm where she worked. This was going to suck big time. I hadn't spoken to her all week and now I was showing up to ask her to help me find her attacker. I was stopped at a new security checkpoint in the lobby and asked where I was headed. Then they called up to Cece to ask if I was allowed to be sent up. I was glad to see the new changes in place. Hopefully, it made Cece feel safer here.

I took the elevator up to her floor and walked over to her office. She stood when she saw me coming and had a smile on her face. Shit. She thought I was here to see her in a friendly manner. Not that my visit was unfriendly, but I had a specific purpose in mind. She stepped out from behind her desk and walked over to me.

"Hey, Logan. I was surprised to hear you were downstairs."

Her tone had changed a lot since her attack. The once *always confident* Cece was barely there anymore. I saw glimpses of her, but right now, she looked uncertain. That killed me. I wondered briefly if I had given in to her that night, would she still have that confidence? Did I help strip that away from her?

"How are you, Cece?"

Her smile faltered a little. Over our brief time together, I had gotten used to calling her sweetheart a lot. Now wasn't the time to think about that. She pulled herself together and smiled again.

"I'm good. It's a little strange being here, but it's gotten easier every day. The new security measures are great."

"That's good."

"So, what did you want to see me about?"

"Um, well Sean has an idea, and I'm here to see if you want to go along with it."

Her smile died and she walked back behind her desk and sat down. Shit.

"Okay. Lay it on me."

"Well, Sean showed the sketch down at the club, and the bartender said that your attacker is usually there on Fridays and Saturdays. He thinks we might be able to draw him out if you were there."

Something crossed her face that looked a lot like fear. I didn't have time to decipher it because she straightened her back and her face went blank a moment later.

"Of course. Anything to catch this guy, right?"

"Cece, you don't have to do this. This could be dangerous, and I don't want you to do anything that you're not comfortable with."

She cut me off, looking up at me with defiance and resignation on her face. "It doesn't matter whether or not I'm comfortable. If I ever want to feel safe again, this guy needs to be caught. So, tell me what the plan is and let's get on with it."

"Basically, the plan is for you and me to go to the club, and Sean and a few other officers will keep an eye out for him."

"You're going to be there?" She looked at me in confusion.

"Of course. I'm not going to let you go there by yourself."

"But if you're there, he won't try to approach me."

"No. You can go to the club with me, but I'm not leaving you alone where he can get to you. Sean won't have enough officers to watch the exits and look for him, so we have to be smart about this."

"I want to talk to Sean about this. It doesn't make any sense to go there, but not allow him to get close to me. We'll never catch him that way."

"If he gets close to you and I'm not there, he could easily grab you without anyone realizing."

"What are you talking about?" She threw her hands in the air as she tried to keep her calm. "We'll be in a crowded club with a couple hundred witnesses. He wouldn't try anything."

"Are you really that naive? That's the easiest way for him to get to you. Do you know how little people pay attention when they're out partying? He could drag you away and nobody would think anything of it. He could spike your drink and then carry you off, and people would think you're drunk and he's trying to help you. There are so many things that could go wrong and we wouldn't know it because there won't be enough police officers at the club to keep eyes on you at all times. We do this my way or I'm telling Sean we're not doing it."

I must have put some fear in her because I could swear I saw her lip tremble for a second. I didn't want her scared, but I needed her to realize how dangerous this could be. She swallowed thickly, then blinked a few times, regaining her composure.

"Tell Sean that I'm good with it. I'll go home, get dressed up, and be ready when you pick me up." She turned back to the paperwork on her desk, effectively dismissing me. I turned for the door, pissed off that we were actually going through with this. It felt wrong to do this to her, but she agreed and there wasn't anything I could do about it.

"I'll be at your place at eight o'clock. We'll check in with Sean and then head to the club. His team will already be waiting there."

"See you tonight." She didn't look up as she said it. I didn't know if she was pissed at me or trying to seem indifferent, but I didn't like her reaction. She was way too calm about the possibility of seeing this guy again. I had some work to finish up at the office, so I headed back there, but honestly, I wasn't very productive. I kept worrying about how things would go tonight. Ryan came into my office and talked to me for a good five minutes before I realized he was in there. I filled him in on what was going down tonight and he told me to go home. He knew my mind was somewhere else and I would be of no use the rest of the day.

I headed home and got ready for tonight, then headed over to Cece's. I was a few hours early, but I thought she might need a distraction for tonight. When she answered the door, she looked pale and I seriously questioned whether this was a good idea.

"Are you okay? You don't look so good."

"I think I ate something bad, but I'll be okay."

"Cece, you don't have to do this."

"I'm fine. It's really..." She took off for the bathroom, and moments later was puking in the toilet. I walked in behind her and held her hair as I rubbed her back.

"I think we should call Sean and cancel. This isn't good for you."

She wiped her mouth and stood as she flushed the toilet. "No, what's not good for me is knowing that asshole is out there and probably has a hard on for me. I can handle this. I just need to get my shit together."

"Would it make you feel better if Vira was with you? Maybe we could have Sean and Vira together as a couple and then there would be an excuse for Sean to be closer all night."

"I don't want to put Vira in any danger."

"Sean would be with her the whole time.

"Only if she's okay with it. I don't want to guilt her into anything."

"Okay, I'll call Sean and see if that plan works for him. You call Vira and see if she's available."

After a fifteen minute call with Sean where he argued against involving Vira, I finally convinced him this was the best way to keep eyes on Cece and keep her comfortable. Sean wasn't too thrilled that I suggested Vira tag along. In fact, he was quite adamant that it was a stupid idea, but I needed to keep Cece from freaking out and Vira was probably the best thing for her right now.

We had a few hours before we left and I did my best to distract her, but it wasn't going so well. She paced around the apartment, not able to focus on doing any one thing. She tried to start some laundry, but forgot to add the clothes. She made dinner, but forgot to set the timer and it burned. She wouldn't have eaten anyway. She was way too keyed up. When Vira got home, she distracted her with picking out outfits and doing her hair and makeup. It helped a little, but knowing what she was dressing up for was a mood killer.

Sean showed up at the apartment a little early, but when he saw how upset Cece was, he decided that we might as well leave early and see if we could loosen her up a little. She was determined to go through with this, so we headed for the club. Vira and Cece got us in with no problem and we headed straight to the bar. The bartender was aware of what was going on and was being compensated to let us know if our guy was spotted. He was to send us each a vodka tonic as a signal that our guy was around.

Cece almost fell over her feet several times just walking over to the bar. She was anything but relaxed. If her attacker spotted her looking this agitated, he might think something was up and head out. I grabbed her hand and headed to the dance floor. I needed to loosen her up a little.

With the next song, I got her to laugh a little at my moves, but she was still stiff. "Hey," I said, cupping her jaw. "It's just you and me. Forget about him."

She huffed out a laugh. "That's kind of hard to do when he's the reason I'm here."

Her eyes darted back around the club. This wasn't working. I needed her to focus only on me and forget everyone else. That was the only way we could make this look natural.

I pulled her against me, grasping her hands in mine, and ran them up her body and over her breasts and up through her hair. When she lifted her hair off her neck, I leaned in and started to suck her delicate skin. Her body shivered in response and I took that as a sign that I was taking her in the right direction. I ground my hips against her ass and lowered my hands to her hips, following her movements. My mouth trailed along her shoulder leaving wet kisses along her smooth skin.

Turning her around, I moved her arms around my neck and kissed her hard on the mouth. My tongue slipped in her mouth and my hands trailed her body, my body vibrating with need. She felt so right in my arms and I forgot all about why we were here. A week without her had been torture for me. The more her body moved against mine, the more I knew I couldn't give her up yet. I needed to fight for every kiss she would give me, for every touch. She was mine, and she may not realize it yet, but she would not be walking away from me again.

CHAPTER 19

CECE

LOOKING into Logan's eyes as he danced with me, I felt my body coming alive again, my spirits lifting. Coming here tonight had been one of the hardest things I'd ever done. My emotions had been all over the place this week. Sometimes I felt like myself, while at other times, I felt like a scared kitten. I couldn't figure out which way was up and it was exhausting. I hadn't slept all week. Every noise made me think that my attacker was back to get me. I didn't think I would ever feel safe again, but Logan changed all that the moment he pulled me into his arms. He knew that I needed some way to find myself, and he made it happen.

Then he kissed me and I about cried at the relief that swept through me. I hadn't realized how much I needed him. This was probably what he was talking about that night, the night I walked away from him. He wanted to help me in a different way, and I was hell bent on doing things my own way. It helped, but the relief was only temporary. In the long term I hurt us both, and I didn't feel any better about myself or feel any safer. If I hadn't pushed him away, he probably would have been with me the whole week, helping me chase away my demons.

As the music changed throughout the night, I continued to dance with Logan, and every dance made me feel more and more like my old self. I caught him glancing around the room from time to time, but he mostly looked at me, his eyes trailing the curves of my body.

Vira and Sean were dancing close by, but I never really paid attention to them. Logan assumed that I needed Vira by my side to get through this, but he was wrong. I loved Vira like a sister, but he was the one that made me feel safe. It was closing in on the end of the night and we still hadn't seen the creep, so we decided that it was time to head out and try again tomorrow. I hadn't gone to the bathroom all night, so Vira and I headed to the bathroom with Sean and Logan trailing closely behind.

Vira and I were chatting as we entered the ladies room, but as soon as Vira entered, she stopped in her tracks leaving me to run into her from behind.

"What the hell, Vira? A little warning next time."

I looked up to see none other than my attacker standing off to our left pointing a gun at Vira's head. He reached behind me and turned the lock on the door, blocking our only escape.

"Brought some friends with you tonight, did ya?"

My body shook as I looked at the man who had assaulted me a week ago. I reached forward to grasp Vira's hand, hoping that it would bring me a little comfort. Her grip was tight and it helped to ground me when panic threatened to take over.

"I just came here to have fun. What are you doing here?"

"Have fun, huh? I saw the cops at the doors and your friend here is dating one. I've seen them together several times. Did you think I wouldn't notice you stepping out on me?"

"What are you talking about?"

Panic was clawing at me and I did my best to hold it together. Maybe I could talk this guy down or at least get him to point the gun away from Vira. If I stalled him long enough, the guys would come looking for us.

"My girl doesn't get to screw other guys. I saw you here last weekend and you left with two guys, you slut!"

This guy was off his rocker. His girl? I had never met this guy before in my life and he was acting like the disgruntled boyfriend.

"Look, I don't know…"

"Shut up, you bitch. We're leaving. Go open that window or I'm gonna put a bullet in your friend."

As I tried to step away, Vira squeezed my hand. Her eyes pleaded with me not to go, but there was no way I would let her get shot. All that would accomplish was a bullet hole in her and me still at his mercy. I stepped to the window and pushed it open as much as possible. Hopefully, one of the cops would see us making our way out and save me before this asshole took me and cut me up into little bits.

"Crawl out the window and wait for me. If you try anything, I'll kill your friend."

"Vira, Cece, let's go," Sean called to us as he pounded on the door. I heard him try to push the door open and he cursed when it wouldn't budge. "What the fuck? Why is the door locked?" There was more pounding and the asshole walked over to Vira and whispered in her ear. She paled and then turned her head towards the door.

"We're almost done. Chill the fuck out." It had all the attitude that Vira normally spoke with, but I could hear the shaking in her voice. Apparently, so could Logan and Sean because they started slamming into the door, trying to break it down.

The asshole pushed me to climb out the window, and when I was out, he quickly followed behind me, stopping on the sill. He pointed the gun at Vira and took a shot before I could do anything. I leapt toward him, pulling on him, hoping I could catch him off guard.

"No! You asshole!" As he fell to the ground, I climbed on top and started punching him. I lost all sense as I thought of my friend lying on the floor dead or bleeding out. Red swarmed in front of my eyes. I could kill this guy right now and have no regrets. When my fists hurt from punching him, I stood, ready to kick him. He grabbed my ankle and twisted, causing me to fall to the ground. I caught myself, but scraped my hands as I fell to the ground. He grabbed me by the hair and in seconds was hauling me away from the club. We were in an alley away from the exits and there was no one around to witness anything. His gun was pressed in my side as he pulled me to the end of the alley to a dark street. There was an old beater on the side of the road that he threw me into from the driver's side. I tried to get to the passenger side, but he held the gun against my head.

"Try anything and I'll put a bullet in you. No bitch of mine gets to fuck me over. You need to learn your place."

I knew you were never supposed to get in a car with someone, but if you did get taken, you had to fight, because there was a smaller chance of being found once they got you to another location. But as I looked around, I knew this wasn't my chance. I needed to be somewhere more populated. I needed a distraction so I had my shot to get away.

He was very good, staying inconspicuous as he pulled into traffic. We drove through the city for a few miles, but the further we went, the more my stomach knotted. There weren't many people around, and if I didn't take the chance soon, I wouldn't get away. I was on the verge of a breakdown, but I couldn't break in front of him. I wouldn't.

His gun was still aimed at my head, but he wasn't watching as closely anymore. It was like he knew he was going to get away. It was either take my chance and risk dying or not try at all and die anyway. And I wasn't going down without a fight.

I flung my left arm up, pushing his gun toward the back seat and thrust the heel of my right hand up into his nose as he turned to me. I was momentarily stunned that it had worked that it took a second for my brain to come back online. I flung open my door and threw myself into the street, rolling several times. His car was swerving all over the road, so I took my opportunity to make a run for it. It didn't look like any of the shops on this street were open, so I ran down the closest alley, sticking as close to the buildings as possible. I heard his tires squealing and quickly turned the corner to another street. I had to find someone to help, but it was past one in the morning. No one was out. I didn't have my purse on me, and there were no pay phones anywhere that I could see. I zig zagged through several streets, trying to stay in the shadows and off one street for too long.

I was just coming around the corner to another street when I saw his car creeping down the road looking for me. Turning, I ran until I saw a fire escape and started climbing to the top. Hopefully, he wouldn't look up and would look only at the street. When I got to the top of the building, I watched from above to see where his car had gone. Luckily, he kept driving. He hadn't seen me. Just as I thought I was safe, he pulled over and got out of his car, looking around the street. I held my breath as he looked up and down both sides of the street and then walked back to his car, kicking his tire and cursing. I could feel his anger from up here on my perch.

He drove away and I watched his taillights disappear down the road. I waited for about a half hour, making sure that he didn't circle back. The longer I sat there, the more I came down from my adrenaline rush. I started to feel every ache in my body from jumping from the car.

As I sat there, the cold seeped into my bones. I didn't have a coat on, and my outfit was too skimpy to keep me warm. I knew I needed to get moving, but fear had paralyzed me. I needed to get to Logan.

Logan. Just get to Logan. I need Logan.

I had wasted so much time with him and it was over something that happened ten years ago. I felt like such an idiot. Logan was a good man and I could have had him back, but I pushed him away. If I got out of this, I swore that I would find a way to tell him the truth and get him back.

I wasn't sure how much longer I sat there, but it must have been a while because I was completely numb. It finally registered in my brain that if I didn't get down from this roof, I would probably freeze to death up here.

I made my way over to the ladder and started the climb down. It took me a long time because I had to concentrate to get my fingers to wrap around the rungs and to make sure my foot was actually on the step. I was about five feet from the ground when my foot slipped on the rung and I lost my grip. I fell to the ground and pain shot up my leg. I couldn't tell what had happened because my mind was in such a fog. I just knew I needed to get someplace safe. I hobbled down the street until I came to a cross street that had a few cars. I hurried over and waved down a few cars, but none of them stopped.

Finally, I was able to flag down a cab. The driver was older and had a kind face. He got out of his car and came to my side.

"Ma'am, are you okay?"

"No," I managed to whisper. "I need to go to the hospital. Can you take me?"

The cabbie didn't say another word. He ushered me quickly into the front seat and got back in the car, speeding off to the hospital. I knew that if Vira had been shot, she would have been taken in, so I would start there. I needed to make sure she was okay.

The cabbie cranked up the heat and ten minutes later, we were pulling up to the emergency room entrance. He hurried out of his car and helped me out. I gripped on to his arm as we walked through the doors. I wasn't sure how much longer my legs would hold me up, but I was hoping it would be long enough to find Vira.

There was a flurry of activity as we walked further into the ER. People in scrubs came running toward me and started asking me questions. When they started grabbing at me, my heartbeat picked up and I started to scream. I didn't want anyone touching me. I just wanted to find my friend.

"Cece! Cece!" Logan's voice broke through the chaos and I sighed in relief when I saw him running toward me. When he wrapped his arms around me, I finally broke, collapsing into his body. My legs wouldn't hold me up any more, so I let Logan pick me up and carry me over and set me down on something. The ceiling was moving above me as I felt myself being wheeled down a hallway. Logan stayed by me and held my hand, concern marring his handsome face. I had never been so happy to see anyone in all my life.

Tears spilled down my cheeks. If I hadn't escaped, I might have never seen him again.

As we went through some doors, I heard someone tell Logan he wasn't allowed back with me. He started arguing with the nurse, but she told him she would call security if he didn't go to the waiting room. I wanted to fight for him to stay, but exhaustion was pulling me under and my eyes slid shut.

When I woke, the first thing I noticed was that I was warm again. The second thing I noticed was that my body hurt everywhere. Opening my eyes, I was grateful the room was dark. Even the small light in the corner burned my retinas. I closed my eyes and mentally took stock of my body. My hands ached and were wrapped in some sort of gauze. My whole right side hurt, but I couldn't remember what I had done to cause it. It must have been when I jumped from the car. I didn't feel anything at the time, but I most likely didn't escape that jump unscathed. My right thigh felt tight, like it should hurt, but that was all I felt. As far as I could tell, that was all as far as injuries, but my whole body ached, like I needed a lot of rest.

I opened my eyes once again and looked around the room. Logan was sitting in the chair next to my bed with his eyes closed. I should probably let him sleep, but I needed to find out about Vira. Moving felt like it was too difficult, so I had to use my voice.

"Logan." My voice came out raspy and low, so I cleared my throat and tried again.

"Logan."

His gorgeous eyes opened and looked right at me. We stared at each other for a moment before he leaned forward and grabbed my hand, blowing out a long breath.

"I didn't think I'd ever see you again."

"How's Vira?"

"She's doing okay. He shot her in the shoulder."

I breathed a sigh of relief, staring at the ceiling. It could have been so much worse. I had seen him pointing that gun at her, and all I could think was that my best friend was dead and it was all my fault. Tears filled my eyes, but I took a deep breath, willing my body not to break down right now.

"How are you feeling?"

"My body aches, but I think I'll be fine in a few days."

Logan stood up and leaned over my bed, his eyes finding mine and forcing me to look at him. "I'm so sorry I wasn't there. We thought you would be safe in there together."

"Please don't blame yourself. We're both okay, and that's what I want to focus on."

He sat down on the edge of my bed and held my hand, brushing his fingers over my wrist. It was awkward because I didn't know what we were doing. I mean, we had been fighting, but then something happened in the club and I felt like things had changed, but now? Now I had no clue if he wanted me back or if he was just helping me to stay calm in the club. Part of me didn't want to know. I liked the idea that I could imagine that he wanted me back, because if he didn't, I wasn't sure my heart could handle that right now.

We sat in silence for a few minutes and I felt myself dropping off to sleep again. I wanted to stay awake and look at Logan some more, to see for myself that I was really back here where I was safe. I was afraid that the next time I woke up, I would be back on that roof or worse, in my attacker's presence again. I fought to keep my eyes open, but they kept drifting shut, only for me to jerk them back open.

"Go back to sleep. I promise, I won't leave."

"Will you lie down with me?"

"I don't think I'll fit in this bed."

"I'll scoot over."

I tried sitting up to move over, but pain shot through my body and I moaned at the movement.

"Hey, let me help you." He walked around to the other side of the bed and worked his hands under my body and gently pulled me over to the side of the bed. Then he walked back around and kicked off his shoes before climbing in with me. He moved his arm behind my body and pulled me in close. I rested my head on his chest and let my eyes drift closed. I needed him more than I was willing to admit at the moment. The only question was, would he still want me once he found out who I really was?

We were waiting for my release papers and Logan was fussing over me, making sure I was warm enough. He had gone to my apartment and gotten me some sweatpants, a sweatshirt, and some warm, fuzzy socks. It wasn't exactly stylish, but at the moment, I was fine with comfort. We had fought over where I was going to be staying over the next few days. I wanted to go to my apartment and be with Vira, but when Logan figured out that was the reason, he started laughing. Apparently, Sean had plans to take Vira back to his place so he could watch over her, so there was no reason for me not to go with Logan.

I was discharged after being in the hospital for a day and a half. I had been out of it for the first day, and luckily, my injuries weren't enough to warrant a longer stay in the hospital. I ached all over, but what I really needed was rest. When I slipped into the bathroom to get dressed before I was discharged, I took a good look at myself in the mirror and saw that my entire right side was covered in bruises. I also had a deep puncture wound in my thigh from when I fell off the fire escape. I had fallen on a piece of metal and it had torn a deep hole, but luckily didn't cause much damage. I was on antibiotics for the next ten days and they gave me some pain pills, which I gladly took. I wasn't into that kind of pain. If something hurt, I wanted to feel better.

It could have been so much worse. Every time I closed my eyes, I was back in that car or running down alleys, trying to escape the madman. My eyes slipped closed and tears welled in my eyes. I quickly brushed them away. I needed to be strong. I wasn't this girl anymore. I wasn't weak. I had become stronger over the years, and I wasn't about to change all that now. I would get through this.

Taking a deep breath, I was startled by a knock at the door. "Yes?" I asked, hoping the shaking in my voice was hidden.

"Are you ready?"

"Uh...I just...I need a minute."

The door opened a moment later and I spun around, hiding behind my sweatshirt that I held up in front of me. But it was too late. Logan got a good look at all the damage, and the rage on his face was crystal clear.

"Logan, it's not as bad as—"

"Don't," he said, his voice deadly quiet. He shook his head slowly. "I never should have let you go. I knew it was dangerous."

"Well, it was my decision. I was the one that wanted to do it. I knew what might happen." My voice cracked on the last word and Logan didn't miss it.

"It was my job to protect you."

"Logan, if I didn't try and that guy attacked more women, I would never forgive myself. We'll catch him."

"How can you be so sure?" he huffed out a laugh. "Christ, Cece, this guy has it out for you. We got lucky this time. What if we're not together next time? I can't lose you!"

The first tear slipped from the corner of my eye and I quickly swiped it away. "Logan—"

"No, don't act like it didn't happen."

"I'm not. I just...I messed up so much with you. There are so many things I wish I could do differently, but I can't go back."

"Hey," he said, wrapping me in his arms. His hand ran up and down my back. I clung to him, needing him now more than ever. I needed to tell him everything. I needed to be honest with him. "It'll be alright. We'll take it one step at a time, okay?"

I nodded and allowed Logan to help me get dressed. It was more difficult than I imagined. The bruising on my side hurt like a bitch, and with my hands all scraped up, it would have been nearly impossible to do this on my own.

Logan brought in the wheelchair for me and took me down to his truck where my luggage was waiting. He had already planned to take me home with him and had packed accordingly. An officer had stopped by my hospital room this morning, but Logan told the officer he could find me at his place later today. I was happy with the interference because I didn't want to make a trip down to the station. In fact, I mostly wanted to stay indoors, away from prying eyes.

When we got to his house, I opened the door of his truck, ignoring his swearing at me getting out on my own.

"Cece, just let me help you."

"No, I need to do this."

"Why?"

I couldn't explain it. Maybe it was pride or maybe it was just sheer stubbornness. I wasn't sure, but I knew that I needed this.

He sighed and took my arm. "You're always so damn stubborn."

I grinned slightly. "But you wouldn't like me as much if I didn't make things at least a little difficult."

He huffed out a laugh. "You know, just once you could pretend that you need me."

I wanted to tell him that I did need him, but maybe that needed to be saved until after I told him the truth. It wasn't fair to lay all my feelings out there before he knew what I had done. And maybe that was for the best, because I had no idea how he would respond. He might kick me out of his life.

By the time I was inside, I regretted walking. My leg was killing me, but it was the combination of all my injuries that made me feel so terrible. I plopped down on the couch, sighing with relief. I should have just taken his help.

Logan stared at me, probably angry at the state I was in. "I think you need to call in to your boss and take a few days off work."

"I don't think I can," I sighed. "I've already taken time off and I'm still the new employee. I don't want to give them a reason to fire me."

"That's bullshit. You were attacked at the office. It's not like this is all happening outside of work. Call them and request some time off." I gave him a stern look that said I wasn't going to do what he said. "I'm serious. You call now and do it, or I'll chain you to the bed and call myself."

"Logan, I don't need you to tell me what to do. I'm perfectly capable..."

I didn't get to finish my sentence because he covered my mouth with his hand, stopping me from saying what I wanted to. His eyes darkened as he brought his whole body closer to mine. I could feel his breath on my face as he practically sat on top of me.

"I don't want to hear one more time about how you are capable of taking care of yourself. You proved that the other night. Please. Do this for me. I need to take care of you and make sure you have everything you need. Stop running from me and just go with whatever's happening here."

My throat constricted and I had a hard time getting anything to come out, so I nodded my agreement. "Does this mean I'm forgiven?"

"There was never anything to forgive. I'll admit, my ego was a little damaged, but nothing I can't recover from."

I placed my hand on his cheek, shaking my head slightly. He might not think I needed forgiveness, but I knew differently. "I'm so sorry that I did that to you. When I was on the roof, waiting for him to leave, all I could think was how much I regretted pushing you away. I was afraid that I would never see you again."

We hadn't really talked yet about all that happened, but I had given him a general idea. The police had to come by this afternoon, so he would hear everything then.

"I'm not going anywhere."

His hand ran down my face, caressing the bruises from my fall. He leaned forward and placed a gentle kiss on my lips. I needed more from him, but he was trying to be gentle until I was healed. He pulled back and sat down next to me on the couch, linking his hand in mine and pulling me down to lie on his lap. We laid in silence with me drifting in and out for most of the morning. I looked around his house, noticing that there was a lot of new stuff.

"Why did you get new furniture?"

"The old stuff was damaged when the house flooded. It might have been okay, but I didn't want to risk getting mold. I got new carpeting also because the other stuff had a weird smell, but the wood dried out and was salvageable."

I felt horrible. I was an evil person. My need for revenge had taken me too far over the edge. I didn't even recognize myself anymore. Sure, I had changed over the years, but I used to be a sweet girl that took into consideration everyone else before myself. Now I was destroying Logan's life all in the name of revenge. I was about to tell Logan who I really was when there was a knock on the door, which was no doubt the police coming to take my statement. Logan eased me into a sitting position and got up to answer the door.

Two officers were standing in the doorway glaring at Logan like he was a murderer.

"Logan Walker?"

"Yes."

"You are under arrest for destruction of property at Disco Fever last night. Officer Calloway, cuff him and read him his rights."

The officer yanked Logan's arms behind his back and started reading him his rights, while the other officer smirked at him. I could see the anger pouring off Logan. I didn't understand what was going on. I got off the couch as quickly as I could and walked over to the door, trying to figure out what was going on.

"Excuse me, what are you arresting him for? He was trying to rescue me last night."

"Ma'am, you need to step back before we arrest you for interfering in an arrest. Now stand back."

He put his hands on me and pushed me backward on my bad leg. Pain shot through me and I teetered falling into the officer putting cuffs on Logan. I tried to grab his arm so I wouldn't fall down, but I wasn't fast enough and I fell into him, knocking him to the ground. In a flash, the second officer had me on my stomach and was wrenching my arms behind my back. Logan lost it and was struggling against the cuffs, screaming at the officers not to touch me. I heard Officer Sawyer get on his mic and request backup for two suspects resisting arrest.

Everything went by in a flurry after that. Police officers showed up at the house, Sean being one of them, and Logan and I were hauled into separate police cars. We were taken to the station, but I never saw Logan. My body ached as they shoved me into a holding room.

"What's going on? I don't understand why I'm here!"

"Ma'am, you were read your Miranda rights. I suggest you remain silent."

"But what did I do? Please!" I yelled as he slammed the door, leaving me alone.

I sat down in the chair, my whole body aching. The chair wasn't comfortable, and as I sat there, wondering what the hell happened, I realized this was my fault. Vira and I had the officers harassing Logan. That had to be what this was about.

There was a flurry of activity in the hallway, shouting and loud bangs that had me jumping. Then it got quiet. Sean came into the holding room about fifteen minutes later, removing the cuffs from my wrists.

He was pissed, and I wondered briefly if Vira and I were caught. Did her officer friends say something? Crap, if they outed us before I had a chance to tell Logan, there was no way I would have a shot with him.

"Don't speak until we're outside," Sean said, holding out his hand for me.

I nodded, relief flooding me. Maybe he didn't know anything. I limped along behind him as he guided me through the station to the chief's office.

"Ms. Baker, I'm very sorry for what happened," he said as he stood. "Please, take a seat. I did as he asked, partly relieved and partly terrified. "Can you please tell me what happened?"

"Um...the police were supposed to stop by this afternoon at Logan Walker's house to take his statement. When he answered the door, they said they were arresting him for destruction of property at the club last night. I tried to explain that he broke down the door to get to me, but they wouldn't listen. One of the officers shoved me back, but it was my injured leg, and I ended up falling into the officer cuffing Logan."

The chief sighed, tossing down his pen. "I'm very sorry this happened. Unfortunately, this is not the first incident with these officers, but I want you to know that they've been placed on suspension."

I ducked my head. I knew the real reason they had done this. And even if they had done it to others, I hadn't helped things. But confessing would only put Vira in the line of fire. I couldn't do that to her. I had to find a way to make this right without ruining her life. I'd have to talk to her as soon as possible. After I was attacked, I talked to Vira and asked her to stop the officers from taking things further. And she had, so why were they still going after Logan? I had to be missing something here.

"I hope you're feeling better soon, and if you have any further problems, please bring them directly to me."

The chief stood and I took that as my sign that it was time to go. I followed Sean out of the police station, relieved to see Logan waiting for me. I walked right into his waiting arms, but guilt took over as he comforted me, because I knew the truth. Everything crappy that had happened to him in the past month was my fault, and if I had any hope of having a future with him, I was going to have to tell him the truth. I would talk to Vira and we would try to figure this out, but one thing was certain, I was either telling him the truth or walking out of his life forever.

CHAPTER 20

LOGAN

I COULDN'T FIGURE it out. For some reason, these assholes had it out for me. All the other officers in the police department were great cops, but these two seemed to have it out for any citizen they didn't like. Harper had been on the receiving end of their anger also. If Sean hadn't heard the call, I'm not sure how long we would have been stuck there. Not to mention, Cece had already had a shit couple of days and then she got manhandled by two asshole cops. I could tell she was hurting when she walked out of the police station with Sean. She was limping pretty badly, and Sean looked like he was ready to pick her up and carry her.

When she collapsed in my arms, it took everything in me to not walk back into the police station and beat the crap out of Sawyer. He was the one that cuffed her like a criminal after he pushed her. I needed to get her home, and getting thrown in jail was not the answer right now. I just wanted to lie down in bed with her and hold her in my arms. Once we got home though, that didn't happen.

"I hate to do this after everything that's happened, but I need a statement about what happened the other night."

"Can we do this another time?"

"No," Cece cut in. "It's fine. Let's just get this over with."

I watched as she hobbled over to the couch, obviously in pain. It was all my fault. I had let her down. I should have followed her back to the bathrooms and gone in with her. But we'd assumed it was fine. It was a bathroom. What could go wrong? No one had seen the guy all night. The bartender had watched for him, but seen nothing.

When Sean tried the door and it wouldn't open, I went ballistic. I heard the fear in Vira's voice as she told us to chill out, and that only made me hit the door harder, but it was a metal door. When we heard the gunshot, my heart practically stopped right in that moment. Sean was able to get the door open, but it was too late.

I still felt guilty, because when I saw Vira laying on the floor in a pool of blood, I was just relieved it wasn't Cece. What kind of person did that make me? I ran to the window, but she was already gone. I ran out of the club, trying to find her, but she was gone, in the hands of a psychopath, and I didn't know if I'd ever see her again. I'd let her slip right through my fingers.

"I'll make some coffee," I said, shaking myself out of those thoughts. I headed into the kitchen and went through the motions.

"Are you alright?" Sean asked from the doorway.

"I'm not the one that was attacked by an officer after just escaping a madman."

Sean stepped further into the kitchen, shoving his hands in his pockets. "I know what you're feeling. I felt the same way too when I saw Vira laying on the ground."

I swallowed hard, remembering driving around looking for her. "When I couldn't find her...I didn't know where to look. I failed her."

"If you failed her, then we all failed her. It was on all of us. We all knew the risks going in."

"I just left her out there," I said quietly.

"You looked for as long as you could."

"Not long enough," I bit out. "She was out there, freezing and terrified. You saw her when she wandered into the hospital. Her skin was blue, Sean. I swear to God, when I saw all that blood running down her leg, I wanted to kill someone."

"I'll pretend I didn't hear that."

"You don't know what that's like, to see the woman you...to not know where she is and if she's hurt."

"You think I didn't feel the same way with Vira, when I saw her laying on the floor?"

"It's not the same. She was right in front of you. You could help her. I was fucking useless."

"You weren't useless. You did everything you could for her. And don't you remember what I went through with Cara when she was missing? I was in hell for ten days, terrified that she was dead. I got lucky. We *both* got lucky. Don't dwell on the things you can't change."

I leaned against the counter, my head hanging low as I tried to calm down.

"Have you told her yet?"

"Told her what?"

"That you love her."

I scoffed, shaking my head slightly.

"Don't even deny it. When a man has to hold another man back from killing anyone in his path at a hospital, it's not just fucking. She means a lot to you, maybe more than you're ready to admit. But I knew, as soon as I had to hold you back, I knew this wasn't just a fling. You love her, and you should tell her before it's too late."

He walked out of the room, leaving me to get the coffee. I knew he was right, but now wasn't the time. I brought everything into the living room, setting the tray down on the table. Then I saw how Cece was curled up, looking cold, and it reminded me of the hospital. I grabbed a blanket from the back of the couch, wrapping her up in it.

"Are you hungry?"

"A little."

"I'll get you something to eat," I whispered, kissing her cheek. I quickly grabbed some crackers for her. She probably didn't want anything too heavy right now. I glanced at the clock and grabbed her medication, handing it to her. She still didn't look comfortable, and it ate at me. She needed to be taken care of, not reliving this shit.

Looking at the tray, I saw there was no cream or sugar. I started toward the kitchen when Cece stopped me.

"Logan. What are you doing?"

"I forgot the cream and sugar. I'll be right back."

"Wait. Please come here."

I turned to look at her and saw a sympathetic look on her face. I didn't understand it.

"I don't need you to get me stuff. I just want you to be here with me when I give my statement. I just need you."

"Why?" I asked, disgusted with myself. "You got taken because of me. You got manhandled today because of me."

"No, I got taken because a psychopath was after me. I got manhandled because two assholes have a vendetta against you. None of that was your fault. Come sit with me."

Against my better judgement, I sat down next to her and spent the next half hour reliving what she went through the other night. She gripped my hand when she recounted details of her escape, her terror shaking through her body. I wrapped my arm around her shoulders, pulling her close to me. When Sean finished with her, he stood to leave.

"Sean, how's Vira doing?"

"She's fine, sweetheart. In a few weeks, she'll be almost new."

Something crossed Cece's face and I couldn't place it, but then she got up and went in the other room, leaving me alone with Sean.

"What are we gonna do about this guy, Sean? I can't be with her all the time and she can't be walking around alone with this guy after her."

"I can put a protective detail on her, but it won't be for long. The department won't let her have protection forever." He sighed, running a hand over his face. "We've had no luck with identifying him. No one saw him at the club or around her building. I'm gonna check traffic cams where she said she was taken, but that's not a good area and there aren't as many cameras. Chances are, it'll amount to nothing."

"She can stay with me until this guy is caught. Will Vira be staying with you?"

"For now. That woman is so stubborn."

"What's going on with you two?"

He huffed as he looked at me. "Not a whole lot. I told her I wanted to date her exclusively. She's pretty wild, ya know? She told me she would consider an open relationship, but that she doesn't do anything exclusive."

"Ouch. Sounds very much like Cece. Where did these girls come from? I have never met a woman that didn't want to string me up by my balls."

"I don't think they were wanting a relationship if they were going to string you up by your balls."

I flipped him off as I stood. "You know what I mean."

Laughing, he stood and started walking for the door. "I'll be in touch after I look into the traffic cams. Don't be surprised if you see cops hanging out on the street."

It had been three weeks and we were no closer to catching this guy than we were the night Cece was taken. Frustration was building with both Cece and me. Cece, because she didn't appreciate my hovering and me, because Cece didn't listen to a thing I said. She was always taking off without me, insisting that the police were watching and she would be safe.

Cece had grown more distant from me during the past several weeks, and I could only assume that's why she was always trying to get away from me. I wasn't sure if it was the attack that had her backing away or if she just needed space, but no matter how much I tried to get her to confide in me, she just pulled away further.

The good news was that I hadn't been harassed since Sawyer and Calloway had been put on suspension. The department was looking into a shit load of complaints from people who claimed they were harassed by one or both of them. It was all great for me because I had a big meeting coming up and the last thing I needed were two rogue police officers coming after me with bullshit traffic tickets.

Ryan and I were scheduled to meet with Cassandra this morning about the funds that were being raised for VAS. She hadn't clued us in on the phone whether or not she got all the funds needed or if we were even hired for the job. Ryan and I were both antsy to get to the meeting and find out what was going on. My body was practically vibrating with the tension running through me. We were driving over to Cassandra's office, and Ryan was driving me crazy tapping the steering wheel.

"Would you fucking stop that?" I was on the verge of losing my mind in the car with him.

"Stop what?"

"That tapping. You're driving me nuts."

"And you think your leg bouncing isn't driving me crazy?"

"You should have just fucked her. Maybe then we wouldn't be waiting to find out if we got the job."

"Is that your solution to everything? Just fuck her? Shit, I thought we wanted to get the job based on our merits, not whether or not I could please her in bed."

"If you're questioning whether or not you could please her in bed, then it's a good thing you didn't sleep with her yet."

"You're such a fucking asshole."

I grinned at him. Our back and forth had released a little tension for both of us and we were ready to go by the time we walked into her office. Cassandra was sitting behind her desk wearing a pair of glasses that made her look like the naughty librarian. I smirked at Ryan when he attempted to talk and croaked instead. I stepped forward to cover his inability to speak.

"It's good to see you again, Cassandra. How did it go with the investors?" I asked as we both took a seat.

"I'm pleased to tell you that all the investors are in and we actually raised money for more than what is needed because some of them thought we should expand further than what was planned. One of the investors suggested that we have some kind of work program on sight. There are studies that show that veterans who participate in work therapy have a better chance of working through their issues and coming out on the other side ready to acclimate back to civilian life."

"What exactly are we talking about with work therapy?"

"Well, some people do art therapy or music therapy, which could be included in this facility. Some veterans may need something that they can do with their hands that's more like work."

Ryan sat forward with an inquisitive look. "Like rebuilding cars?"

"Something along those lines. There's not one thing that would work for every veteran, but we could have several small programs if I work the financing the right way."

"We have a friend that does woodworking with his father. It seems to be something that really helps him with his issues."

Her eyes lit up. "That sounds like it would be perfect for the facility. Would you be able to add on to your current plans for a shop room?"

"I'm sure that wouldn't be a problem," I said, feeling the excitement growing. This project could be huge for us, but it also stood to help a lot of people.

"Maybe I could have veterans incorporate their woodworking into the building somehow. What kind of woodworking does your friend do?"

"Mostly furniture. He mostly does custom orders for people. Some come to him with a specific design, while others ask him to come up with something unique."

"Would he be willing to donate some pieces to the facility?"

I looked at Ryan and he nodded. "I think so, but he's got some stuff that he's dealing with right now. I'm sure by the time the facility is up and running, he could have some pieces for you. Let me talk to him and see what he says."

"Sounds perfect. Now, Ryan, let's talk about when we can break ground."

"This is going to be great for us. What do you say we go out and celebrate tonight?" Ryan suggested.

"Yeah, we could head over to The Pub. Why don't you ask Cassandra to join us? You know, to celebrate VAS getting off the ground," I raised an eyebrow, knowing that he really had a thing for her and would jump at the chance to invite her out to celebrate.

"Sure. That sounds good. I'll give her a call."

"I'll see if Cece is available to go out."

We all met up at The Pub that night and had a great night drinking and celebrating. Cece was still being a little reserved with me, and I had big plans to find out what was going on with her. When we left, I drove straight back to my place and pulled her inside, slamming her up against the door.

"Are you gonna tell me what's wrong? You've been different for the past three weeks."

"Nothing's wrong."

"Really? You seem like you're holding back about something, but I can't figure out what it is. What aren't you telling me? Is this about the attack?"

"No. It has nothing to do with that."

"Then tell me what the fuck is going on."

She looked away from me and looked so vulnerable. I wasn't used to this Cece. I wanted the old Cece back. I turned her around and slammed her front into the wall, then ran my hands down her breasts to her pussy.

"If you aren't going to tell me what's going on, then I'm going to fuck it out of you."

I heard her whimper as I shoved my hands down her pants and stroked her wet pussy. I ground my erection into her ass as I grabbed her hair and yanked back her head. Nipping at her neck, I slid down her body, yanking her pants down. I pulled her around to face me and threw her over my shoulder, her pants were still down around her ankles giving her no room to move. I threw her on the couch and took off my belt, cinching it around her wrists. I spread her legs at her knees and crawled up between them. With her pants still around her ankles, she had no way of escape.

"Are you going to tell me what's going on?"

"Nothing, I swear."

I tore her panties off her body, then undid my pants and shoved them down my waist. I lined up my throbbing cock with her pussy and looked at her one last time.

"You sure you've got nothing to tell me?"

She shook her head and I slammed inside, not giving her another minute to think this over. I rammed into her so hard, it felt like my dick would fall off, but the sensations were amazing. She moaned as I continued to thrust inside her. I reached forward and grabbed her tit through her bra.

"Eyes on me, sweetheart."

Her eyes popped open, but there was something hiding behind her lust for me. It was so clear to me. I pulled out and picked her up, toeing off my boots and wiggling my pants off. I almost took her down doing it, but managed to stay upright. Walking over to the bookcase, I held her up against it as I slammed back into her. Books and pictures fell to the ground. Something made of glass shattered at my feet, but I kept thrusting into her.

"Oh, fuck!" She screamed as I rammed her harder and harder, her bound arms wrapped around my neck.

"Are you going to tell me the truth?"

"I am."

"You aren't," I growled. "Tell me or I won't let you come."

She glared at me. "You wouldn't dare."

I pulled out of her and rubbed my dick against her clit. Her eyes shuttered as I felt her body tremble against me.

"Oh, God. Logan, yes!"

I pulled my dick away from her and her eyes popped open. "Put your cock back inside me."

"Not until you tell me what's wrong."

"Do it now or I'll never fuck you again."

"Sweetheart, I've got you trapped against my dick right now. I don't think you're in the position to make demands." My mouth moved to her neck and I whispered against her ear. "I could slip back inside you right now and make you come so hard that you'll forget your name. Or, I can tease you with my dick and keep pulling away right before you orgasm. What's it gonna be, sweetheart? I've got nowhere to be."

I rubbed my dick against her again and felt her breath hitch as need roared through her.

"My name is Cecelia Clark," she yelled as I slammed my cock back inside her and stilled an instant later.

I pulled back slightly and looked at her face. Uncertainty crossed her features and I finally saw it. Before she reminded me slightly of Cecelia, but now I could see it in all her features. She wore her hair differently and it was a different color. She wore makeup now and she held herself differently. Her body was definitely different. She had filled out in all the right areas and toned up in others. I felt like such an ass for not seeing it earlier, but she had changed so much in ten years.

I didn't waste another minute as I fucked her hard against the bookcase. I had once thought I loved this woman, and now she was back in my arms. I didn't want to contemplate how I felt about that right now. I had her back and I would think about the rest later.

She squeezed me tight with her legs and her pussy clenched as she came. I slammed into her one more time as I came, biting her shoulder and leaving my mark. Slowly, her legs became limp and her arms hung loosely around my neck as her breathing slowed. I walked back over to the couch and slowly extricated myself from her, then took my belt from around her wrists. Rubbing my hands over the red on her wrists, I brought them to my mouth, kissing the red marks I had left behind. Then I pulled her shoes and pants off and carried her up to my bedroom.

I laid her down in bed and stripped her of her t-shirt and bra before taking off my own shirt. I pulled her close to me and kissed her temple. There was so much I didn't understand, and I wasn't sure I would like her answers, but I needed to ask.

"You've changed a lot."

She was silent for a minute and I didn't think she was going to say anything, but then she finally spoke.

"When you left me, I changed everything about myself. The thought that I wasn't good enough really cut me deep. I met Vira and she helped me become the person I am today."

My callous words to her that day rang in my mind. I had been young and stupid with no thought for how my words might affect her.

"I was stupid and afraid. I'm sorry I said those things to you."

"What were you afraid of?"

"I loved you, and I thought I was too young to be in love. I didn't want to be tied down to one person yet. I had this stupid idea that I needed to experience more women, to find a woman that could give me more."

"Well, you certainly got that," she sniped at me.

"I had no idea that what I said would hurt you so much. I'm more sorry than I can put into words."

"It wasn't just that you hurt my feelings. You made me question everything about myself." She sat up and glared at me. "I changed who I was so that no one could ever make me feel as small as you did that day. I'm not the same girl I was back then. When I said I didn't want a relationship, I wasn't lying. I haven't been with a man more than once since I was with you ten years ago. I've fucked a lot of men and I enjoyed every minute of it. I will never be that woman again."

"I know, and I will never be that kid again. I can't change what happened ten years ago, but that doesn't mean we can't move forward as the people we are today. I would be lying if I said that I wasn't attracted to the woman you've become. You have to admit we have great chemistry. Before, we just didn't have that."

"I don't see any reason why we can't continue our relationship the way it is, or lack of relationship." She ducked her head, like she didn't want me to see her face. "I wouldn't mind continuing to fuck you, but don't get any ideas of more."

I had the feeling that she was lying, but I let it go. It had to be hard to lay herself bare like she just did. And it was my fault that she had changed everything about herself. This was something I needed to ease into with her.

"Fair enough. So, why did you change your last name to Baker?"

"My dad cheated on my mom. Actually, he had been cheating on her for years. I decided that I didn't want anything to do with him, and that included having his last name."

"You must have thought I was a real ass when I didn't recognize you in the club."

"Honestly, I was relieved. I kind of panicked when I saw you there. When you didn't know who I was, my confidence came back. No girl wants to run into an ex-boyfriend and be a bumbling idiot."

"No guy wants to fuck a girl and realize later he's fucked her before."

She chuckled and then climbed on top of me. "Well, the solution to that is to just keep on fucking her."

CHAPTER 21

CECE

I WOULD BE LYING if I said I wasn't enjoying my time with Logan. In fact, we could hardly keep our hands off one another. I felt this desperate need to have him all the time. If we were home, we were screwing, and sometimes when we were out too. I knew he wanted me just as much as I wanted him. After the attack, something changed with me. I wanted him the way I used to have him, but I couldn't allow that to happen. Would it even work between us? We were different people now.

Besides I wasn't sure that I was ready to start things up with him again, I also had a huge secret hanging over my head. While he knew about who I really was, he had no idea about my revenge. I wanted to tell him so badly, to have no secrets between us, but I couldn't without exposing Vira. And the only way forward for us was if there was complete honesty between us. I just didn't see this going anywhere, no matter how much I wanted it.

When Sean finally let her out of his sight for more than five minutes, we met up at the apartment for some alone time. I hugged her at the door, even though we normally wouldn't be so touchy-feely.

"God, it's so good to see you," Vira said, squeezing me back. "My jailor is driving me insane. You would think the *fuck off* I gave him would have pushed him away, but no such luck."

"Well, Logan seems to be just as determined to have his own way."

"Yeah? What's he doing?"

"You mean besides following me everywhere I go?"

"So, has he convinced you to stay?"

I groaned, walking over to the couch and flopping down. "Is it too much to ask for five minutes of peace without him banging on the door?"

She snorted. "Yeah, I wish I could get five minutes. I swear to God, if I ever get shot again, it'd better be deadly. I can't take anymore of Sean's attitude."

She grabbed a bottle of wine and brought it over, along with some glasses.

"This is the first time I've been able to drink. Sean's all worried about me drinking, despite the fact that I'm not taking pain pills. He cleaned out all the alcohol from his house."

"Then we'd better drink hard and fast," I laughed.

"So, what's really going on with you and Logan?"

Sighing, I got right down to it. "Well, I finally told him who I am."

"Was he completely pissed? He's still looking out for you, so I'm guessing not."

"He was actually pretty great about it. I just feel like I'm still not being honest with him."

"You mean you want to tell him what we did."

I sat there picking at the non existent lint on my pants. My feelings were at war with one another. I had no idea what the right thing to do was.

"I don't know. If I tell him, that means telling him about flooding his house and it implicates you in what happened with the police. I'm not sure how he would react to that and I'm not willing to get you in trouble."

"But..."

"But if I don't tell him everything, we can never really have anything more than what we already have. It would eat at me to keep those secrets from him."

"I thought you didn't want anything more than you have?" Vira asked, giving me a knowing look.

Sighing, I drank my wine. "I'm not sure I want anything with him. It's fun with him, and I really like being with him, but can we ever go back? I mean, there's no erasing what he did to me. I'll always remember that, and if he finds out about what I did, he would never move on from that."

"Would it really be so bad if he never found out?"

"Okay, he might never find out about me flooding his house, but what if Sawyer came out and told the police chief that he was asked to pull Logan over and harass him?"

"Why would Sawyer tell the chief though? What's in it for him?"

"Well, the chief is looking into all his cases where he was accused of harassment. I'm sure he knows by now that you and Sean are together."

"We are *not* together."

"It doesn't matter. If he can get to Sean through you, don't you think he would?"

"Hmm. I'm not sure. If it comes out, it comes out. I'm not going to worry about it right now."

"If I tell Logan, there's a chance he'll forgive me, but if I don't and he finds out because of something else, I don't think he would forgive my deceit."

"On the other hand, he might not forgive you at all if you tell him, but there is the chance that he'll never find out from Sawyer. Babe, you have to decide what's best for you here."

"I don't think Logan would go to the police over a few tickets, but do you think Sean would turn you in for asking Sawyer? He seems very black and white to me."

"He hates Sawyer, so I don't know. Wouldn't it be like taking a bribe or something?"

"Something like that. I doubt it would be very good for Sawyer."

We sat there contemplating things for a few minutes when I finally came to a decision.

"I'm not going to say anything. If Sean finds out about Sawyer, we'll cross that bridge when we come to it, but I don't want to give him any ammunition."

"Are you sure?"

"Definitely. This thing with Logan is new. I don't even know if it would go anywhere. I'm not willing to risk what could happen to you if Sean ever found out. I think it's best this way."

"Under one condition. If you change your mind, you come talk to me. I'm sure I could find a way to persuade Sean to keep his mouth shut."

I grinned at her. "Deal."

It had been close to two months since I confessed who I really was, and we were heading out for New Year's Eve at The Pub. I had done my best to keep things with Logan purely sexual. If I thought of him as anything more than my sex toy, my feelings would get in the way of everything else.

Vira was joining Sean at The Pub tonight, which made me think there was more going on there. Her part in my revenge was over, so there was no need to stick around. She seemed to really like him, but she was still seeing other men. I wasn't sure if Sean was doing the whole open relationship thing with her, or if he was just screwing her when she felt like it.

When we walked in The Pub, Logan's friends were already seated at a table. A big round of hoots went up as we walked towards the table. Sean and Vira were right behind us and she was stunning as ever.

"Cece, these are my friends. You met some of them when we went paintballing, but now you can actually seen them. This is Jack and his wife, Harper."

"Nice to see you again. It's about time we hang out with the woman that's had Logan all tied up. We haven't see much of him lately," Jack said as he shook my hand.

"I definitely have had him tied up a time or two. How else does a girl get exactly what she wants?"

"Oh, damn. Logan I think you need to watch your back. One day you'll wake up tied up and alone."

Logan punched Jack in the shoulder. "It's already happened. Maybe you should worry about your own woman." Then he turned to me. "Harper over there is quite feisty. I think you two will get along well."

"Men are such neanderthals." Harper stepped forward and shook my hand. "Stick with me and I'll help you survive this group of cavemen."

"This is my friend, Vira. She's with Sean."

"Actually, I came with Sean, but I'm not *with* anyone."

Sean rolled his eyes, and Harper chuckled under her breath and smiled. "Good to know."

Logan pulled me over to another man that was as huge as a truck. He was extremely sexy, but he didn't really smile, except at Harper. "This is Drew. He's Harper's part time lover."

"Logan, you know he's not, so shut your mouth or I'll shut it for you," Harper growled.

"Hey, I had your back when you were making threats against Jack. You just remember that."

There was some crazy dynamic that was going on here and I had a feeling I was way out of the loop. Drew gave me a chin lift, but other than that, was pretty quiet.

"This is Ryan, my business partner."

He gave me a quick handshake and said hi, but his eyes assessed me, like they were looking for something deceptive. I quickly looked away because I felt exposed under his gaze.

"This is Cole, and his girlfriend, Alex, is tending bar tonight." He pointed over to a small woman behind the bar. She was beautiful, just like her boyfriend. In fact, all of these men were extremely good looking.

"This ugly fucker is Sebastian." He had to be shitting me, because Sebastian was one of the most handsome men I had ever seen. My panties practically melted when he looked at me.

"It's nice to meet you all."

"So, you know Logan from a long time ago, right?" Ryan gave me a smile, but his voice said something completely different.

"Yeah, we knew each other ten years ago."

Logan handed me a glass of something and I gripped it tightly as Ryan narrowed his eyes at me.

"So, you knew our boy from the start, but chose to keep who you were a secret. Why is that?"

"Dude, chill out. It's water under the bridge. I've made my peace with it, so just shut the fuck up and let's have a good night."

"Just looking out for you, man. Seems a little strange that she would hide who she was." He shrugged and downed the rest of his drink, but his eyes continued to watch me throughout the night. I had a feeling he saw right through me and he wasn't buying what I was selling.

The rest of the night went by pretty well. Vira and I partied with Harper, who was completely awesome, but wasn't drinking because she was pregnant. She ragged on Jack with so much ease, but I could tell that she truly loved him. Their friends, Anna and Luke, showed up later and Anna joined us in drinking away the night.

I was well and truly tipsy as midnight approached and we were all having a great time. Cole excused himself a few minutes before twelve to go find his girlfriend, and that's when all hell broke loose. Fire alarms screeched all around us and before we could move toward the door, thick smoke started to pour out of the back of the bar, most likely from the kitchen. Panic erupted around us as people pushed toward the exit. We were in the far corner, so it didn't seem like we would ever get to the exit. All the men around us gathered the women and started ushering us to the door.

One minute Logan was holding my hand and the next, my hand was wrenched from his when someone knocked into me and shoved me to the ground. I barely had time to register what happened before a body pressed on top of mine and hot breath flooded the side of my face.

"You've been well guarded, Cece. You won't always be protected, though."

Fear tore through me when I recognized the voice. I prayed that Logan was nearby and trying to get to me, but even as I laid there scared, I could feel people shoving around me. The weight suddenly lifted from my body and disappeared from sight, but people were stepping on me, keeping me from standing. I pushed myself to my knees, but a shoe connected with my stomach and a person fell on top of me, smashing me back into the floor. More people fell around me, and I felt the air being pushed from my lungs as the pile on top of me grew.

The air was getting thick around me, and with the people laying on top of me, it was nearly impossible to breathe. Black spots appeared in my eyes and I was sure I was about to pass out. There was a person lying across me and their shirt was close to my face, so I buried my nose into the material, hoping that it would protect my lungs from the smoke.

"Cece!"

I prayed I wasn't imagining Logan's voice, but a second later, he appeared in front of me, kneeling and talking to me.

"It's okay, Cece. I'm gonna get you out of here." I felt the weight being lifted from me, little by little, and then Logan had me in his arms and was carrying me out of the bar. My head lulled against his chest as the cold air hit my face. My head was fuzzy and the lights and sounds around me left me just as dizzy as when I couldn't breathe.

Logan placed me in the back of an ambulance where a paramedic placed an oxygen mask over my face. Logan climbed into the back of the ambulance with me, though now that I was out of the smoke, I wasn't sure I needed to go to the hospital.

Pulling my mask down, I tried to reason with Logan. "I'm fine now." But I barely got that out before I was coughing again.

Replacing the oxygen mask, he shook his head. "Cece, don't be stubborn. We're going to the hospital."

I tried to argue, but he wasn't having it. Before I knew it, the doors were being shut and Logan was holding my hand as the ambulance drove off. But when I got to the hospital, Logan wasn't allowed to come back with me to the room, and that's when I started to remember what happened. I hated being alone in the room, and every time someone walked past my curtained off area, I froze, thinking it was that man.

By the time I was done being poked and prodded, I was exhausted.

"Well, I would say it's okay for you to head home now," the doctor said with a smile. "You were lucky. If they hadn't gotten you out when they did, you would be looking at an overnight stay at the very least."

"Wasn't that an overnight stay?" I said dryly. "The sun is coming up."

He looked out the window with a laugh. "Very true, but since it was after midnight, I can say it wasn't an overnight stay."

I shook my head, not that it mattered. Logan came back just as the doctor was leaving, a big smile on his face. "Well, that was a close one."

"I'd like to just forget it and move on."

"I can help you with that. The nurse said she'd be right in with the discharge papers, and then we can blow this popsicle stand."

"Thank God, I could really go for a popsicle right now."

"Really?"

"Well, if it was made with vodka."

We were walking toward the exit when we saw all of Logan's friends and Vira in the waiting room. This couldn't be for me over a little smoke inhalation, which meant that someone else had been injured. I noticed that Cole and Alex weren't in the waiting room.

"What happened?" Logan asked as he looked at all the stricken faces.

"Alex was attacked. We don't know for sure what happened yet, but she was in the back and when she was brought out, she was bleeding pretty heavily from her head. They don't know if she's gonna make it. Cole was carrying her out, but he passed out when he was almost to the door. He's being treated for smoke inhalation, but he isn't awake yet."

I looked at Logan and saw the devastation on his face. He closed his eyes as he looked up at the ceiling. I gripped his hand firmly in mine and prayed they would be okay. Vira walked over to me and pulled me into a tight hug.

"Are you doing alright, sweetie?"

"Yeah, I'm just a little sore."

She pulled away quickly. "Oh my gosh. I'm so sorry."

"It's okay. I just need to lie down for a little bit."

Logan wrapped his arm around my waist. "How about we get you home." I looked up at him and saw the battle in his eyes. He wanted to stay and find out what was going on with his friends, but he also wanted to get me home.

"Hey. Vira can take me home. We'll be fine. You can stay here and wait for news on your friends."

"No, I want to take you home."

"Okay, how about you take me home, and then Vira will hang out with me. Honestly, I'm just going to sleep."

He glanced at his friends and back at me. I knew he really wanted to be with his friends, and I didn't blame him. I would feel the same way if it was Vira.

"I won't think less of you for not staying with me, Logan. Your friends need you right now."

He nodded and we all said goodbye as the three of us walked out the door of the ER. Logan got us home in no time, and it took me fifteen minutes to convince him to leave us. I didn't really want to be alone, so Vira and I snuggled up on the couch for a little bit.

"Are you sure you're okay? You've got quite a few bruises."

"Yeah, I'm mostly tired." I had been sitting there a few minutes when I remembered the creep on top of me. With everything that happened, I had completely forgotten about him. "When I was knocked to the ground, that guy was there."

"What guy? You mean *the* guy?"

"Yeah."

"Why didn't you tell anyone sooner?" Her eyes were bugged out at me, and I had the silly thought of poking her eyes back into her head.

"Honestly, I forgot about it until just now. I mean, I remembered in the hospital, but so much was going on, and then we found out about Cole and Alex. It kind of didn't seem important at the moment."

"Maybe not as important, but he needs to know and so does Sean. Do you think it was pure luck that he ran into you?"

I shook my head. "I'm not sure that me falling down was an accident. I think he was there watching and he pushed me down. He said that I had been under protection, but I wouldn't always be."

"You need to tell Logan or Sean."

"I know, but not right now. They have enough going on with their friends. I'll talk to them in the morning. All I want right now is a hot shower to wash all this grime off me."

"Alright, I'll be here. We'll watch a movie when you get out."

"Sounds good."

I took a long shower and washed away the night, then got in some comfy clothes and went out to snuggle with Vira. We were watching *Dirty Dancing* when we both drifted off to sleep. The credits on the

TV were rolling when I heard a click that brought me out of my slumber. I looked over at Vira to see if she heard it, but she was still sound asleep. Looking over at the front door, I saw the door handle moving slowly. If it was Logan, he would have come right in. He had a key to the apartment ever since I was attacked, in case I needed him. I slapped Vira on the arm to wake her from her slumber.

"Ow, bitch. What did you do that for?"

"Shh. Someone's at the door," I whisper-hissed.

She got to her feet and stared at the door as the handle continued to move around. "Someone must be trying to pick the lock."

At first, I felt a twinge of fear, but then I decided enough was enough. This man was torturing me, driving me insane, and trying to ruin my life. He turned me into some sappy sack of shit that cried all the time, and that's not who I was anymore. This was going to end tonight.

"I'm sick of this shit. Let's take care of this fucker. Grab something and we'll surprise him when he comes in."

I crept towards the kitchen and grabbed the skillet off the stove that still had remnants of eggs from breakfast. Vira grabbed an empty wine bottle from the island and went to stand behind the door. I stood against the wall where the door opened and pushed myself up against the wall as much as possible.

A moment later, the door knob turned all the way and the door slowly creaked open. I held my breath waiting for the intruder to enter, thinking maybe this wasn't the smartest idea, but it was too late to back out now. He stepped slightly inside the door and I grabbed his jacket, pulling him into the room. I swung the skillet with all my might and whacked him upside the head. Vira came roaring out from behind the door and smashed the bottle on top of his head. I hit him one more time in the face before he went down, falling in a heap on the floor.

"Who says drinking is bad for you?" Vira dropped the neck of the bottle at her side and then turned to me. "Quick, grab some duct tape and we'll tape his wrists."

"Do we have duct tape?"

The skillet was dangling from my hand as I questioned her about the duct tape. We were not handy girls, so why we would have duct tape, I had no clue. I heard the guy moan and I immediately jumped, spreading my legs wide, crouching low, and swung my skillet one more time at his face. Then I rested the skillet over my shoulder as I stood tall. I grabbed my pants with the other hand, hefting them up and then spit on him.

"I could so play baseball."

Vira burst out laughing, and then I did also. I supposed that I should be on the ground in a ball shaking, but I was through being scared of this guy.

Vira went to the living room and grabbed some cords from behind the TV. "Here' let's tie him up with this."

We tied his wrists as best we could and then his feet.

"You know, I think I should grab my taser just in case. We don't want to be caught unawares."

She smirked and then walked into the other room. I went and got my phone, trying to decide if I should call Sean or Logan. Sean was the police, but Logan would kill me if I didn't let him know what happened. I decided that I would call Logan.

Vira came back out just as I was getting ready to place the phone call. She charged her taser and held it at the ready. I took a good look at the man lying on the ground and confirmed that he was the guy that had attacked me in the office. The guy came to and started struggling with his bonds. I dialed Logan's number and he answered immediately.

"Cece, are you okay?"

"Yeah, I'm okay, but we had an intruder."

"What?" His voice exploded through the phone. Vira pointed the taser at the guy on the floor and pressed the button. The guy on the floor screamed and started writhing in pain. "Cece, talk to me. What's going on?"

"Vira tasered him. He was starting to wake up."

"Okay, Sean and I are on the way over. Just stay calm. We'll be there soon."

"Really, Logan. We're fine. We'll see you soon."

I looked at the man on the floor in disgust. "Do you have any more cartridges for that?"

"Yep. I'll go get one." Vira walked away and returned a minute later, reloading the taser. She handed it to me with a smile on her face. "Don't waste that. Make sure he's awake and can feel every second of it."

"Not a problem."

We stood there for a few minutes as the man tried rousing himself. He wiggled a little, but I wanted him wide awake when I used the taser on him. Logan and Sean made their appearance a few minutes later, barging through the door with anger on their faces. They looked down at the man on the floor that was now staring at them instead of fighting his bonds.

"What the fuck? You did this?" Logan asked incredulously as he looked at me.

"I told you we were fine."

"Is this the man who attacked you?" Sean asked.

"Yep. That's him." I glanced at the man on the floor. "You're not so tough when you don't catch me by surprise."

"Alright." Sean pulled out his phone and told the person on the other line his badge number and then told them he needed a squad car at this address. Sean was about to pull the guy to his feet, but I hadn't had my turn yet. I quickly pointed the taser at the man and pushed the button, watching in satisfaction as he screamed and then peed himself.

"He's already incapacitated, Cece." Sean shot me a disapproving glare, but I just shrugged.

"He looked like he was trying to get loose to me."

"Me too. I saw him trying to get out of his restraints," Vira added. "You get to clean up the mess since you tased him."

"Totally worth it."

The police came a few minutes later and hauled the guy off to the police station. Logan stayed behind, not wanting to leave me alone. Sean stayed also, getting our statements, which I had a feeling wasn't going to turn out well for me.

"So, what exactly happened?" Sean asked after everyone was gone.

"Well, I woke up to the sound of the door handle being jiggled. I woke Vira up, who almost gave us away with her loud mouth—"

"It's not like I knew there was an intruder. Besides, who had the taser?"

"Who knocked him over the head with the skillet?"

"Who smashed him over the head with a bottle of wine?"

"My skillet skills were much better than your bottle skills. I got in three shots."

"And if I had the skillet, he would have been out in one," Vira taunted.

"Would you two shut up?" Sean shouted. We both turned and stared at him. "Now, you heard the knob turn..."

"And I decided I'd had enough of his shit. At least here, I could defend myself."

"Why the fuck would you decide to go after him? He could have hurt both of you," Logan roared.

"So we should have cowered in the other room while he broke in here and tried to attack us? What would you have had me do, Logan?" I crossed my arms over my chest, and when Sean went to intervene, Vira shot him with a death glare.

"If you want to keep your balls, you'll keep your mouth shut," Vira hissed.

"What is it with the women in this town always threatening our balls?" Sean turned to Logan and rolled his eyes.

"So, anyway, he came through the door and Vira and I took turns hitting him until he was down. We tied him up—"

"Which was totally my idea," Vira smirked.

"And then Vira went to get her taser—"

"Also my idea."

"And that's when I called you."

"So, why did you tase him the first time?"

Vira looked innocently at Sean. "Why, we're just two little women trying to survive. You have no idea how terrifying it was. So, when he moved, I didn't feel I had any other choice but to defend myself."

Sean shook his head and looked at me. "And the second time?"

"Hey, he twitched. The last thing I wanted was for an officer, who serves this city so proudly, to be attacked whilst trying to help out two women that had just been almost raped and murdered."

"We were standing right there," Logan said dryly.

"But I had the taser. And he twitched."

"I'd swear to it in court," Vira grinned.

Sean sighed as he stood. "Alright. We'll get him booked and I'll let you know what we find out about him. Vira, do me a favor and put the taser away for the night. Logan's here, so you won't be needing it."

"Since when do I let you tell me what to do?"

"Women. I need a drink," he muttered as he walked out the door.

Over the next few weeks, Logan and I grew closer than ever. With my attacker out of the picture, I moved back to my apartment, which really bothered Logan, but I wasn't about to keep living with him. I still had this nagging feeling in the back of my mind that he would do something stupid and I would end up hurt. Luckily, he didn't fight me on it too much.

Sean had interrogated my attacker, John Keen. Apparently, the guy had seen me at the club several times with Vira and had developed a sick obsession with me. He had been following me for weeks, and I had been totally oblivious. He was in jail now, so I didn't have to worry about him for a while.

Vira and I met up at The Pub on Saturday night to let loose from the work week. We were drinking beer when Vira shocked the hell out of me.

"So when are you moving in with Logan?"

I almost spit out my beer at her question. She knew me well enough to know that I wasn't the type to just move in with a guy, not any more. I valued my independence and enjoyed not having anyone at home waiting for me. It was liberating to answer only to myself, and while I really liked Logan, we weren't there yet. No matter how much I thought I was falling for him, we needed time to figure out who we were apart from all the drama. Not to mention, he still didn't know of my revenge.

"Why would you think I'm moving in with Logan?"

"Oh, come on. Two lovers reunited after all this time? The chemistry is off the charts with you two. I just figured that you would want to take that next step with him. It's pretty much the natural progression in a relationship nowadays."

"Really? So, should I expect you to be moving in with Sean soon?"

She rolled her eyes at me, but conceded my point. "Point taken, but it's a little different with you and Logan. You know that I'll never settle down with anyone, but I always figured that you eventually would."

"You'd have to actually love the person you're with in order to take that next step."

She was about to take a drink, but halfway to her lips. "You don't...you mean to tell me that you aren't in love with that man?" Her jaw was hanging open and I had a strong desire to reach across the table and close it.

I wasn't sure why I lied to Vira in that moment. It felt like if I told her the truth, it was admitting to being a fraud all these years. Even after all this time, he could still draw me in and change me. I didn't want Vira to see me as weak. She was the person who helped me become this woman. I just couldn't imagine telling her that I might want something different.

"I'll always see him as the man who completely devastated me when I was younger. He changed me, and I can't help but look at him that way. He's great in bed and I have fun with him, but he's a good time. That's it."

Vira looked at me with a sad face. It was the last thing I was expecting coming from her. She and I were alike in every way, so when she looked at me with those pitying eyes, it just made me angry.

"Don't you even look at me that way, Vira. There is nothing wrong with the way I live my life. I get to choose who's in it and who I fuck. I've kept him around a lot longer than any other man before him. He'll understand when our time is up. I never promised him more than some fun."

"I'd just hate to see you miss out on something great."

"I'm not missing out on anything. That something great is what we have right now. Anything more is just a mess I don't need."

She changed the subject like any good friend would, but Logan was on my mind the rest of the night. I lied to Vira for the first time that night. She had always been the one person I was honest with, but I couldn't tell her that I had already fallen for Logan. I was so afraid that if I admitted it, things would end and I would be devastated again. I knew it was silly to think that way, but I couldn't handle being hurt like that again. What Logan and I had would end eventually, and I just had to keep my head on straight until then.

CHAPTER 22

LOGAN

RYAN and I were meeting at the bar tonight for a few drinks. Things were going great with Cece, but I knew I couldn't spend all my time with her. She was a very independent person, and when I pushed too much, she pulled back from me. Every day I thought more and more about what it would be like if she moved in with me, but I knew I couldn't ask her yet. If she was ready to make that commitment, she wouldn't have moved back to her apartment a few weeks ago. I had to make her see how much she meant to me, but I couldn't just come out and tell her that I loved her, even though I was dying to. It would take time and patience to show her what we could have.

I walked into The Pub and saw Ryan waiting for me at the bar. He was already started on a beer, so I ordered one for myself and sat down on a stool. "Hey, man. How's it going?"

"Shitty."

"Why's that?"

"Let's just say that a certain woman is on my mind and it's making my life difficult."

"If this is about Cassandra, just go for it. I know you wouldn't do anything to put the company in jeopardy. She doesn't strike me as the vindictive type either. If things don't work out, I can deal with her."

"I don't know," he shook his head. "I'd still rather wait until the deal is done. How are things going with Cece?"

"Good," I said with a smile. "I think I'm gonna ask her to move in with me soon."

"Really?" he asked in surprise. "Things are that serious?"

"They are for me. She's going to be more difficult to convince."

"Even after she lied to you?"

I waved him off. "I know you don't trust her, but...it was a different time, for both of us. She didn't want to tell me because she thought I'd break her heart. I can't blame her."

"And now?"

"I love her."

He grinned at me. "Have you told her yet?"

"No, but I will be soon. I'm trying to keep things slow with her."

"Well, you know, there's no time like the present," he said with a smirk.

"What do you mean?" I glanced around the bar and saw Vira and Cece sitting slightly behind a wall. They obviously hadn't seen us yet. I jerked my head in that direction and we both stood, walking over to them. I stopped when I was just about to them, because it sounded like they were talking about Sean and me. Eavesdropping wasn't something I normally condoned, but it was like pulling teeth to get Cece to have an honest conversation with me.

"Really? So, should I expect you to be moving in with Sean soon?"

"Point taken, but it's a little different with you and Logan. You know that I'll never settle down with anyone, but I always figured that you eventually would."

"You'd have to actually love the person you're with in order to take that next step."

Knives to the chest wouldn't have hurt more than that. It wasn't so much that she said she didn't love me, but the vehemence in her voice as she said it.

"You don't...you mean to tell me that you aren't in love with that man?"

"I'll always see him as the man who completely devastated me when I was younger. He changed me, and I can't help but look at him that way. He's great in bed and I have fun with him, but he's a good time. That's it."

I pushed back against the wall to keep from being seen. Glancing at Ryan, the firm set of his jaw told me exactly what he thought. He never trusted her. I didn't know what more I could do to convince her that I wasn't that man anymore. That *kid*. I was young and stupid when I met her, but I knew what I had now, and I had wanted to make something great with her. But it seemed that I was the only one.

"Don't you even look at me that way, Vira. There is nothing wrong with the way I live my life. I get to choose who's in it and who I fuck. I've kept him around a lot longer than any other man before him. He'll understand when our time is up. I never promised him more than some fun."

"I'd just hate to see you miss out on something great."

"I'm not missing out on anything. That 'something great' is what we have right now. Anything more is just a mess I don't need."

I felt Ryan pulling me away from where they were seated, and a few seconds later, the cold air from outside slapped my face, bringing sanity back once again. The last thing I needed was Cece to keep me around for a good time. I wasn't the same person I was before I met her months ago. Sure, I had known her much longer than a few months, but this woman was the woman I had truly fallen in love with. To know that she was going to continue to use me until she'd had enough about tore my heart out. I couldn't deal with it for one more second, but I also couldn't just storm in there and let my emotions get the better of me. I would find a way to end it with her and break her just like she had just broken me.

I turned to see Ryan looking at me with concern on his face, his hands shoved in his pockets. "You okay?"

"I'm fine."

"Logan, I know how you feel about her, so don't try to bullshit me. That was rough for me to hear, and I'm not the one in love with her."

"What do you want me to say? You've never trusted her." He started to shake his head, but I cut him off. "Don't pretend you did. I saw it every time you looked at her and when you talked to her on New Year's Eve. You were right. I shouldn't have trusted her, but I did, and now I have to deal with that."

Ryan didn't say anything for a moment. There really was nothing left to say. I started walking back toward my car when Ryan called out to me.

"Logan, what are you gonna do?"

I turned and faced him, no longer feeling anything. Ice had seeped into my veins and all that was left was a cold-hearted man. "I'm gonna end it."

I didn't respond to Cece at all that week. When she called, I ignored her. When she texted, I ignored her. When she showed up at the same coffee house as me, I nodded hello and then headed out the door to work. It wasn't hard to ignore her. I really did have a lot to get done this week. The VAS project was taking off, so I had to focus my attention on that. Still, at some point I would have to address the problem with Cece.

After much debating, I decided that I would take her out to her favorite club on Saturday, and then leave her the same way she left me that first time. That would be my final goodbye to her. I could just end things and not tell her why, but part of me wanted one last taste of her before I threw her away.

"Are you sure you want to do this?" Ryan asked after I told him my plan. He had been nagging me about it all week instead of ignoring the situation like a good friend would.

"Hey, she knew who I was that first time in the club. It's only right it should end the way it started."

He sighed, shaking his head. "I know she broke your heart—"

"Don't," I warned him.

"But if you do something like that, you might not be able to take it back."

I hung my head, feeling like shit. "I already did something I can't take back, and ten years later, I'm still paying for it. I know what you think of me," I accused. "I know you think I'm just some playboy that'll stick his dick in anything, but I loved her."

His face fell. "Logan, you know I think you're a great guy, but you have a reputation."

I nodded. "And that's on me, but what I had with her, I thought that was real."

He patted me on the back uncomfortably. "You'll find that again, only it'll be better. The woman you get will deserve you. I saw the way you were when she was attacked. You were terrified for her, and even after she...well, you know, you were still there for her. That takes a really strong person."

I huffed out a laugh. "But it wasn't good enough, was it? Every single thing I did to show her how much I cared didn't make any difference. She never cared about me, so she used me and got what she needed. I won't make that mistake with any woman ever again."

"Hey, don't do that. Cece is not like every woman out there."

"You're right, but I fell for that. The way she was with me, that's what I loved about her. She brought out this need to be with her all the time. Most men wouldn't like how independent and confident she is, but I loved that about her. It was what attracted me to her. So, if I ever settle down, it's gonna have to be with a woman that's nothing like her."

He opened his mouth to say something, but I just shook my head and walked out of his office. The last thing I needed was someone trying to make me feel better. I had done this to myself, and now it was time to end it. I pulled out my phone and texted Cece to meet me at the club because I was working late. I wasn't, I just didn't want to ride with that bitch.

I walked into the club about a half hour after I said I would meet her and immediately dragged her out to the dance floor. I didn't say a word to her, and I could see it was on the tip of her tongue to ask me what was wrong. I danced with her and teased her body all night long before I decided I'd had enough and needed to end this night.

Pulling her from the dance floor, I wound my way through the club, back to the bathrooms. A dirty bathroom seemed a fitting way to end our time together. I opened the girls' bathroom and after checking for other occupants, closed the door and locked it. I thrust her up against the sink and lifted the dress from her body. There would be no going slow or kissing this time. I felt no passion for this woman, only a need for revenge.

I ran my fingers over her slit once and when she moaned, I took that as a sign that she was ready enough. I yanked my cock from my pants and rammed into her so hard that I was sure it hurt her. I didn't care right now, though. I pounded into her with all the rage that had been building inside me over the course of the week. I saw her eyes in the mirror questioning the change in me. While we had always been rough with one another, there was passion involved. This was nothing but cold, hard fucking. I took what I wanted and didn't wait to see if she finished.

When I grunted out my release, I tucked myself back in and zipped up, heading for the door. She hurried to get her dress down before calling for me.

"Logan, what's going on? You haven't been yourself this past week."

She stared at me with hurt in her eyes, begging me to talk to her. I considered telling her what I had overheard, but that would be like admitting that I was hurt and felt used. I didn't need her pity, and I sure as shit didn't need her excuses. I walked closer to her and stared at her with no feeling at all.

"Cece, you're a great lay, but I think it's time we end this."

Her head reared back like I had slapped her. "Excuse me?"

"What's the problem? You said from the beginning this could never be more than what it was. You told me you don't do relationships, so what's the problem?"

"I just...I thought that...with everything we've been through..."

"You thought we would all the sudden become this couple that would get married and have kids?"

Anger and indignation took over her features and fighting Cece came out. "Don't pretend like we didn't have something more. I know you felt it just like me. What happened?"

I wasn't about to tell her what happened, but her argument did provide me with the perfect way out. It would be cruel, but effective.

"You are right about one thing. I do want more, but you're not the girl I used to know. That girl, I could have built something with. But let's face it, you're a bit of a slut now. Not exactly marriage material."

I saw the tears build in her eyes at my low blow, but the next minute, she pulled it back and stiffened her spine.

"I never said I was anything else. You're right. I take whatever men I want, when I want. It was getting a little stale with you anyway."

I turned and walked out of the bathroom and left the club, jumping in my truck and driving away. It had been horrible of me to throw her sexual history in her face. After all, I had originally broken up with her because she wasn't experienced enough and now I accused her of being too loose. Really, what right did I have to judge anyway? I was a man-whore myself. Still, I felt better as I drove away from the club knowing that that chapter of my life was over.

I wanted to tell myself that I was fine. I wanted to believe that everything that Cece and I had really had meant nothing to me, but the fact was, I was drowning in my own misery. I couldn't stop kicking myself for falling for a woman that could disregard me so callously. Yet, I couldn't blame her either. She was the way she was because I had done the same thing to her first. My pride was wounded and that really rankled me.

Just keep moving, that's what I told myself. I had better things to do than waste my time thinking about Cece or Cecelia, whatever she wanted to call herself. I knew that Cece was nothing like Cecelia anymore, but at times, I would catch a glimpse of the girl I once knew. I was well informed now on who exactly she was.

I went back to my old habits within a week. I needed something to wipe her from my memory and getting lost in new pussy was exactly what I needed. None of them were nearly as good in bed, though I tried to tell myself that I wasn't thinking about her when I was with them. Still, if I kept on, over time I wouldn't think about her so much.

Then I started seeing her more and more around town. She was everywhere I went, though I don't think she knew it. She never paid attention to anyone around her, so she didn't see me. I did all I could to avoid her, but she was still always there.

Which was why it really sucked when I ran into her and Vira at The Pub one weekend while I was out with the guys. Jack, Sebastian, Ryan, and I were all hanging out drinking beer when they walked through the door and headed to the bar. I must have been seething because the table got quiet. When I looked back at everyone, they were all staring at me like I would explode. I hadn't told any of the guys about what happened with Cece. Only Ryan knew and he was keeping my secret. It wasn't something that a guy wanted spread around.

"So, you haven't talked to her at all?" Jack asked. Jack was probably my least favorite fan. He'd always thought that I was a screw up, and though he didn't agree with my asshole ways, he was still a friend that supported me. Most of the time.

"No. There's nothing to talk about. We had fun and now it's over."

Sebastian took a pull on his beer and then started in on me. "Don't you think maybe it's time to stop dickin' around and take someone seriously? I mean, you guys were perfect together. You seemed to really be into her and then you ran."

Ryan started to speak up, but I cut him a harsh look. "When I'm ready to stop dickin' around, I'll let you know."

The last thing I needed was Ryan telling the guys how I was pussy whipped and then got my heart broken. I didn't need their sympathy and their sad looks. I just wanted to hang out and have a good time.

"Logan, not to get all mushy, but you two were perfect together. I don't get why you dumped her. She was just like you, except with a vagina."

"Jack, just because you found the woman you want to spend your life with doesn't mean the rest of us have to be tied down to one pussy the rest of our lives. I like fucking different women, and while she was a good time, I don't need the complication of a girlfriend."

Luckily, Ryan came to my rescue and changed the subject. "Anyone hear from Cole? How's Alex doing?"

Sebastian, who had been protecting Alex before this attack, was taking this whole situation especially hard and made sure he always knew what was going on with her now. He had taken on the role of protective brother where she was concerned.

"I went by to see her yesterday. She's coming along okay. Her speech is a lot better, still a little slow to come at times. I see it more when she's tired. She's still struggling to move a lot, but the physical therapy is helping."

"That sucks. I wish there was something we could do to help."

It made me feel like absolute shit that Cole was going through this and there was nothing I could do to help. Alex had been seriously injured New Year's Eve during the fire. Some psychotic detective from her past had attacked her, leaving her with a traumatic brain injury. She could barely function most days. She had to learn how to speak all over again, and when she tried to move, a different area of her body would move than what she intended. She was basically left to the care of others all day and night.

"Well, there is something you can do. She needs Cole to give her some space."

"She doesn't want him around?" Ryan asked.

"No, it's just that he's always there with her, and she thinks that it would do him some good to start doing other things. She has his mom to help her during the day, so she asked me to have us help her get him out of the house."

"Well, we did talk to him about making furniture for VAS. I can talk to him about that again."

"That'd be great."

The conversation turned back to more light hearted topics, and I did my best to not stare at Cece the whole time.

CHAPTER 23

CECE

I SAT on my couch staring at the TV. It was off, so that should have been my first clue that I wasn't holding it together all that well. I still hadn't told Vira what happened. Honestly, I didn't think she would understand, not after I had just told her that I didn't want Logan long term, anyway. Then he fucked me in the club and walked out like I meant nothing.

"Girl, you need to tell me what's wrong right now," Vira said as she walked into the living room.

Sighing, I shook my head. "Nothing. I'm fine."

"You are not fine. You've been staring at the TV for like two hours. And it's been like this all week. What the hell happened?"

It didn't seem like I could hold it back from her anymore. I couldn't just go on pretending that nothing happened. Eventually, she would find out, either from Sean or because she would realize Logan wasn't around anymore.

"Logan and I are over."

"Shut. Up." She plopped down on the couch, staring at me incredulously. "What happened? Did you end it?"

I laughed humorlessly. "You would think that, but no, he's the one that ended it."

She gaped at me. "I don't get it. He loves you."

"Apparently not. I'm pretty sure after last weekend that he never felt anything for me."

"Is this because of you not telling him who you were?"

"I don't think so. I don't really know what happened. He was...he ignored me all week, and then sent me a text to meet him at the club because he was working late."

"Wait, you mean this happened last weekend and you're just now telling me about it?"

I sighed, not knowing what to tell her. "It's embarrassing."

"Well, what happened at the club? Did you dance with another guy or something?"

I shook my head. "No, we danced and it was just like before. Come to think of it, he never actually said anything to me at the club. He just grabbed my hand and dragged me out onto the dance floor. And then he dragged me into the bathroom."

"That's hot," she said weirdly.

"It might have been, but not this time. It was fast and hard, but not in a good way. He didn't get me ready really, and then he just plowed into me. It reminded me of those fucks I had when I first met you."

She grimaced, remembering some of the stories I had told her about guys that were into the quick and hard, but had no idea how to make a woman come.

"It was unlike anything that ever happened between us. That's why I was so confused. He didn't make sure I came. He just fucked me and zipped up."

"Ouch," she grimaced.

"I didn't know what to do." I shook my head, still in disbelief over the whole thing. "I told him that I thought we were moving in a different direction, that maybe we could make something real."

"What did he say?"

I turned and looked at her, still not believing it. "He said that he might have with the old me, but the new me was a slut."

She gasped, reeling back. "No!"

"Yes."

"I don't believe it!"

"It happened."

"But he loves you. Sean said that everyone knows it."

I shook my head. "I could be wrong, but I don't think a man calls the woman he loves a slut. Like I said, I could be wrong."

She sat back against the couch, just shaking her head. "I can't believe that prick. After everything that happened to you, he had the nerve to say that to you."

"You know, I knew something was wrong at the club. When he didn't speak to me, I should have known, but I guess I thought that he was just having a bad day. But then in the bathroom..." I laughed slightly. "Things have always been hard and fast for us, but there was always this passion with us. It wasn't there. I should have stopped him, but I just kept thinking something else was going on. I was completely blindsided."

A stray tear slipped from my eye, falling down my cheek. I quickly wiped it away.

"You know the worst part about all this? I wanted my revenge on him, and then I fell for him again."

"Well," she sighed. "I thought that might happen."

"Yeah, but he did it to me again! He shattered my heart and made me feel completely worthless. I was so stupid," I said angrily. "I knew better. Why did I fall for it again?"

"Because deep down, you're not just like me. I hate to tell you this, but as much as you've changed, you're still that girl that just wants the boy to love her."

I swiped at the tears that kept falling as I laughed. "God, I hate her." Taking a deep breath, I pulled myself together. "It doesn't matter. In the end, I was never good enough for him. At least, not in his eyes. I was too naive before, and now I'm too much of a slut.

There's nothing I can say or do to be what he wants. He's still the selfish prick that left me ten years ago."

Vira smiled at me, gripping my hand. "So, you move on with life and forget about him. You had your revenge on him. He doesn't deserve your tears, and he sure as hell doesn't deserve your body."

I shook my head. "No, he doesn't, but at least he taught me something. I'll never be so stupid as to fall in love again. It's not worth it."

A few weeks after my break up with Logan, I was at work going over a new marketing campaign when one of my bosses, Mr. Johnson, came into my office with a rather large file folder.

"Mr. Johnson, what can I do for you?"

"Hi, Cece. We're getting ready to meet with Cassandra Crawford about marketing for the new VAS building. This is the pro bono job I was telling you about when you signed on."

"Yes, of course, I remember. Are those the files?"

He handed me the folder with a smile. "Everything you need to get started is in there. The meeting will be next Friday afternoon. I'll expect you to have some ads drawn up by then. Not anything concrete, but give her a taste of what she can expect from you."

"I can do that. Is there anything else?"

"That's it. Thank you, Cece."

He walked out of my office and I opened the folder to go over all the material for VAS. Something niggled at the back of my mind, but I couldn't remember what it was. I pushed it away and spent the better part of the day going over the folder and making notes about possible marketing strategies. I was almost done for the day when I came across some notes about the builders they were hiring.

A huge grin spread across my face when I saw that Jackson Walker Construction was in charge of construction and design. Logan had unknowingly placed himself directly in my line of fire. I had so many contacts in the marketing world that I could make sure he never got another job again. I wouldn't even feel bad about it. Well, I felt bad about the people that may lose their jobs, but Logan had brought this on himself. He had toyed with my emotions one too many times, and I wasn't going to take it anymore.

I called a few friends in the marketing industry and spread small tidbits of gossip into the conversation that would eventually trickle down to VAS and possibly get them fired from the job. If not this job, future jobs would be difficult to obtain.

Smiling to myself as I drove home, I walked into my apartment happier than I had been in a long time. Vira was sitting on the couch watching TV when she saw the ginormous smile on my face.

Holding her hands up in front of her eyes, she mocked me. "Ahh. You're blinding me with that smile. Stop! It's too much."

"Haha, Vira. I just had a fantastic day."

"Nooner at work?" she said as she waggled her eyebrows at me.

"Nope."

"Went to the gas station and had the attendant fill your tank?" she added suggestively.

"Not even close."

"Spontaneous orgasm from the vibrations in the car!"

I laughed at her humor. "Sorry, nothing to do with orgasms."

"Well, then this story isn't going to be nearly as good as I hoped for."

I plopped down on the couch and let out a contented sigh. I leaned back into the cushions and twirled a piece of my hair around my finger, imagining my handy work taking place right this minute.

"Bitch, don't hold out on me. Tell me what happened!"

"I got my revenge on Logan."

Vira stared at me for a moment. "How?"

"Remember that one of the stipulations for my job was to work on a pro bono project?"

"Yeah."

"Well, it's this new building in town for a private military foundation called VAS. Guess who the contractors are?"

An evil smile curled her lips. "No way."

"Yes way. I called a few people in marketing, and I may have slipped a few rumors about the company. I wouldn't be surprised if they lost the job, but it most definitely should hurt their future contracts."

"Remind me not to get on your bad side."

"Hey, he had this coming. I let him push me around the first time, but he won't get away with it again."

CHAPTER 24

LOGAN

SOMETHING STRANGE WAS GOING on over at VAS. We were scheduled to meet up with Cassandra to go over some final details for the project, but she put us off, saying the investors were having second thoughts. We waited for a few days without hearing anything further and I called back on the fourth day. If we were going to get this project off the ground, we had to get moving.

"Cassandra Crawford's office. How may I help you?"

"Hi, this is Logan Walker at Jackson Walker Construction. Can you please put me through to Ms. Crawford?"

"One moment please."

I waited on the phone, trying to figure out why the investors would be backing out of the deal at this point. They had loved everything we had presented to them, so this must have to be more to do with Cassandra's end.

"Mr. Walker, I'm sorry I haven't gotten back to you. We're in a bit of a mess over here."

"I'm sorry to hear that. Is there anything I can do to help?"

There was a pause on the line that gave me a bad feeling. "I'm afraid we're going to have to go with a different contractor. Some things have come to light and the investors are not willing to go with your company."

"What things?"

"I'm sorry, but that's all I'm willing to say right now."

"No. We have a contract. If you're backing out, then you're going to tell me why. Otherwise, you will stick with the contract, or we'll take you to court."

Again, there was a pause. My gut was churning, wondering what could have happened to make them back out of our deal.

"We've heard some disturbing things about your company. There have been people saying that your company has been overcharging for materials and keeping the difference. There are also reports that you don't build to code, but nobody has been able to prove it yet."

"That's all bullshit. Who's been saying that?"

"I'm not sure. It's coming from the investors. I haven't heard anything first hand, but the investors insist that we go with someone else. I have to start looking all over again. Mr. Walker, I really hope these rumors aren't true, but the damage is already done. I really thought your ideas were fantastic, unfortunately I am under obligation to the investors."

"How much time do you have to find a new contractor?"

"I have a few weeks."

"Will you give me that time to find out what's going on? Don't hire anyone else for the next few weeks. Just give me some time to investigate these accusations."

"Mr. Walker, I can't promise you anything, but I'll give you the time. You'll need proof that these accusations are false for the investors to come around."

"I understand. Thank you, Ms. Crawford."

I hung up the phone and slammed my fist down on the desk. What a clusterfuck. Who would do this to our company? It had to be the competition. Nobody else would have a reason to do this. Now I had to go tell Ryan the bad news and then get on finding the source. I walked down to Ryan's office and sat down in front of his desk. He looked up at me and frowned when he saw my face.

"We have a huge problem."

"What's that?"

"I just spoke with Cassandra. She said the investors don't want us anymore for VAS. Apparently, there are rumors going around about us padding material expenses and not following building code. They don't want to take the chance that it's true."

Ryan threw his pen down on the desk and ran a hand over his face. "Who the fuck would do that?"

"I'm guessing a competitor. Cassandra has a few weeks to find a new contractor and she told me she wouldn't hire anyone in those weeks. We have that long to come up with proof that these accusations are false."

"Shit. This is bad. This could destroy our business."

"I know. I'm gonna get on the phone and start to figure this out."

"Alright. Keep me updated. I have a few people I can call also."

I left his office and spent the rest of the day trying to figure out what the fuck was going on. Other companies were calling and starting to question us also, so I told them I would show them invoices for their materials and answer any questions they had about building codes. Most of them were willing to hear us out. All of my time on the phone with those other companies was that much time I couldn't spend investigating. Ryan was having the same luck on his end. Even employees were starting to come to us. Word spread fast and we had to find out what was going on now and plug this leak or we were going to sink fast.

It was a week later when I finally got some answers. Apparently, the source of the rumors was coming from someone over at JNP, the company Cece worked for. I didn't even stop by Ryan's office to let him know what was going on. I was pissed and I was going to find out within the next hour what she thought she was doing.

I stormed into her office building, forgetting that I had to bypass security first. I didn't want to alert her that I was coming, so I had security call her boss and tell him that I was here to surprise Cece. He let me up, probably not knowing that we weren't together anymore.

I stormed into Cece's office and she stared at me in shock before finally coming out from around her desk.

"What are you doing here, Logan? I don't want to see you."

"Yeah, well I'm not too fond of seeing you either. But see, there are rumors going around about my company that is set to destroy every contract we have and tank our company. Do you know how many people would be out of work?"

She quirked an eyebrow at me, but didn't give anything away.

"I know it was you. I have contacts too and they tell me the source is out of this company. Now, who would want to do damage to my company other than you?"

She paled a little at that. Yeah, I'm betting she was thinking she wouldn't get caught. She didn't look so self-assured now.

"Nothing to say? Do you really hate me that much that you would destroy a company that Ryan and I built from the ground up?"

She didn't say anything, just looked away as she crossed her arms over her chest. I stalked up to her and got in her face.

"You hate me that much for breaking up with you? I had no idea you were so vindictive."

"You broke me," she yelled at me. I could feel the anger emanating off her now. I took a step back and huffed out a laugh.

"I broke you? I heard you that day in the bar with Vira. I heard you tell her that you didn't love me and I would always be the person that hurt you." My voice grew louder with each word. "I heard you tell her that you were using me until you had your fill. That's why I broke up with you. I was ready to ask you to move in with me. I was going to tell you that I loved you. After all that went on between us, I meant nothing to you."

She took a step back and dropped her head. When she looked up at me, there were tears in her eyes.

"You broke my heart the first time around and then you did it again to me. What was I supposed to think?" she whispered. "I only told Vira that stuff because I was scared. I thought for sure you were going to walk away from me like you did the first time. I was trying to protect myself."

"Well, you did a good job of that."

Her head snapped up to me again. "It was a private conversation. You weren't meant to hear me."

"But I did. You didn't think Vira might say something to Sean? That maybe it would get back to me either way?"

"Vira would never betray me. If you had told me you loved me, I would have come around. It was a mistake."

I laughed humorlessly. "Yeah, well too little too late. You need to find a way to fix this. We could lose everything if you don't. The investors for our VAS project need proof that this is all a lie. You do whatever you have to do to convince them that it is, or I will be sure that your boss hears every last word of what you did to us. There won't be a hole you can crawl into to hide from this."

Her head bobbed in a jerky nod, then moved to look at the door. Her mouth fell open and her face turned deathly white. I turned to see her boss, Mr. Johnson, standing in the doorway with a guarded expression.

"Mr. Walker, I don't appreciate you talking to my employee in this manner. I think it's time for you to leave."

"Mr. Johnson, this is a misunderstanding on my part. Logan was just informing me of it. I assure you, everything is fine."

Mr. Johnson didn't say any more, but moved to the side of the door frame as if to tell me he expected me to leave. I turned back to Cece one more time.

"I expect a call when this is fixed." I turned and stalked out of the office and headed back to inform Ryan of the newest developments. I was beyond pissed, but at least now I had a chance of fixing this mess.

CHAPTER 25
CECE

MORTIFICATION DIDN'T EVEN BEGIN to describe what I was feeling at the moment. Not only was I responsible for potentially destroying Logan and Ryan's company, but the whole office witnessed our argument.

Logan stormed out of the office, leaving me with my boss. "Are you alright?"

I put on a fake smile, needing to get away. "I'm fine. I promise. Just a misunderstanding."

He didn't look like he believed me, but he nodded and left my office. As soon as he was down the hall, I headed for the bathroom, ignoring all the stares from my coworkers. Locking myself in the bathroom, I pulled out my phone with shaky hands and dialed Vira. I was on the verge of collapse.

"Hey, chica!"

"Vira, I'm so fucked."

"What's going on?"

I could hear the panic in my voice. I was near hysteria. "I fucked up so bad. Oh my God. This is so bad."

"Cece, calm down and tell me what happened."

"Logan came to the office. He knows I'm the one that spread the rumors."

"Good. Now he knows what it feels like to get kicked in the balls."

"Vira, he was at the bar that day we went to lunch. He overheard our conversation. That's why he broke things off with me."

"Oh...Shit."

"God, how could I be so stupid?"

"Just take a deep breath. We can fix this."

"Really?" I snapped. "Because I'm not sure how I can fix destroying his company."

"Okay, let's start small. Who did you contact?"

My hand shook as I pressed it against my forehead. I was sweating so bad and my heart was racing out of control. I was so fucked. "Everyone I knew. I mean, anyone that might spread the word back to investors. Vira, I practically went through my rolodex. Even if I call them all and tell them the information was wrong, that's not proof. It won't change anything for them!"

"Then you need to find a way to convince the investors."

I closed my eyes, trying to calm my nerves. I felt like I was going to throw up. Vira stayed on the phone with me as I took deep breaths and calmed down.

"Okay, I think I have an idea. I'm not sure if it'll work, but I'll get started on it."

"Alright. We'll talk tonight when you get home."

"Okay."

I took a deep breath and flushed some water on my face. Nothing else mattered right now but fixing this situation. I wished I could go back in time and change everything. I had fucked so much up. All this time, I was getting revenge and Logan was just trying to help me. And then when he broke up with me, I behaved like a fucking teenager throwing a temper tantrum. I hated myself right then, but there would be more of that to come, and I was pretty sure by the time this was all done, so would everyone else.

I was exhausted by the time I walked through the door. I needed a lot of alcohol and for this day to be over.

"Hey, did you figure it out?"

"I called Cassandra over at VAS and asked her to set up a meeting for the investors. I told her it was a marketing meeting."

"So, you have a plan."

I nodded. "The meeting is set for Monday, which means I have the whole weekend to think about all the stupid decisions I've made in my life."

"Don't be so hard on yourself. Let's just focus on the last ten years," she joked.

I laughed slightly, but I knew after the weekend, nothing would make me laugh again. And what about Logan? Would he ever forgive me? I wasn't sure I would ever forgive him if our positions were reversed.

"So, what's going to happen after Monday?"

"Well, after I basically tell everyone what I've done, I'm pretty sure my boss won't want me around anymore. Word will spread pretty quickly about what I've done. I'll be fired from my job, because if they kept me on, it would spread distrust through the company. Not to mention that nobody would work with the company if I stayed on. Mr. Johnson wouldn't keep me on anyway. I would fire me too. Then, I'll be blackballed from the industry, which is the least of what I deserve."

"So, do you have a plan for after all this?"

I shook my head slowly. "I haven't even thought about it. I was too worried about fixing all this. But I know it's coming. I have some money in savings, but what kind of job will I be able to get?"

"Maybe a change of careers is what you need."

I glanced over at Vira. "Nobody will hire me. I mean, any legitimate company would take one look at my resume, and want to know why I was fired. After they found out, my resume would be tossed in the trash without a second look."

She sighed, shaking her head. "I'm so sorry."

"What do you have to be sorry for?"

She stared at me like I was stupid. "Cece, I was the one that came up with the whole revenge plan. Let's face it, you're not mean enough to come up with that on your own."

"Maybe not, but I'm the one that decided to go along with it."

"Yeah, but this isn't just you getting revenge. You're going to lose everything, and that's all my fault."

I patted her hand, loving that she thought this was on her. It was so Vira. She was always on my side to the point of taking the blame for something that she shouldn't.

"Vira, there is absolutely nothing you could be accused of besides trying to help your friend. I could have told you no to everything. And besides, you suggested going after his company in the beginning and I said no. I knew that would be cataclysmic, and I still did it. It was a spur of the moment decision, but it was the stupidest thing I could have done, and now I'm going to pay the price. That's all on me. Play stupid games, win stupid prizes."

CHAPTER 26

CECE

BY MONDAY MORNING, I was a wreck. I knew what I needed to do, I just wished I was allowed to bring alcohol with me. It would make this so much easier. I dressed in my most professional outfit, remembering my first day at the office and how excited I was. This was a fresh start for me. I just didn't realize it would be so short-lived.

I didn't bother with coffee or anything to eat. I couldn't stomach anything if I wanted to. I was a nervous wreck. Grabbing my purse, I headed for the door.

"Now, you wait just a minute," Vira yelled, storming out of her bedroom. "You don't get to just leave today without saying anything."

"What's left to say?"

"Well, fuck, I don't know. Shouldn't we have some kind of mourning song playing or something? Something to commemorate this day?"

"Sure, you can play taps for me."

"You're not in the military."

"Funny, I feel like I'm facing the firing squad."

"Well, you are," she pointed out. "Not that I'm trying to be insensitive, but by this time tomorrow, you'll be lounging around in your pajamas, eating Cheetos, and ruining the body that you've worked so hard for."

"Somehow I doubt that one morning of Cheetos would ruin my figure."

"Hey, it's a slippery slope. First it's Cheetos, then Pringles, and then we move to chocolate. Within a month, you'll be blown up like a balloon."

"Well, Pringles have like thirty percent less fat. And I could always go for Three Musketeers. They're supposedly light on fat."

She nodded. "Well, I'll have the wine on standby for tonight."

"You'd better make it a few bottles. I'll call you when it's all over. I need to get into work and explain myself before I head off to my meeting."

"Good luck, sweetie." She stood up and gave me a hug before I slipped out the door.

I decided over the weekend that the best thing to do was go into work and be straightforward with my boss, explaining what I had done and apologize profusely for it. Then I'd hand in my resignation and explain my plan to correct my actions. He was sure to be pissed, and would probably sit in on the meeting just to make sure I didn't fuck it all up.

As I drove into work, I thought about what my parents would say when they found out. They would be so disappointed in me. They hadn't liked the changes in me over the years, but they accepted that I was an adult and could do things the way I liked. They never really got over the fact that their baby girl had changed so much, but they tried to be supportive. But that was when I was successful in life. Who knew what I would become now. Maybe I'd be able to get a job as a waitress.

As I pulled into work, I realized that I was more disappointed in myself than anything else. I had let ten years of heartache fester to the point that I stooped so low that I almost destroyed another person's life, along with everyone associated with him. I had no one to blame but myself.

Stepping out of my car, I ran my hands over my suit. It would most likely be the last time I wore it. I would never step foot inside a professional building again.

I took the elevator to my floor and went straight for Mr. Johnson's office. I didn't feel it was necessary to involve the other two partners of JNP. He was the person I answered to most often, so I thought he would do.

"Excuse me, Mr. Johnson. Do you have a minute?"

"Yes, please come in." He waved me in and I walked forward, standing in front of his desk.

"I need to talk with you about what happened on Friday with Mr. Walker."

"Of course. Sit down."

I took the seat across from him, clearing my throat. I was so nervous, despite the fact that I already knew the outcome. It was the disappointment that I couldn't stand seeing.

"Mr. Johnson, I've done something that I'm not proud of. I recently spread gossip about Jackson Walker construction, which has led to them losing a lot of contracts, including the one with VAS."

He frowned, sitting up in his seat. "Why would you do that?"

"The reason doesn't really matter. The point is that I did something unbelievably stupid, and it's hurt a lot of people. I'm well aware that my actions are a poor reflection on the company, so I've written up my resignation and I will be out of the office within the hour. I have a meeting with VAS to explain myself so that Jackson Walker Construction can hopefully salvage the account. I was also planning to hand over the marketing strategy I had done up for them as a sign of good faith on behalf of JNP, if you give me permission to do so."

He studied me for a minute and then gave a curt nod. "I'm disappointed. You showed great promise in the company. I would like to say that you still have a job, but you're absolutely right. Your actions make us look like we can't be trusted. You will be terminated without severance and without a reference. If you put us down for a reference, I'm afraid you'll only get a negative one."

I nodded and swallowed hard. "I know. Thank you for your time. I'll pack my things and be on my way."

I stood and turned to go, but then looked back one last time. He was studying his blank desk and I hated that I had let him down.

"I want you to know that I regret what I did and I'm very sorry for what I did to the company. I know it doesn't mean much to you now, but I still wanted you to know."

I turned and walked out and down to my office. I collected my things and walked out with my head held high. People were staring and gossiping, but I couldn't think about that now. I had one more stop to make before this day would be over.

The drive over to the hotel where VAS and the investors usually met left me on the brink of tears. It was a ten minute drive over, which left me plenty of time to think over how I had royally screwed up my life. By the time I reached the hotel and found the meeting room, I was a jumbled mess. It was one thing to admit my transgressions to my boss. It was another to admit them to a room full of men that would now look at me as a woman scorned who took things a step too far. On top of which, Cassandra would be there to judge me also. It was just too many people judging me in one room. Still, I was no coward. I pulled my shoulders back and walked into the room that was filled and ready for the meeting to begin. I walked to the head of the table, where they were expecting me to give my presentation.

I set down the marketing boards I had brought with me and cleared my throat.

"Thank you all for coming today. I know you all think that this is a marketing meeting, and it is to an extent, but I am here to talk to you about another matter. I recently made some very unwise decisions that I'm sure will affect your opinion of me, and whether or not you would like me to continue my work with your foundation.

"I found myself in the position to spread some awful gossip about a man I was dating....Spreading gossip wouldn't be correct. I made up some awful things about his company and used my marketing contacts to spread my lies. I felt I had been wronged and took advantage of a situation that I saw available. It was reprehensible and has now left him in a precarious situation with his own company." I took a deep breath and looked at all of their wary faces. "The man I was dating was one of the owners of Jackson Walker Construction. I was the one that manufactured the lies about his building codes not being up to par and them padding their pockets with outrageous material costs.

"I want you all to know they are an honest company with good employees that would never do such reprehensible things. This project actually means quite a bit to them because two of their friends are vets. One of which had a difficult time when returning from war. I'm sure Cassandra could go over some of the wonderful things they had planned for this facility that would have been implemented by their friend."

One of the investors interrupted me, leaning forward in his seat. "How do we know that any of this is true? You could be doing all this to save your boyfriend's ass."

"As of this morning, I was terminated from my job. I went to my boss before I came here and told him what I had done. I will never have a job in marketing again after this, and I am sure the only job I would be able to find would be as a waitress. Still, it was the right thing to do. Many people could lose their jobs because of what I did, and I can't live with that. You can confirm my story with my boss if you'd like. Also, he gave me permission to hand you my marketing plans I came up with for the project. If you would like to use them and would like to discuss them, my boss will have someone from the team take over for me.

"As for my boyfriend, we haven't been together for a while. Yes, I am trying to save his ass because he doesn't deserve what I've done to him. I hope that you reconsider having Jackson Walker Construction as your contractors. They were your first choice for a reason, and I ask you to remember that."

I gathered my things and quietly walked to the door. No one said anything to me and I couldn't tell what they were going to do. I caught Cassandra's eye as I left and saw disappointment on her face. The men all looked disgusted with me and I couldn't blame them. I walked to my car and drove home, finally breaking down when I stepped foot inside my apartment.

Vira found me curled up in a ball on the couch when she got home. That's where I spent the next week, crying over the loss of Logan, my job, and frankly, my sanity.

It turned out that I was pretty spot on concerning my job prospects. I interviewed at several places for a receptionist position, but when they asked about my previous employment and why I was leaving marketing, I was forced to tell them the truth. I wasn't about to lie and have it come back to bite me later. It turned out, nobody wanted me anywhere near their company, which I had expected.

After a week of job searching, I decided that getting something temporary would be best for now. I went down to a diner that was usually busy and applied for a job there. I figured that at least I could earn some tips that way. I didn't dare apply at The Pub. While I would probably earn better tips, I didn't know how to bartend and that was a favorite hangout of Logan's. It was best at this point to avoid him at all costs.

The owner of Maggie's Diner took me back to the office and sat down behind her desk, waving me toward another chair. I sat down and looked around the office. It was definitely a far cry from where I was working, but then again, maybe I deserved to be knocked down a peg or two.

Her name was Sylvia and she was a beautiful woman in her fifties, I would guess. She had dark brown hair that was pulled up in a bun and she wore jeans and a t-shirt that advertised the diner. Her expression was no nonsense as she looked me over. Straight forward was definitely the best route with this woman. If this didn't work, I would have to move to a town that didn't know anything about me.

"So, I see you have quite a bit of education listed. May I ask why you are applying for a job as a waitress?"

"Basically, I got revenge on my boyfriend in a very inappropriate way and I have now been blackballed from any marketing company or any company that has any information that would be sensitive to them."

"Did he deserve it?"

"I thought so at the time. It turns out I was wrong. I corrected my mistake, but it was at the expense of my job."

She stared at me, looking me over and judging me. I was really tired of being judged at this point and just wished I could blend into the wallpaper.

"Well, men always need to be taught a lesson. I'm sure he learned his, right or wrong. I have no problem with you as long as you don't bring that into my diner. I expect a professional attitude and all drama to be left at home. You arrive to work at least five minutes before your shift and always have a smile on your face and you'll be fine."

I smiled at her, happy that I at least had a job to go to now. "I can do that. When do I start?"

"You'll work the morning shift into the afternoon. Come in tomorrow at five in the morning. We open at six. I'll show you around and teach you how to set up. Then we'll get you on the schedule for mornings every day. If you want overtime, you let me know. I can always use extra hands. Some of my girls aren't always reliable. Wear jeans and comfortable shoes. I'll give you a few t-shirts to take home with you."

She stood up from her desk and walked over to a box, grabbing a few shirts. She handed me three and walked to the office door. "If you want more than three, let me know. They're ten dollars a piece."

"Thank you so much. I'll see you in the morning."

I went out to my car and drove home. I was happy to have a job, but the hours would be killer. Still, it was a job and that was more than I had yesterday.

CHAPTER 27

LOGAN

I LEANED back in my chair, digging the heels of my palms into my eyes. I was fucking tired. Clients were constantly calling to ask questions about the rumors that plagued us. I knew we were fucked. There was no way we were coming out of this unscathed. If we were lucky, we could rebuild our business. Most likely, we were finished. Even the clients that believed us still had a certain level of distrust.

Ryan walked into my office, looking just as bedraggled as I did. His tie was loosened around his neck and his jacket was all rumpled. Sighing, he sat down across from me. Pulling the bottle of whiskey out of the drawer in my desk, I grabbed two glasses and poured us both a drink. He nodded, taking it from me and swallowing it in one gulp. Surprised, I poured him another.

"So, any luck?" I asked hopefully.

"Same as you," he said sullenly. "Some of them believe us, but some don't want to be tainted by association."

Resting my elbows on my desk, I rubbed one hand across my forehead. This was all my fault. "I'm sorry, man."

He snorted. "I wish I could say that I don't blame you, but you did stick your dick in a crazy lady."

"If I had known she was that vindictive..." I shook my head. "What a clusterfuck. I'll buy out your half of the business," I offered.

He shook his head. "It's not going to come to that. We'll dig our way out of this."

"Will we? Because I gotta be honest, I'm a little skeptical right now."

"Well, we didn't start this business from nothing to stop now because of some bitch."

I was a little surprised at the way he was talking. Ryan was kind of the softy of our group, always the first to defend someone. But after what happened, if he wanted to call Cece a bitch, I guess it was well deserved.

Ryan laughed across from me, scratching at his stubble. "You know, this brings new meaning to the old phrase *hell hath no fury like a woman scorned.*"

I chuckled along with him, not because it was funny, but what else was there to do? "I should have seen it from the beginning. I mean, no woman fucks that good. It was like she was hate fucking me every time we were together."

"And that made it better?"

I shot him an incredulous look. "You haven't been truly fucked unless you've been hate fucked. It's all nails and scratches and...lots of passion. You know, she left me tied to the bed with only a coffee filter covering my dick?"

"And that was a fond memory for you?"

"Before all this? Hell yeah. Sean had to come untie me," I laughed. "It's not exactly a position I ever thought one of you would find me in."

"I'm not all that surprised. What exactly did you do that pissed her off so much? You still haven't told me."

Huffing out a long breath, I decided it was time to tell him. "I fucked her in the bathroom at the club, didn't make sure she came, and then I told her we could never have any kind of relationship because she was too much of a slut now."

He winced, shifting in his seat. "Wow, that's..."

"Harsh?" I nodded. "And get this, that conversation we overheard in the bar? She didn't even mean it. She just didn't want Vira to know she had fallen for me."

"You mean to tell me that this could have all been avoided if you just hadn't heard that conversation?"

"More like if both of us weren't acting like idiots. I believe this is the point where you tell me I'm an immature asshole."

"I won't deny it," he said quickly, "but let's just say that this was a series of very unfortunate events."

"Right," I laughed, taking a drink. "So, I act like an idiot for months, take revenge on a woman for a conversation I was eavesdropping on, and destroy the company. Oh, and let's not forget that I ruined any chances you have with Cassandra. But you're right. Let's call it a series of unfortunate events."

My office phone rang and I picked it up, certain it was another client calling to dump us. "Logan Walker."

"Mr. Walker, this is Cassandra Crawford at VAS."

My eyes widened and I pointed at the phone, mouthing that it was Cassandra.

"Uh...yes?"

"Mr. Walker, the investors have had a change of mind. They'd like you to continue on with the project."

I stared at Ryan, unable to speak.

"Mr. Walker?"

"Uh...yes. Yes, um...What happened? What changed their minds?"

"Your ex called a marketing meeting requesting all the investors be there. Then she told them all about how she had sabotaged you in an effort to get revenge. She even handed over her marketing plan for the building before she left."

"And they believed her?"

"Well, they made some calls and found out that what she was saying was true. They're back on board and send their apologies.

They'd like to get the project up and running again as soon as possible. Time is money, you know."

"Sure. I'll talk to Ryan and we'll get going on the project again. Cassandra, I can't say how sorry I am for this. This could have really hurt the project."

"I understand. Let's just hope from here on out there are no more hiccups. I'll talk to you later."

"Sure. Bye."

A grin split my lips as I shook my head with laughter.

"What happened?"

"You're not going to believe this."

"I will if you actually tell me what the hell is going on."

"Cece called a marketing meeting and confessed to everything."

"What? That would be career suicide."

I nodded, just realizing that Cece had just ended her career. For me. "Why would she do that?"

Ryan snorted. "Isn't it obvious?"

"Not to me," I grumbled.

"Logan, she just fell on her sword for you—"

"Now, let's not make her out to be some hero. She did almost destroy our company and put everyone out of work."

"I'm not denying that, but she did this for you. She won't get another job working in marketing ever again. Hell, I'd be surprised if she got any job ever again. She just walked into a meeting and admitted that she purposely sabotaged our company for revenge. There is no fucking way anyone hires her again. Well, unless that's what they're looking for. She could make a good career out of destroying others."

I had to agree with him. Her plan was very effective. "Well, don't feel too bad for her. She did try to screw us over."

And despite the fact that I felt that way, a part of me still loved her and hated that she was losing everything. Which was insane, because I almost lost everything, along with everyone that worked here. I shouldn't feel a thing for her, but I did.

"On the other hand," Ryan said, picking up on my conflicted feelings, "for a woman to give up everything she's worked for to save a man, even though she's the reason he almost lost everything..." I shot him a look that said to shut up. He raised his arms in concession. "I'm just saying, that doesn't sound like a woman that doesn't love you. That's a good woman that did some terrible things for the wrong reasons."

"A good woman?"

"Well, I mean, part of her is good. She's decent at the core. If she wasn't, she would have let us drown."

"That doesn't excuse anything."

"No, and I'm not making excuses for her. You know I've never trusted her, and I'm not saying that I suddenly want to invite her over for Sunday dinner, but she did the right thing in the end."

I leaned forward in my seat, staring at him. "Ryan, the woman is batshit crazy."

"And you're in love with her."

"And you could just look past the fact that she almost destroyed our future. You could sit beside her and accept her, even though she's a conniving bitch?"

"If she made you happy and you wanted to be with her, I'd learn to live with it."

Ryan stood, slapping my desk. "Well, now that we have the contract again, we need to get to work."

I nodded at him absently. I wondered if he would really be able to get past what she did. I wasn't necessarily anxious to see her again, but my chest filled with some emotion that I couldn't quite describe. She had done that for me, or at least, I was pretty sure she had. But before I got too overjoyed, I had to be sure that she didn't find some way around this. For some reason, it would take something away from her gesture if she found a way to keep her job. I didn't want her to be out of a job, but I also didn't like the idea that she could get away scot free.

I called her office and asked to speak with her, but I was told she wasn't working there anymore, so I asked to be patched through to Mr. Johnson.

"Mark Johnson speaking."

"Mr. Johnson, this is Logan Walker. I'm calling in regards to Cece Baker." I heard a grunt on the other end, so I continued. "I understand that she confessed some things about a situation at a meeting she was attending for a client of yours. I'm wondering if you could tell me how that went?"

"Let's not bullshit here, Mr. Walker. Cece came in here and told me that she spread lies about your company to get back at you. Then she turned in her resignation and went to the meeting to tell our clients what happened."

"You didn't fire her?" I asked in disbelief.

"No. She quit before I could do it. She knew there was no way we would keep her on here after what she'd done. However, the situation is taken care of and she is no longer employed here. I'm sorry she used our company to attack you."

I was baffled. She hadn't even tried to plead her case. She knew exactly what would happen and took it all. I didn't know if this was because she felt guilty or she did it to save my company, but I would be finding out very soon.

"I appreciate your candor. Thank you for your time."

I hung up the phone and stared out my office window. I needed to go talk with her and find out exactly where she stood, and then I needed to make some decisions. I didn't know if I could forgive her, but I also didn't know if I could live without her if she truly loved me.

CHAPTER 28

CECE

I WALKED through the door of the apartment, tossing my keys on the counter. Adjusting to this new schedule was killing me, along with my feet. It was worse than wearing heels all day.

"Long day?"

"You have no idea. My shoulders are killing me."

"That'll happen when you carry a tray of food all day."

I slumped down on the couch, closing my eyes. "I don't remember it being this hard when I was in college."

"That's because you were younger and more agile. Now you're fragile."

"Haha," I said drolly. "Seriously, this job sucks. The customers are rude half the time and I can't even go out on Saturday nights anymore."

"You could always ask for a Sunday off."

"Yeah, I could if I wasn't worried about money. This isn't like working at the firm. The money sucks." Sighing, I kicked off my shoes, rubbing my feet. "How do grown adults make money doing this?"

"They don't. That's why it's meant for college students."

"Yeah, well, it's not very likely that I'll suddenly find a new career. At least not around here."

"Are you thinking of moving?" Vira asked, sitting up quickly.

"I don't know. I'm not sure I can really move on here. Logan hates me. I won't ever hear from him again."

"Do you want to?"

I shrugged, but it was a lie. I desperately wanted to see him. I wanted to apologize and beg for his forgiveness, but I knew he didn't want to see me. I had ruined everything between us, and now I had to live with that.

"Cece, you're a terrible liar. I knew from the start that you wanted him back. You can't hide that from me, no matter how much you try."

"It doesn't matter," I said tiredly. "That's all over now." It was strange to think that just a few weeks ago, I was happy. "You know, when I moved back here, it was supposed to be this great new beginning for me. Now everything's ruined. Oh, and to make matters worse, my mom called. She wants me to come over for dinner tonight."

"Does she know what happened?"

"She knows I lost my job. I called her the day after and told her, but I didn't tell her how I lost it. She's been patient with me, but it's been two weeks. She's not going to wait any longer."

"Do you want me to go with you?"

I snorted. "You know my mom's not your biggest fan. I think that might make things worse."

"I'm sorry," she said sympathetically. "I wish I could make this better."

"It's okay," I said, hauling myself off the couch. "I'd better get ready to leave. I'll talk to you later. You'll be home, right?"

"Yeah, I'm not working tonight."

I nodded and headed for my room. I was grateful I had Vira with me. She might not be everyone's favorite person, but we understood each other. She was the only person in my life that always supported me.

After much procrastinating, two hours later, I walked up to the house I grew up in and tentatively knocked on the door. My mom answered the door and wrapped me in a hug. She always had a way of making me feel better, but she was only going to be disappointed by the time dinner was over.

"Hey, Mom."

She rubbed my back. "Cecelia, it's so good to finally see you. I swear, after you took that job, I thought I would see you more, but you're always busy."

There was something fantastic cooking on the stove and the aromas drifted out of the kitchen and wrapped around me.

"Well, I'm here now."

Mom walked us into the dining room and pushed me towards a chair. "Come on in. I was just setting the table for dinner."

I took the seat that I always sat in while Mom fussed over setting the food out and making sure we had everything we needed. She finally sat down and approximately four seconds later, the inquisition started.

"So, are you going to tell me why you got fired from your job?"

"Okay, before I tell the story, you have to keep quiet and let me finish before I answer any questions."

She nodded and I told her most of what happened since I moved here. I left out the details she didn't need to know and a few things that only Vira knew about. She knew nothing about the guy that was after me or being kidnapped. I had asked Sean not to say anything to her. Our town was plenty big, and unless someone said something, chances were she would never find out. Besides, it was all over with now, so there was no point in scaring her.

When I got to the part about now waitressing because it was the only job I could get, my mother pursed her lips and minutely shook her head. I could see the disappointment all over her face.

"I don't understand. This is not the woman we raised. What happened to you?" my mother asked.

"Mom, people change and make mistakes. I know what I did was wrong, and as much as I'd like to go back and change things, that's not going to happen. I did this to myself and now I have to live with it."

She looked at me, though it was more like she was looking through me. "I can't believe this. I just...I can't believe that you would throw your life away like this. All that money that we spent sending you to college. Did you even consider that you were throwing all that away?"

"Honestly, at the time I wasn't thinking about that. I was thinking about payback. I know that doesn't even matter now, but at the time, it was all I could see."

My mom stood from the table, her face turning red. "You are not my daughter. My daughter was a kind, loving girl that would have never hurt anyone else for any reason, let alone revenge. This person you've become is ugly and I want nothing to do with you." She shook her head at me as tears fell from her eyes. "I don't want to see you anymore. Get out of my house."

I was shocked. I had known she would be less than thrilled, but to tell me she didn't want to see me was a hard pill to swallow. I looked at my mom and felt my heart split in two. She didn't look at me like her daughter whom she loved. She looked at me like a stranger that disgusted her.

"Mom, I know what I did was wrong, and I'm sorry." Tears clouded my eyes as I pleaded my case to her. "I can only try to make up for that now. I'm starting over, but I need to know that you will stand beside me and help me get through this."

"Ever since that boy broke up with you, you've been a different person. I've tried to understand, but this? This is too much. You tried to destroy a person's life along with all the other people that would have been affected. Tell me, if someone had done that to someone in your family, would you have forgiven them?"

I looked down. There would be no convincing her that I could ever make up for this. I was evil in her eyes, and to some extent, I believed that of myself too. Still, she was my mom and she was supposed to love me unconditionally.

"You need to leave now," my mother said cooly, taking dishes to the sink and cleaning up.

I couldn't look up at her. I had already seen the hate in her eyes. I knew she didn't want me here. I could pray that in time she would forget her anger toward me, but for now, the best thing to do was leave. I gathered my purse and jacket and made my way out to my car. I don't know how I managed to make it home with how hard I was crying, but I somehow made it and walked back up to my apartment. Vira was there and hugging me before I could even say anything.

"Do you hate me too, Vira?"

She pulled away from me. "What? How could you even ask that? If your mom chooses to hate you because of what happened, then she doesn't deserve you."

"You should have heard the things she said to me. I know I deserved it and so much more, but she said she never wants to see me again."

"Fuck her. People make mistakes and if she can't forgive them, then she isn't the Christian person I thought her to be."

"But she's right. What I did was unforgivable."

"Maybe to Logan, but sweetie, your mother's supposed to forgive you your mistakes. Sure it may take some time, but she should still be there for you. Besides, how could I hate you? I'm the one that came up with the idea to begin with."

I sniffled and made my way to the couch. "I guess this is my life now. Working a dead end job with one friend to my name and the rest of the town hating me."

"Not the whole town. Just about half."

I laughed at her teasing. It was only about half. Not bad for six months' work.

CHAPTER 29

LOGAN

THE FIRST PLACE I looked for her was her apartment, but I had no luck when I got there. Either she wasn't answering or she wasn't home, but I would bet that she wasn't home. I didn't hear any movement on the other side of the door. The next place I tried was the cafe we met at every morning. It was a long shot, but I really didn't have any other ideas.

I finally broke down and gave her a call, but she didn't answer. The more time it took to find her, the more my desire to talk to her grew. I was getting impatient and my skin was crawling with the need to see her. There was still one person I could try.

"Sean, I need your help with something."

"Sure, whatcha need?"

"I need you to get ahold of Vira and find out where Cece is."

There was a pause on the other end. "Logan, I don't think that's a good idea. You guys are over. No sense in beating a dead horse."

"Sean, I need to find her. Please. Do this for me."

I heard a sigh on the other end and I knew it was going to be tough to convince him to do this. "If you're just trying to find her so you can harp on her some more..."

"That's not..."

"Because you've said enough. Look, I know what she did was horrible, but you have to let it go and move on from her. You guys are toxic to each other."

I was about to argue with him, but his words stopped me in my tracks. Were we toxic? I had always thought we had explosive chemistry, but to the point of being bad for each other?

"What? Why would you say that?"

"Logan, seriously, you two get revenge instead of working out your issues. It's not a normal relationship."

"She did something for me, something that really helped me, and I need to talk to her. I need to know why she did it. I need to know if she still loves me," I said fiercely.

"Fine. I'll get in touch with Vira, but if she says no, that's the end of it. I'm not getting involved any further than that."

"Thanks, man."

I hung up the phone and sat in my truck, waiting impatiently to hear back from Sean. I knew I should be at work, but this was too important and I wouldn't be able to concentrate anyway. I waited for fifteen minutes before my phone rang and my heart kicked into overdrive.

"Yeah," I barked into the phone.

"She's at Maggie's diner, but..."

"Thanks, Sean. I owe you one."

"Wait, Logan..."

I hung up before he could finish. I didn't need to hear about how I should think about this first or I should just leave her alone. I needed to see her and it had to be now. I was across town so fast, I was surprised I didn't get pulled over. I parked and all but ran into the diner, my gaze sweeping the booths for her. When I didn't see her, I was so disappointed. I had missed her.

I turned to leave when I heard her voice float across the restaurant. Turning, I saw her coming out of the kitchen with a tray in hand with plates on top. I stared in confusion and then it dawned on me.

Sean was trying to tell me that she was working here. I wasn't sure if I should stick around or leave. She may not want me here seeing her working here.

Before I could make a decision, she looked up and our eyes locked. Her face paled and shame filled her eyes. She swung around quickly and ran straight into a customer, spilling the food everywhere and causing the plates to shatter on the floor. She knelt down immediately and started gathering the broken plates and food from the floor while apologizing to the customer that was now covered in food.

I rushed over to her to help her clean up as an older woman walked out and stared at the mess on the floor. "What happened here?"

"I'm so sorry, Sylvia. I was clumsy and dropped the tray. You can take it out of my pay."

"Don't worry about it, honey. Accidents happen. Let's just get it cleaned up. What were the orders? I'll take them to the kitchen to get them whipped up real fast."

She spouted off the orders and then continued picking up, all while ignoring me. Her hands were shaking and she looked close to tears. When we finished, she picked up the tray and brought it into the back as the woman, Sylvia, came back out front.

"Excuse me, Sylvia is it?"

"Yes." She eyed me skeptically.

"Could I borrow Cece for a minute? It's important."

"Are you the guy?"

"Excuse me?"

"The guy she ruined her career over."

I blew out a breath and looked away. "Yeah, that's me."

"What makes you think she wants to see you?"

"I don't know that she will, but I have to talk to her. I just found out what she did for me and I need to talk to her."

"You're not here to start trouble are you? Because she's a good worker and I don't want you running her off."

"No, ma'am."

She walked into the kitchen and I heard her telling Cece to take a break. A minute later Cece walked out of the kitchen looking very uncomfortable to see me. She was fidgeting and wouldn't look me in the eye.

"Can we go talk for a few minutes," I asked.

"I don't think that's a good idea. I think we've said enough to each other."

"Please."

She looked up at me and after a minute, nodded in acquiescence. We went over to a table in the corner that was in a secluded part of the restaurant. She took a seat, but refrained from looking at me.

"I heard about what you did."

She shrugged. "It was the right thing to do. You didn't deserve that and neither did your employees."

"Is that the only reason you did it?"

She looked at me with tears swimming in her beautiful eyes. "I made a huge mistake letting my past with you dictate my future. I will always be sorry for that. I ruined something great between us."

"Yeah, well, I did a pretty bang up job of helping you with that. I should have talked to you about what I overheard." I shook my head as I continued. "I said and did some horrible things to you at the club. No matter how hurt I was, that wasn't the way to handle it."

"No matter how awful you were to me, there was no excuse for me trying to destroy your company. That was...the most despicable thing I have ever done in my entire life. I lost you, my job, my mom..."

"Your mom?"

"She wasn't exactly thrilled to know that her daughter could be so evil. She basically told me not to ever step foot in her house again."

I was shocked. I mean, I was the one who was hurt by all this, and yet I was sitting here talking with her. "I'm sure she'll come around. She loves you."

She scoffed. "No. Apparently, I have been a disappointment to her ever since I went off to college."

"Did you tell them why things changed? What I did to you?"

"It wouldn't matter. She wouldn't want to hear it anyway. Besides, I have no right to plead my case to anyone."

"Even me?"

Her eyes narrowed in on me. "Especially you. I don't even understand why you're here talking to me right now."

I didn't know what to say. I wasn't sure what I hoped to get out of this either. I wasn't sure if anything she said would change my mind or not. I just knew I had to hear what she had to say for herself.

"Just tell me one thing. Do you love me or did my actions ten years ago ruin everything for us?"

Something like hope sparked in her eyes. "I don't think I ever stopped loving you. I wanted to hate you, but this time around was different. There was a strong connection between us that I don't think we had ten years ago. I was just a kid then, and I was naive to think that we would be together forever. This time though, I knew who I was and I liked who I was with you. I just wish I would have trusted that."

"I want to believe you. I want to just take you in my arms and pretend none of this happened, but I don't know that I can and it wouldn't be fair to get your hopes up. I have to be sure I can get past what you did."

She nodded, but I saw the hope die. There was nothing I could say. I couldn't just magically forgive her. I needed some time to wrap my head around all this. I stood from the booth and looked down at her.

"I need to sort this all out."

"Don't, Logan. I think we've run our course. I'm through hurting you, and I think it's about time I moved on. It'll be too hard for me to do that here. Maybe I need to start over somewhere else. Everyone here knows what I did. The only chance I have is to move somewhere people don't know me."

Damn it. I wanted so badly to tell her to stay, but I couldn't. I didn't know if I had anything to offer her, and she was right, moving on in this town would be difficult with everyone knowing what she did. She wouldn't ever be able to get a better job than she had now.

"Take care of yourself, Cece."

I walked out of the restaurant and out of Cece's life. It was time to get back to my own and get it back on track.

A week had passed since I made the decision to move on with my life. Cece was still part of my thoughts throughout the day, but I made my best effort to push her away as much as possible. She'd made her choices, and now I had made mine.

Thursday night was poker night at Jack's house and Cole was going to be there. I hadn't seen much of him lately because he was helping Alex recover from her injuries. She had a long road ahead of her, so we rarely saw him. Alex had convinced him that he needed a guys night, so this would be my opportunity to convince him to help us out with VAS.

I started in on him right away, not wanting an opportunity to slip through my fingers. Ryan also took a few turns trying to convince him, but the thing that really worked in our favor was the suggestion Cassandra had.

"The woman running the project, Cassandra, thinks it would be a good idea to start a work program at the center. The idea is that we would set up a workshop and have veterans do what you've basically been doing for the past two years. She wants you to run the shop since you're a veteran and it's worked for you."

"I don't know that it worked. Alex was the driving force behind me getting better." Cole played his hand as the conversation continued around them.

"Do you think you would have ever met Alex if you hadn't been working in your dad's shop? Would you have been strong enough to help her?"

"I don't know. I don't think I'm in any position to help others, though."

Ryan threw down his cards. "Who better to help them get through their shit than someone who understands what they're going through. None of us were really able to pull you out of what you were going through. Sean dragged you out of bed and got you out of the house, but you did the rest on your own. That's what these guys need is someone to help guide them through their shit."

The other guys grunted their agreement. I knew we were getting through to him, he just needed to figure it out for himself. We didn't push too hard and changed to other topics, hoping that what we said sank in.

"Vira tells me that Cece is moving out of town next week. Didn't say where she was going, but said that Cece felt she needed to get out of town so she could move on," Sean said as he played a hand.

I grunted. I already knew all this. "What's your point?"

Everyone at the table stilled. It was so quiet, you could hear a pin drop. I looked up from my cards to see all the guys glaring at me. I furrowed my brows trying to figure out why they all looked so pissed at me.

"What?"

"You really are a dumbass," Ryan said.

"I'm the dumbass? She practically destroyed our company. What do you want me to do?"

He shook his head and Jack groaned. "You have so much to learn."

"You have something to say, Jack?"

"Yeah. You're fucking stupid. Correct me if I'm wrong, but you love this woman, right?"

"I...yeah, I love her, but the things she did...I can't forgive them."

"You can't or you won't?"

Drew, never one to get involved in matters of the heart, piped up, shocking the hell out of me. "She gave up a career to clear your name. Yeah, it was the right thing to do, but she wouldn't have done it if she didn't love you. She condemned herself to a life of being a waitress so that she could save your company."

"A company she put in jeopardy," I interjected.

"She's making crap money working as a waitress, moving to another town so that she can move on. She could have screwed you over, stayed in her cozy, good-paying job, but she didn't. She gave it all up for you. If that ain't the love of a good woman, I don't know what is."

I didn't know what to say. Good woman was not the term I would have used to describe Cece. She used to be a good woman, but now she seemed to be the devil incarnate.

"I don't get it. Where does this sudden adoration for Cece come from? A few weeks ago she was a bitch and now you guys are shoving me at her."

Sebastian was the one to speak up. "I'm not saying she's perfect. I would have paddled her ass weeks ago, but we all make mistakes. We're all human. She did everything possible to rectify what she did."

Then Ryan said something that totally baffled me. "You know I'm not her biggest fan after what she did, but I've never seen you happier than you were with her. I'd hate for you to miss out on something because you feel you need to be mad at her. I'm not gonna think less of you if you want to be with her. Don't hold back because you feel you have to."

"Why would I feel I have to? This has nothing to do with what I feel I have to do. I don't trust her, and I'm not asking her to wait around until I decide if I can."

"Bullshit," Cole said. "You're holding back because she made a fool out of you, and you don't want to risk it happening again. You already know if you can trust her. She already proved what she was willing to do for you. Now you just have to open your eyes and see it for what it is."

I had nothing to say to that. Probably because it was true. I didn't want to be made a fool again, but if I didn't take the chance, I would probably be alone the rest of my life. Cece was a once in a lifetime match for me. I didn't think I'd ever meet someone as good as her. Someone who fit with me the way she did.

"Shit. When is she leaving, Sean?"

"Don't know for sure. Vira said in a week, so I figure you got a few days to come up with a way to convince her to stay. You know you can't just walk in and ask her to stay. It won't work. Go big or go home."

CHAPTER 30

CECE

I WAS PACKING MY STUFF, trying to ignore Vira huffing and puffing in the next room. She was pissed at me for leaving. I knew she understood why, but she didn't want me to go. I couldn't blame her. I didn't want to go. I was only leaving because she was the only thing holding me here, and I needed more than that in my life. I wanted to be happy with my job and live where people didn't know every negative thing about my life.

"Vira," I said, approaching her like a feral animal.

"What?" she snapped.

"Please don't be mad at me."

"How can you ask that? You're leaving me!"

"You know why."

"Yeah, well, I thought we were closer than that. But you decided to up and leave when things got rough."

"That's a little unfair," I said angrily.

She sighed. "I know. I'm sorry. I'm just...We've been together for ten years. And now you're just leaving. I don't know what I'll do without you."

"Hey, we'll still see each other."

"Yeah," she snorted. "When you get your new waitressing job in some podunk town and scrape together enough money to visit. Sure, we'll have a blast."

"Don't be defeatist. It's not like you."

"Maybe I could move with you," she said hopefully.

"And do what? You love your job."

"Not that much," she grumbled.

"Look, if you really want a change, then you do it for you, not for me. I don't want you moving across the country, only to end up hating it."

"I just hate that you're leaving. And you didn't even pick a fun place to move. Nebraska? Seriously?"

"I think my wild days are over," I reminded her.

"Yeah, but this town is tiny. Do they even have a fast food restaurant? I mean, where are you going to go for fun?"

"I'm sure I'll make my own fun. Besides, it's not the end of the world. The apartments are cheaper there, which means I'll be able to save a lot more money than I could here. Maybe I'll even meet a nice man, someone who knows nothing about my past."

"He won't be Logan," she grumbled.

"No, he won't, but maybe that's a good thing. No one could compare to Logan. He's...special. I'll never meet someone that makes me feel the way he did."

"Maybe you could talk to him one last time before you leave, see if he's changed his mind."

"I think I've done enough talking. Vira, I can't change his mind. He told me that it would take time, and he wasn't sure he could move past it. That's not exactly a winning endorsement."

"Then make him see what he's missing!"

"Vira, it's over! I'm sorry, I know you want me to stay, but I can't. I can't be in the same town as him, to see him around town and know that I messed up one of the best things that's ever happened to me. He was right all along. I was the one that fucked things up."

She sighed and sat down on the couch. "When are you leaving?"

"Saturday. I was thinking maybe we could have one last night of fun."

She gave me a half-hearted smile. "Sure. Did you tell your mom?"

I nodded. "Yeah, for all the good it did. She didn't answer my call. I left her a message, but she didn't bother to call back. I'm sure at some point she'll tell my brother and sister, but we haven't been close in years, so I doubt they'll care that much."

"It's just so sad. All the friends you made here, and you're just leaving them behind."

"They're not my friends. They were all Logan's friends, and I bet they're congratulating him right now on his escape. But you're right. It is sad. I wish it didn't have to be this way, but it is what it is."

"Just promise me you won't run off and find another friend."

"I probably will, but whoever she is, she'll never be as awesome as you."

I worked as many shifts as I could at the diner this week to set aside money for my trip. I was only taking what I could fit in my car because renting a truck would be too expensive and I wouldn't have anyone to help me unload.

By the time Friday came around, I was emotionally exhausted. Part of me just wanted to move today and get it over with. This long, drawn out week was just making it more difficult to say goodbye to Vira. Still, I got dressed up in the same outfit I wore the night I first saw Logan. Call me sentimental, but I wanted to feel like he was there with me tonight.

Vira and I left for the club around nine, and I tried to be in a good mood, but my heart wasn't in it. I was moping around and I couldn't even get into dancing. I wasn't trying to be a Debbie downer, but I couldn't choose to be happy the night before I left the one place I truly felt at home.

She dragged me out on the dance floor for song after song, and I eventually loosened up enough that I didn't look like I was there against my will. Vira was obviously looking for her next hookup, as she continued to glance around the dance floor searching for someone.

"Vira, I think I'm ready to go. You stay and have some fun. Find a hot guy to take home."

"What? No, you're just starting to loosen up. Please, just stay for one more song."

Her pouty face had me agreeing to one more song, but I was a little confused when the song *Cecelia* played in a disco club. I gave Vira a strange look and she just shrugged her shoulders and started dancing. I looked around at the confused faces of the other dancers and watched as most of them walked off the dance floor toward the bar.

It was then I saw Logan as he stalked out onto the dance floor, his eyes burning into me. He reminded me of a panther stalking his prey as he strode up to me and wrapped me in his arms. I was so shocked that I didn't know what to do. He started swinging me around the dance floor, his body moving swiftly and lightly, but his gaze stayed trained on my face.

I could barely hear his voice over the music, but the moment I heard that smooth croon coming from his lips, I smiled, resting my head on his shoulder. He pulled me tighter against him, bringing tears to my eyes. I swear this man brought me to my knees. I didn't know what exactly he was saying by showing up here tonight, but I knew he was trying to tell me something. I didn't want to hope that he was asking me to stay, because it would break my heart if that wasn't it.

When the song finished, he pulled back slightly and looked me in the eyes. There was a glimmer of danger in his eyes. Danger that said I shouldn't fuck with him right now. He pulled me off the dance floor, his body vibrating with an intensity that I didn't quite understand. His hand gripped mine as if he were afraid I would take off at any moment. He took me to the private boxes upstairs that were reserved for VIP guests. He shut the door and stalked over to me, pushing me backward into the couch.

He fingered the strap on my halter as he spoke to me for the first time tonight. "Here's how this is going to go. We're going to leave this club, and you're coming back to my place. We've been dancing around each other long enough and it's time to stop that. Your stuff is already back at my place, and you and I are going to live together and make this work."

"What? No...That's not..."

"That wasn't a question. This is going to happen. We aren't going to give ourselves another reason to fail. We're sticking together this time and we're gonna work shit out instead of working against each other. I love you and I'm telling you that you're staying here."

I stared at him with a gaping mouth. Logan had never been quite so demanding before.

"Say it." I didn't say anything right away. He pushed against me, his erection pressed against my clit. He leaned in and kissed my jaw up to my ear. "Say. It. Tell me that you're staying. No more running. Tell me you're mine."

I shook my head slightly. "Logan, why will it work this time? Shouldn't we just admit that we're bad for each other and move on?"

"We're not bad for each other. We just need to work our shit out. And there's no way I'm moving on from you. Maybe I didn't see it before, but that was my wounded pride talking. Cece, there's no one else in the world I would rather fight with. You're the one for me, and the sooner you admit that, the sooner we can move on and be happy."

"I want that," I whispered. "But I'm scared."

His hand slid up to cup my jaw. "You think I'm not scared? I'm terrified, but I want this more than I want to walk away. I need you. Say you need me too, that you'll stay."

It was insane. I knew I should run for the door and never look back. We had both hurt each other so much, but I wanted him. I needed him more than I had ever needed anyone in my life. He was it for me.

"I'm staying. I won't run."

He crushed his mouth to mine with such force that I toppled backward onto the couch. He landed on top of me and ran his hands up my thigh and straight to my shorts. He tore at the buttons and ripped them down my legs. Before I knew it, he was sheathed inside me, pounding me into the couch. My legs wrapped around him as I pulled him deeper into me. It had been too long since we'd been together and I needed him like I needed air.

"Oh, God, Logan. Don't stop."

I clung to his back and then worked my hands up to his hair, pulling his face to mine for another kiss. We didn't do gentle when we were together. Everything between us was explosive, and this time was no different. He thrust into me until I was left boneless on the couch with him panting above me as we both came down from our highs.

"That wasn't supposed to happen here. I was going to take you back to my place, but I saw you in this outfit and I just had to fuck you."

"I'm glad you didn't wait. I needed that."

He pulled off me and hauled me to my feet, then handed me my shorts. "Get dressed. We're going home and I'm going to fuck you properly."

I had to admit. I liked this side of Logan. He was no nonsense, and I found I liked knowing he wasn't giving me a chance to run, to think things over. He was telling me exactly what he wanted, which cut out all the guesswork and didn't leave room for misinterpretation. There was one more thing I needed to do though if I was going to move forward with Logan. I had to tell him the whole truth.

"Logan, I need to tell you something first."

"It can wait, sweetheart. I need to get you home and in my bed." He started to turn, but I pulled on his hand, stopping him where he was.

"This won't wait. You might not want me after I tell you this." I could see the flash in his eyes that said he didn't want to know, but I couldn't live with myself if I didn't tell him. "Your company wasn't the only thing I fucked with."

His jaw clenched and I saw his throat working as he swallowed. "Okay. What else did you do?"

"I flooded your house, I used you to get free coffee, I had Sawyer and Calloway target you, and I fucked those two guys to get back at you."

It all flew out of my mouth so fast that I wasn't sure he understood me, but then he stood and started pacing the room. When he didn't say anything, I gathered my clothes and quickly dressed, sure that he was going to tell me to get the fuck away from him.

"How did you flood my house?"

"I found your spare key and I snuck into your house and turned on the water. The drain stopper was in one side and you had left your plate in the other side, so I just had to turn on the water. I was in and out in under five minutes."

"And Sawyer and Calloway? I wasn't aware you knew them."

"Vira knows Sawyer. He's always had a thing for her, so she used him. Please, don't bring her into this though. This is all on me."

"I don't get it. If you were the one they were doing it for, why did they attack you when they tried arresting me?"

I shrugged. "At that point, I had already asked Vira to call them off, so I don't know what was going on. I assumed they just really had it out for you and no longer cared about me."

"When did you decide you were done fucking with me?"

"The night I slept with the two guys. After you left, it finally dawned on me that you really cared and wanted to help me. I felt like complete shit for how I acted, but it was too late then. I decided that I couldn't keep torturing you without hurting myself. You had become too important to me."

He crowded in close to me, wrapping one arm around my waist and his other hand trailed around my neck, squeezing lightly. "And those fuckheads, were they as good as me?"

"They did the job, but not even two guys could come close to what you do to me."

He gripped my ass, squeezing tightly and pulling me up against him. "No more games. You're mine now, and I won't tolerate that kind of shit anymore. We work out our problems together from now on. Understood?"

I nodded and he swooped in giving me a hard kiss. "Remind me to never fuck with you again."

A small smile played across my lips. "You can fuck with me anytime you want, just expect a little revenge. I'll keep it in the bedroom, though."

He swatted my ass, dragged me out the door, and took me to his house. I didn't say a word, but my eyes didn't leave him as he drove me home. Home. He was taking me to his house where I would now live with him. He did want me. I felt a small piece of my former confident self reappearing and urging me to make myself known.

When he pulled into the garage, I got out and met him in front of the car, but I didn't give him an opportunity to drag me inside. I grabbed his cock through his pants and gave him a kiss that had him throwing me on top of his precious car. He ground himself against me, but I shoved him away to undo his pants. I couldn't wait any longer to have him inside me again.

He was inside me moments later. I didn't remember my shorts being taken off or even my boots, but there he was inside me, making me come all over him. At some point, he picked me up off the car and carried me into the house, setting me on the counter in the kitchen, fucking me hard.

He pulled out suddenly and stepped back. "On your knees."

I didn't waste a second following his command. I took him in my mouth and gagged repeatedly as he roughly fucked my mouth over and over. I grabbed his balls and lightly tugged, but as his thrusting got more intense, I squeezed harder.

"Damn, woman. Don't rip my balls off."

I moaned around his cock, eliciting a hiss from him. I found the spot behind his balls and pressed down, feeling him thrust wildly into my mouth once more before coming down the back of my throat.

"Holy fuck!"

I swallowed everything and stood, staring at him through my eyelashes. In a flash, he threw me over his shoulder and took me upstairs. We spent the night fucking like rabbits and only fell asleep as morning was dawning.

In the light of the morning, doubt started to creep in. I wondered if he would change his mind and decide he didn't want to keep me around. It's not like I could offer that much financially, and he might get tired of that.

"You think too much, sweetheart. Go back to sleep. It's still early."

"I don't think I can sleep anymore."

"What's on your mind, babe?"

"I'm just wondering if you'll truly be happy with me. I mean, I'm a waitress now. I don't have a lot I can offer you. We both know I'm not going to get a better job anytime soon."

"Do you really think I'm with you because of your job? I couldn't care less about where you work as long as you're in my bed at night."

"I just don't want you to be ashamed of me. I mean, when we get together with people, you're successful and you own a company. I'm a liar that destroyed my own career and now waits tables."

"Babe, your job doesn't make you who you are. You are still just as wild and just as tempting as you were when we first met. Our chemistry is still off the charts. Your job didn't change that. I love that sassy attitude that you have, and I love that you're confident. Don't let that die just because you made a few mistakes. You owned up to them, held your head up high, and moved on. That's sexy as hell."

"What about your friends? No doubt they all hate me."

"Actually, I had my head shoved up my ass about the whole thing. I was scared that if I gave you another chance, you'd make a fool of me again. They all practically shoved me back to you. They were impressed by what you did to set the record straight, and they reminded me that we all make mistakes. God knows I've made more than I can count, especially with you. Even Ryan said that he had never seen me happier than I was with you and he wanted that back for me."

I felt horrible because I had not only hurt Logan, but I had assumed that his friends would be just like him. In fact, they were all better people than I gave them credit for. I had been too blinded to see it, though.

"I promise to never hurt you like that again. I want to move forward with you and see where this takes us."

"There is no seeing, sweetheart. I already know where this is going and so do you. There were never two people that were more meant to be together than us. Now, I don't want to discuss what happened with you ever again. It's in the past and we need to move on from that. It's time we get back to where we should have been all along."

"And where's that exactly?"

"With you in my bed and me between your legs. For the rest of our lives."

Logan had once told me that he was going to put a permanent mark on my ass. He had never gotten around to it and I wasn't so sure that he was really serious, but the next day I was dragged downtown to a tattoo parlor where Logan proceeded to tell them I needed a stamp on my ass. I glared at him, but he just continued talking to the guy at the counter.

"I want the stamp to say *Property of Logan*."

"Excuse me, I am not your property!"

"Really? Does that ass belong to anyone else?"

"No."

"Then it's my property. I promised you once I would mark your ass and today's the day. Go sit down in the chair and get it done or I'll do it myself and it won't look nearly as pretty."

Honestly, I didn't really mind having his tattoo on me. I liked the idea of being marked as his. Still, I would give him shit over it as long as I could get away with it. I walked over to the chair where the tattoo artist was preparing the ink. Logan chose a design, and soon I was getting my ass poked by what felt like a hundred tiny needles.

When it was all done, the guy handed me a mirror and I looked back to see the beautiful letters Logan had chosen. The dark look on Logan's face told me we needed to get out of here before he bent me over the table and fucked me right here in the shop.

He leaned over me and whispered in my ear so only I could hear. "Now when I smack your ass, I'll hit you right on that spot as a reminder of who you belong to." A shiver ran down my spine at his words. "Pull your pants up so we can get home. I have plans for you for the rest of the day."

CHAPTER 31

CECE

IT TURNED out that Logan was right. I did belong in his bed for the rest of my life. We only waited another month before taking off to Vegas and eloping. It felt right and neither of us wanted to wait. We figured that would give us too much time to talk ourselves out of something that we knew was inevitable.

We stayed in Vegas for the weekend and that was where we conceived our baby boy. It turns out that some things in life turn out exactly as they're supposed to. If I had continued working at my job in marketing, I would probably have continued to work long hours and wouldn't have had time for a family. Or if I did, I would have worked so much that I wouldn't have seen my children. As long as that job was a part of me, nothing else was that important.

Logan and Ryan's company has really taken off over the past few years and a big part of that is their work with the VAS building. I thank my lucky stars every day that I didn't screw up that contract for him. It really put them on the map and other private organizations have come out to check out the facility and now consult with the director of VAS and Jackson Walker Construction.

It's been five years since we married and we're still in the house

Logan built, but now we have three children that I stay home and take care of. His friend, Drew has horses on his property now and I go over there during the week to help out. I was enthralled with horses when I was a kid and I really missed that about myself. When he rented out his land to a rancher, I couldn't help but ask to help out. It felt good to get back to my roots.

I didn't dress as sassy anymore, but my confidence was still in full swing. I was now more comfortable in cowboy boots than heels, much to Vira's chagrin. I still get dressed up and go out with her once a month so that I don't lose what made me into the person I am today.

After a few months of my mother ignoring my requests to see her, I finally decided to send her one last message in the hopes that we could repair our relationship. I left some flowers on her doorstep with a card sending my congratulations that she would be a grandmother. It didn't even take her twenty-four hours to call me and ask to meet. Things weren't fixed overnight, but by the end of my pregnancy, we were closer than we had ever been before. She absolutely adored Logan and even came over to help the first few weeks that our son was born.

Now, my mother and Logan's parents take turns watching the three kids during the day while I go work at the horse ranch. My dad hasn't been in the picture since I told him he was going to be a grandfather. He tried to reach out to me, but it never felt sincere, so I didn't push a relationship.

It's strange because everything that Logan and I had was something I desperately wanted with him when we were together fifteen years ago. It turns out I got everything I wanted with him, we just took the long way of getting there.

ALSO BY GIULIA LAGOMARSINO

Thank you for reading Logan! I hope you enjoyed Logan and Cece's twisted love story, but it's not over yet. In fact, you'll see them in the rest of the books in the series, but look for them next in Book 4, *Drew!*

Join my newsletter to get the most up-to-date information, along with new content in the Reed Security series.

https://giulialagomarsinoauthor.com/connect/

Join my Facebook reader group to find out more about my obsession with Dwayne Johnson!

https://www.facebook.com/groups/GiuliaLagomarsinobooks

Reading Order:

https://giulialagomarsinoauthor.com/reading-order/

To find the individual series, follow the links below:

For The Love Of A Good Woman series

Reed Security series

The Cortell Brothers

A Good Run Of Bad Luck

The Shifting Sands Beneath Us- Standalone

Owens Protective Services

Printed in Great Britain
by Amazon